InSight

Also by Paul S. Piper

Novels and Short Fiction

The Wolves of Mirr,
The Soul Loves Most What Is Lost
South Fork and Other Stories

Poetry

Now and Then
Winter Apples
Dogs and Other Poems
And Light
Praises

Books of Essays (co-editor)

Father Nature
X Stories
A Flutter of Birds Passing through Heaven

InSight

PAUL S. PIPER

BOOK VIEW CAFE

InSight
Copyright © 2023 by Paul S. Piper

ISBN 978-1-63632-157-8

Cover Art by TK Palad

Production Team:
Editor, Gregory Frost
Copyreader/proofreader, Sherwood Smith
Ebook formatter, Jennifer Stevenson
Print formatter, Marissa Doyle

This book is a work of fiction and all that entails.

Book View Cafe
304 S. Jones Blvd. Suite #2906
Las Vegas NV 89107

www.bookviewcafe.com

Dedication

This book is dedicated to all those attempting to stop the harvest and trafficking of illicit wildlife

1

There was nothing but furious pain and blurred light, and pulsing darkness hovering at the periphery.

The woman lay face flat on wet cement, a traffic light down the block bathing it with green, yellow, and red, successively, endlessly. Her thoughts flew like flocks of birds and left the sky of her mind vacant. The only thing that hovered clearly was the face of the man who'd hurt her. Thick, cruel, and malignant, two gold incisors, curly oily black hair.

The car she'd been thrown from had sped off, rear tires spinning on the slick asphalt. Other cars drove by but no one stopped.

In a moment of clarity, she raised her head, and pulled herself by her elbows across the sidewalk. Once there, she lay panting, sighting her goal. Then crabbing her legs and knees, she climbed three cement stairs. It took every bit of strength she had. But she needed more. The outside door barely opened inward as she pushed against it. But it was enough. She pulled herself through.

The apartment lobby was bathed in yellow light and was warm, almost stuffy. Musty with the faint scent of perfume, cigarette smoke, cooked cabbage. Above her, to her left, a row of rectangular brass mailboxes was embedded in the wall, a tiny white button under each. Newspapers and advertising circulars were strewn on the floor underneath. Across the lobby was a dull-green metal door, worn at points of contact by thousands of hands over nearly one hundred years. Above the door the name of the apartment, *The Royal Arms,* was meaningless.

With a Herculean effort, she managed to clear the outside door and heard it bang shut, shutting out the hiss of traffic, the blare of horns. Now fully inside the lobby, her cheek cool on the black and white tile floor, she managed to raise her right arm and point weakly toward the mailboxes, as if beckoning silent friends for help. Then her arm fell heavily to the floor, and her eyes glazed as she surrendered her soul to the night and whatever lay beyond.

2

"Shit!"

Jack Toyokata slapped the pockets of his ash-grey sports coat. He'd forgotten his cell phone. Again. On the counter. Attached to a charger plugged into the wall. Next to the microwave holding the cup of cold coffee he'd forgotten to remove.

Forgetting things was getting to be a daily occurrence.

Yesterday it was his keys, and he had to rouse his manager from a Mariner's TV game trance.

Over the past two weeks he'd left the stove burner on, forgotten to turn off the TV, several times, forgot where he'd parked his car, forgot to flush the toilet (number two --embarrassing!), turn off lights, and had "lost" several things in the pantry and fridge. Minor things all, except the stove burner, but irritating.

Sure, he was under excessive stress at work, but who wasn't? It was the nature of the job. Gone were the days when you landed a client for life. Now it was a matter of days, weeks, or if you were lucky, months. And after each successful project, after your pat on the back and check, you still had to resume-up for the next project. And the new crops of coders were *SICK*, hybridizing codes like they were pouring cream into black coffee. Creative and brilliant, and clients were always looking for the "new."

AI was emerging as the next Mecca, and although the primary codes were still evolving –Python, R, Lisp, Prolog, Java – code languages language had their own evolution and natural selection. Jack had the feeling lately that some new language would blow everything out of the water. And he couldn't help but think that it already existed. Or the components did. And he didn't have a clue what it would be. But someone did.

Jack walked over to the floor-to-ceiling window, as wide as the living room. Beyond it, Lake Washington, steely in the dusk, stretched east to the far shore of fir and scattered lighted houses. Large homes on large acreage. Bill Gates, Paul Allen, Larry Ellison. Steve Jobs' house had already been sold. These people, and those like them, liked their privacy. They all had heli-pads, gates with guards at the head of their driveways, prison-style fences, and high-end security systems. And they liked living in the forest. They left thousands of trees standing. And that's what Jack liked looking at. The trees. The forest. His mind went there to escape. It was a dark place, and not at all safe, the wild.

It was drizzling out, and traffic moved in fits-and-starts on Lake City Way.

Jack Toyokata was forty-one. Japanese-American. A coder since he'd escaped from college. He'd recently purchased one of the new condos that were popping up like dandelions in Bothell and Kenmore. This particular building, located between the Burke-Gilman Trail and Lake Washington, was a twelve-story, 50 unit, tastefully finished structure with an underground parking garage, and plenty of storage for Jack's bike, skis, snowboard, and various camping and outdoor equipment. Not that Jack had time to use any of the gear anymore, but it was there, waiting.

The floorplan and view had sold Jack. An eighth floor, two-bedroom, L-shaped unit, tastefully painted airy desert colors, kitchen with a center high-polish rose granite counter. All the modern perks – voice command lights, heating, Dacor gas range, LG fridge and freezer.

Jack loved Northwest art. He valued what the Skagit artists did with color and space. These paintings spoke to him. When he had time, he drove up to La Conner, dined, wandered the town, and bought a painting. These now hung in the living room and a hallway.

A corner unit, his views from the living room confronted Lake Washington. The two bedrooms looked north, up-lake, and the forested hills beyond.

While still sparsely furnished, the essentials were in place. The couch, two faux Shaker chairs, a zafu, a chrome-legged coffee table. Lots of space to dance around. Jack couldn't remember when he last danced.

His music situation was insane, to put it mildly.

Jack had love and an ear, but was a technical audiophile. Jack's friend Stan, a minor audio god, had constructed an assemblage of tweeters, woofers, sub-woofers, amps, pre-amps, dacs, cables and wires, some no more than a gossamer suggestion. The net result was sound that moved heaven and earth.

As for content, Jack was an omnivore – Skiffle to Mahler, gamelan to Patsy Cline, Hank Jones to Tool. Et cetera. And an addict for streaming services. Pandora, Spotify, Apple, Amazon, LiveXLive, Deezer. And to fill in the gaps, his extensive collection of categorized, alphabetized CDs, LPs, and cassette tapes filled a wall.

His friend Per told Jack that if "I owned this much music I would never know what to listen to." But Jack loved and lived in music, and no surplus was too great. Just because he couldn't possibly listen to all of it in multiple lifetimes, didn't mean he couldn't try.

He sat down on a blue couch positioned for lake viewing, and lifted a cup of Oolong tea to his lips, blew across it, then set it down. His system was streaming Seattle cellist Gretchen Yanover, a recent find.

He'd gotten home from work around 7:30. It was now a little before nine.

His team was jamming on a large contract and he needed to get back to it. Dinner tonight was a package of Safeway California rolls, microwaved for one minute, eaten in four. But at least he was home, done with the office. He'd work into the wee hours from home.

Jack sighed, watched a small regatta of sailboats clipping across the Lake, sails bulging. He'd always wanted to do that, and mentally added it to a list that grew longer by the day. Things he'd never have time to do until he was too old to do them.

A few minutes later, switching the music to a Brahms piano trio, he moved over to the table, and opened his laptop. Lines of code streamed across the computer screen in a variety of colors. Notes from his programming team popped up, modified, then disappeared.

Processed cups of noodles, pre-made sushi, energy bars, breakfast sandwiches, and the occasional apple made up the bulk of his diet. He just didn't have time to cook and sit properly at a table. His job was a beast that controlled him.

The cell phone, keys, and like were troubling, but what had happened yesterday was more so.

Jack worked for UniCode, a Seattle-based company with satellites in Redmond and Bothell. The Bothell office was his go-to, but he worked all of them including from home.

Jack preferred the offices to home for the social buzz during the day; evenings and night he preferred to work from home. He was basically a social guy who liked the jostle of conversation around him, even if he didn't always participate. His friend the writer, Per Morten, wrote in coffeehouses for the same reason.

Yesterday, Friday, Jack was coding a piece of software designed to inventory the GPS movements of his client's fleet of 2,067 trucks, based on real-time traffic, weather, construction projects, natural disasters, and cheap gas. It continually micro-managed the routes of each vehicle in real-time. The coding was boring and tedious, and he was dying to finish it.

Suddenly he was looking at a computer screen cluttered with letters, numbers and symbols, and he had no idea what any of it meant. Frozen, Jack stared at the blinking cursor until, some indeterminate time later, everything clicked back into place.

Out for a beer after work, Jack confided to his colleague Miguel that he'd blanked, weaving the smaller serial memory lapses into the narrative.

Miguel told him he should see a doctor.

And he'd seen one this morning, had been tasked with getting several blood panels, which he'd done on the way home, and ordered to get a CT scan of his head, which he'd scheduled for the next day.

The doctor hadn't seemed overly concerned.

"Stress causes memory lapse. I doubt it's anything more than that, but in addition to those tests, I want you to start taking 1000mcg of vitamin B-12 a day, and I want you to start getting exercise. Doesn't need to be aerobic, just get out for a walk in nature. Go to a park, or the Burke-Gilman. Saint Edward. Some nice trails there. A good workout, but not too steep. Run if you want, but walking is fine. A couple miles a day. And eat right. Cut the caffeine in half, same with salt. Alcohol. Stop smoking pot, if you do, or anything else. Make an appointment with the desk to see me after the CT."

Maybe it was time to try and clean up his act. Maybe that was the message.

3

The following week, several things happened.

Jack had another blanking incident.

Judging from the outcome, he'd apparently hit a lot of keys on his keyboard. Why? He couldn't remember. But the outcome was that he'd severely damaged two days of coding by his team-mates, Rondel and Curry. And he'd destroyed several days of his own work.

Of course everything was backed up, right? Corporate policy. The computers they used at the UniCode offices captured data every minute, but both Brown and Curry had disabled auto-backup, considering it an intrusion into their creativity. And they never backed up anything manually.

Jack had also disabled auto-backup and had forgotten to back up for over a week.

The net result was that they'd lost huge amounts of code, and would have to start over with older drafts. In a nutshell, even working sixteen-hour bombs, they'd lost two to three days. And Jack was the project lead.

"How the fuck could you let this happen?" Ken Billetts yelled across the oval table.

Jack started to explain, but Billetts interrupted him.

"Shut the fuck up!"

Three upper management, who'd Jack never met, clustered at the far end of the table. Tyler Ryder, CEO of UniCode, sat at the head of the table staring straight ahead impassively.

"Twelve hours, fourteen, twenty, I don't care! If we lose Kloser-Meyer because of you knuckleheads, you're all toast! History!"

Jack saw Curry flinch.

"Now get to work. Do what fucking needs to be done to get back on schedule. And remember," Billetts drew it out, "the program is due next Tuesday by noon. Forget about the word 'weekend.' It doesn't apply here. Now get at it!"

After the meeting Jack called a friend, Alex Noone, a nurse-practitioner at Kaiser Permanente, and told him about the memory lapses.

"You should see a doctor, Jack. Get some tests."

"Done. What else?"

"Vitamin B complex. Eat lots of protein. Get at least eight hours of sleep a night."

"Not going to happen. What else?"

"Have you tried Prevagen? They sell it at Walgreens. No research, but a lot of word-of-mouth. 'Makes me sharper. Don't forget as much.' That sort of thing. Can't hurt."

"Be amazing if it were that simple."

"It's analogous to glucosamine. Some people say it helps; others say it doesn't. Try it. Be rigorous about the results. Don't keep taking something that you think might be working. If you're not improving, it ain't working."

Another thing that happened was the CT scan, and his doctor's almost immediate call to inform him there was nothing wrong with his brain.

"Just wanted to let you know in case you were worried. You don't need additional stress. Now go take a walk."

And the third thing. A woman he'd been seeing sporadically, Samantha, Sam for short, called him and bowed out of their Thursday night dinner date.

"Anything wrong?" Jack asked.

Sam was silent for a long minute.

"We're all busy people, Jack, so there's no use batting around the bush."

"Beating around the bush."

"Whatever. This just isn't doing anything for me. I think we should split."

Jack didn't really think they'd established enough of anything to split, but he said "Um, Okay, if that's what you think."

"That's what I think, Jack. Have a nice life."

And Jack was holding a dead phone.

4

A week went by. His team resurrected the Kloser-Meyer project and completed it Sunday morning, around 4:30 to be exact, celebrating with a breakfast at *Parfait's*, heavy on the Bloody Marys. I'll quit alcohol tomorrow, Jack was thinking, deep into his second Mary.

Jack returned home and fell into bed with his clothes on, asleep before he hit the mattress. He was awakened by a late afternoon phone call. It was Per Morten, his raspy voice raking the fog from Jack's barely crackling brain. "Dinner. My place. In an hour. Can you do it?"

Jack heard him exhale, and could see the cigarette smoke flowing languorously out of his mouth. Technically, it was pipe tobacco smoke, since Per rolled his own, using Captain Black.

"What time is it?"

"Five-thirty-six to be precise. Oh, by the way, we're celebrating. My novel, *Quaint Toys*, was just accepted by Penguin."

"Damn, Per, that's excellent news!" Jack sat up. Per had been shopping the novel, and finally found an agent he liked. The contract had taken another five months, but Penguin was a good fit for Per, since his novels sold well in Europe.

"So, you coming?"

"Of course I'll be there! I'll bring wine. Anything else I should pick up?"

"Some cheese, Gouda, preferably smoked, crackers, and a tin of tapenade. That should do it. I've invited a few others, but no big crowd. Chill people."

"See you in an hourish."

People were standing around a table munching and chatting when Jack arrived.

He'd showered for the first time in days, letting the warm water massage his shoulders and upper back, then shaved. He still had bags under his eyes, but C'est la vie. He forced himself to smile. Passable, he thought.

Per's apartment was seven flat blocks, and Jack chose to walk. He ducked in Delaurenti's for the cheese, tapenade and crackers, and chose a mid-range bottle of Tempranillo, then headed to the Burke-Gilman for a five-block walk.

"Jack," Per loudly announced as he walked in the door. "Meet everyone. Everyone, this is Jack."

Per was solidly drunk, but not at the wobbly stage yet. His feet planted wider than hip-distance apart, Scotch, from the looks of it, in his left hand.

"Jack's a programmer. Damn good one I'm told. But he slums with the creative types now and then. Per waved his right arm at the small crowd. "Jack, you know Marla, my girlfriend. Meet Cheryl, Thomas, Charles, his lovely wife Lal, and Riordan."

Jack walked over and shook hands, repeating their names, getting further information.

Cheryl, a petite woman in jeans and a white linen blouse, was an artist, primarily a children's book illustrator; Thomas, a large black man, was a barrister; Charles and Lal ran a restaurant, *Blondie's*, on Queen Anne Hill; and Riordan, was a rogue with a bush of wild white hair, a photographer, and creator of several well-known Seattle-area coffee table books. *The Way of the Orca. Salmon and Their People.*

Jack joined the three men, who were talking about the odds of the Mariners, how the Seahawks were shaping up.

"What's it like coding for a living?" asked Riordan during a lull. "Sounds bloody boring."

"Sometimes, not always. Depends on the project. More like frenetic, creative, mentally demanding. When I'm in the zone, really there, I forget everything else. There's no room for anything else."

"Sounds Zen. Is it a solo thing?"

"It can be, but I run a team, so nearly everything's collaborative. Pieces and personalities have to fit. And it's a bit like building a house. The end result is something tangible."

"Makes sense I guess," Riordan said. "That's a field I know nothing about."

"Are there coders you would consider artists?" Cheryl had wandered over and joined the group.

"Certainly. Coding can be functional art. Certain coders are known for their creative and imaginative prowess. Others are technicians. There's a gamut. When I put together a team, I need to be aware of the coders' strengths and weaknesses, and match them accordingly."

"I thought computer nerds were socially mal-adapted," said Thomas with a laugh. "You don't seem to fit that mold."

"I guess I should thank you," Jack responded, laughing. "And expanding a bit on Cheryl's question, a coder can be considered an artist for different reasons. There are aesthetics for code, an elegance in code that is well-written, efficient. Just as in a well-constructed sentence or paragraph. But there's also the end result, the program or app. There are programs, think of a screensaver that creates myriad colorful shapes, or collages of photographs."

"You can do that? Create photo collages." Riordan seemed interested.

"Sure," said Jack. "Eezy peezy."

"Tell me about them. The photo collages."

"Well why don't you tell me what you have in mind?"

"Okay. I've been thinking about this lately. I've got, let's say 500 plus photos of people's faces. I've been thinking of a piece of software that can do something interesting with them."

"What do you mean exactly?"

"Well, I can't tell you exactly." Riordan had a contagious laugh.

Thomas and Charles had drifted off, and were sitting on the sofa with Per and Lal. They were talking politics, which is what Per usually ended up talking about. Jack overheard Per exclaiming how fearful of socialism America was, then flicked back on Riordan.

"But perhaps a grid of spaces, each one a face photo, and they change, rapidly or slowly."

"That's easy. You could even do that with a table program."

"I could?"

"I can show you how on Per's computer."

"Huh." Riordan scratched his prodigious nose. "Wow."

"But mind if I build on that?"

"Not at all."

"I was thinking of something more interesting. What if you took those 500 photographs and had them continually blend into each other? No grids. Rather a blurring of boundaries, random, so there's no regularity to it. Parts and pieces of faces morphing into other parts and pieces of faces."

"Wow! I like it. So this would be one face at a time, or what?"

"Could be, but I'm thinking more. Let's call the photos or parts of photos objects. I'm thinking of maybe twenty to thirty objects on the screen at any given time. The spatial requirements, components could be worked out. Or even set to evolve organically."

"So theoretically a screen could contain only eyes?"

"It could, given it's random, although that would probably be a rare occurrence. But if you like eyes, we could filter them out, play around with only eyes."

"Damn, this sounds fucking interesting!" Riordan stuck his hand into the pocket of his khakis and fished around, eventually coming up with a wad of scuffed business cards, one of which he handed to Jack.

"Give me a call. I'd like to talk further about this." "Sure," said Jack, laughing. Maybe I could make a living off rich artists if I quit UniCode."

"You thinking about that?"

"There are days…"

Lal and Charles had catered the event: poached cod with a brandied green peppercorn sauce, steamed broccoli, a beet salad with capers and blueberries, cups of Avgolemono soup.

Riordan gave a speech, then Per gave a speech, then dessert was served, pear halves with vanilla sorbet, topped with shaved chocolate. Snifters of brandy.

Later that evening, Jack found himself talking to Riordan again, confessing to him the job stress he was experiencing, the incidents of forgetfulness.

"Huh," said Riordan. "Memory's a funny thing. It comes and goes."

"Seems like it's going more these days. I even started taking Prevagen."

"Is it helping?"

"I don't know. Nothing substantial."

"Hey, I have a friend, Diedre, that was having bad memory issues. She even thought she might be getting early Alzheimer's. Got a bunch of tests done, CAT scan, the whole nine yards. She was taking that Prevagen a while. It didn't really work. But she found something that did. Cleared her right up."

"What's it called?"

"Can't remember," Riordan laughed. "But I'll find out. She gets it on the Web. I don't think they sell it at stores. Give me your phone number. I'll text you tomorrow."

5

InSight. Google it. It's made by Blu-Pharma, but you don't need a scrip. Pricey though.

Jack texted Riordan back. *Thanks!*

Earlier this morning he'd gone for a walk and forgotten his keys again. He was ready to try anything. He Googled InSight and Blu-Pharma, and pulled up an attractively designed page that obviously had a lot of money behind it. They seemed to specialize in products for the Silver Set, as they called it. Pain relief supplements, fiber supplements. That sort of thing. He found InSight rather quickly, and damn, Riordan was right. It *was* expensive, two bucks a capsule, and the smallest batch was 60, a month's supply. Jack filled in the form, his name, address, phone, email and credit card information, and hit the order button. After a nanosecond during which the screen read "Processing" then a "Thank you for your order" screen replaced it. They'd promised overnight delivery.

It wasn't the next day, but the one after.

When Jack got home from work, a small rectangular white cardboard box was on the shelf under his mailbox. He picked it up, remarkably light, and turned it over. Blu-Pharma was using every design ploy to look legitimate, and who knows, maybe they were.

Once inside he sliced the tape and lifted the clear plastic bottle out of the box. It was filled with grey and green capsules. He pulled one apart and saw it contained multi-colored powder. There was a short, printed paragraph accompanying the bottle. It read:

Thank you for purchasing our products. We at Blu-Pharma adhere to a rigorous safety protocol, and use only the finest ingredients in our products. Everything is natural, and when possible, organic. We use no synthesized or laboratory manufactured ingredients. We hope the product lives up to your expectations, and look forward to doing business with you in the future.

The label, soft violet, repeated some of the same information, gave dosage, two a day, one morning, one evening, and a list of ingredients: Hericium erinaceus, Ashwagandha, Gotu kola, Kelp, Ginko biloba, Seakale, and something called simply organic aesther compounds. Jack immediately Googled it, and got results for both ether and ester compounds. Nothing for aesther.

He ran the tap water cold and filled his glass, then popped one of the capsules, took a gulp of water, and swallowed it. There was a rather astringent aftertaste that quickly dissipated. Well, here goes nothing, he thought.

But the results were rather dramatic. By the second day he was noticeably more acute, more energetic. Before he went out, he automatically generated mental lists and double-checked them. He'd done this before haphazardly, but this was, if he dared call it that, an automated procedure.

At work, lines of code became crystalline, their depth reflecting their purpose. He worked faster, took fewer breaks, returned home later. He seemed filled with renewed vigor and purpose. And after a week went by without forgetting anything, he admitted to himself that *InSight* was actually working.

Well fine. Great even. That little issue was taken care of. Jack added InSight to his daily routine of morning and evening supplements. Vitamin D, Centrum, B12.

One of its immediate impacts was heightening his sensory perception.

Jogging the Burke-Gilman that evening, Jack experienced the songs of various birds in the alder, dogwood and blackberries along the trail – thrushes, towhees, warblers, waxwings, grosbeaks – with startling clarity. And for the first time in a long time he began to stretch out, run, and it was as if the chorus of birdsong, each with its own tone and hue, its own rhythm and cadence, were moving through him, were moving him. A synesthesia of sorts powering him along. He ran effortlessly to its rhythm.

Later than evening, laying the novel he was reading aside, Jack sensed his body humming like a perfect machine. He hadn't felt this good in years. He got up, poured himself a small glass of brandy then turned on the stereo, giving a voice command. Bach's *Cello Sonata in G Minor* flooded the small room, and Jack sank into the sofa, and gazed out over the dark water of Lake Washington, and it seemed as if the darkness of the lake and the music entered him simultaneously, created a synthesis of sound and sight that took him somewhere far, far away.

6

Jack awoke with a start. He was sitting on the sofa in exactly the same position as last night. The brandy glass had fallen to the floor, and the Gabbeh rug was darker blue where it had absorbed the brandy. The stain looked like an outstretched hand. The mantle clock glowed 4:38. Light was leaking into the sky. And as he gazed out the window at incipient dawn, he suddenly remembered a most remarkable and horrifying dream. And promptly vomited onto the Gabbeh, smothering the brandy stain.

After work, he called Per and asked if he could stop by.

"The place is a mess," Per said. "Still haven't cleaned up. How about we catch a drink somewhere. Maybe dinner."

"How about *The Seaplane*? Seven? You sound beat."

"That isn't the half of it."

"See you then."

Jack spotted Per across the room sitting in a booth nursing a martini and reading a magazine. He wove his way through the tables and slipped into the banquette across from him. Per was reading a *New Yorker* and looked up.

"Jack. Hey."

"Hey." Jack took his phone out and placed it on the table. "A couple of guys are working on something with a midnight firing line. I may get called in."

"Ha, on call, like a doctor. Hope you make that big dinero."

"Yeah, right." Jack waved dismissively. "I don't mind."

"I know, it's your life, right?" Per laughed, and Jack gave him a wry grin. "You look, I don't know, off."

The grad-student-aged waitress, tall, with her chestnut hair in a robust ponytail, stopped, and Jack ordered a pilsner.

"You had that 'I need to talk bad' tone of voice. What's up?"

"Ah, you read me like a book. I want to tell you about a dream

I had last night. At least I hope it was a dream."

"What do you mean you hope it was a dream? That sounds intriguing." Per drummed his fingers on the table.

"Well, it was a dream. It had to be." He stared at Per but said nothing else.

The beer came, and Jack waved off the glass, drinking directly from the bottle.

"Let me tell you about it. I'll let you decide."

"Sounds fair," Per said, still smiling.

"Okay, here goes. I was in a dying woman's body, experiencing the remainder of her life. Hearing, seeing, feeling as she did."

"Dying woman?"

"Critically injured."

"Could you feel her pain?" Per asked laughing. "Like a good liberal?"

"Fuck you, Per. This is…" Jack stopped talking, looked down and shook his head, then faced Per. "I could. My body was exploding with it. Knives everywhere."

"Jesus. Go on."

"I, as the woman, was thrown out of a car. The dream started as I/her was lying on a damp sidewalk, but I knew I/her had been thrown out of a car.

"Cut the I/her shit. I follow."

"It was a rainy night. I saw the back of the car, a 1951 Ford coupe, as it peeled away."

"You know your cars," Per quipped.

"I saw the rear of the car as it took off. Chrome bumper, scarlet oval taillights, Ford insignia. I looked it up on the web. The license plate was Illinois. DJU89. I caught the street sign as well. Wabash. So I'm guessing Chicago. There was a bar down the street, *Delaney's*. Blue neon. I couldn't see the intersecting street."

Jack paused and took a long drink from the bottle of pilsner, then lowered it to the table and continued.

"Over the next indeterminate period of time, I, as the woman, crawled up three cement stairs and into the lobby of an apartment building. It was by far the most difficult thing I've ever experienced. The apartment was directly adjacent to where I'd been shoved out of the car.

"The lobby was luxuriously warm. It smelled faintly of cigarettes, dust, lilac perfume. I remember staring up at a row of brass mailboxes. Tiny round pearl-white buttons underneath. The row of mailboxes had a Dutch painterly quality. That light. Like a Vermeer.

"I also remember several newspapers scattered on the black and white tile floor. One was the *Chicago Daily News,* the date was November 2, 1951. The headline was *Atomic Explosion Witnessed By US Troops.*"

"This is strange Jack. Vivid."

"Tell me about it. I remember pointing at the mailboxes, then my arm losing all strength, coordination, falling to the floor. Then it all went black."

"Huh."

"I'm assuming she died."

"This is strange. Very strange."

"I caught her reflection in the lobby window when I was lying there. Pretty. A thin face, pronounced cheekbones, long dark hair, pearl earrings. Her face was gashed on the left side, and scraped from hitting the pavement. Her nose looked broken. Her eyes, deep blue, were terrified, but angry too. She was brave. I could feel that."

"Maybe she operated in that world. You know, one where being thrown out of a car isn't unheard of."

"That's what I thought. She didn't seem innocent, the way a kidnapped college girl would."

The waitress stopped by, and they ordered dinner without consulting the menu. *The Seaplane* was a regular haunt. Fish and chips for Jack, a cup of chowder and a cheeseburger for Per. And another round of drinks.

"So what do you think?" Jack asked after the waitress sashayed off.

"You ever had a dream like that before?"

"Never. At least that I can remember. I'm always myself in my dreams. Never someone else." Jack killed his beer. "And my senses were so acute. It didn't feel like a dream. In retrospect, like I was hyper-awake. And in addition to everything, there was a sense of déjà vu about it."

"Huh," Per said, tipping his martini for the final drop, setting the flared glass on the table with a practiced move.

"But there's more."

"Go on."

"I got curious, so I checked online. *The Chicago Daily News* went out of business in 1978. No online records that I could find. So I called the Chicago Public Library and talked with a reference librarian. A really nice woman named Sara Fields. She's going to check the newspaper records around November 2nd and see if there's anything about the death of this woman. There were apparently four major Chicago newspapers. Two morning, two afternoon. She'll send me whatever she finds."

"Crazy. You think this may have actually happened?"

"I'm beginning to think so. The dream was so realistic, like I was actually there."

"Like you were reliving this woman's memory."

"Well in a way. But if she's dead, there would be no way to tap into her memory, would there?"

"Who knows?" Per smiled. "Despite our science and certainty, there's a great deal of mystery in the universe. Maybe all our myriad consciousnesses are swimming around out there in some celestial ocean, and you just took a swim. Let's wait for the librarian's report."

"To tell you the truth, I'm a bit nervous about this."

"Why?"

"I've had a lot of weird symptoms lately."

"I know you've been mega-stressed. You think it has something to do with that?"

"I told you about the memory lapses, right?"

"Yeah."

"Well, it could all be stress related."

The waitress brought their dinners, had just laid them out, when Jack's phone buzzed. He picked it up and glanced at it.

"Damn." Then called out "Hey" to the waitress, caught her before she'd gotten too far away.

"Can I get a to-go box?"

The waitress said "Sure," and headed off to get him one.

"Sorry dude. Needed on this. I'll keep you posted." Jack stood, as the waitress returned with the box.

"Sorry. Have to go into work, he said to the waitress."

"No problem." She flashed him a vague smile.

Jack threw a twenty on the table.

"Could you cover this if it's more?"

"Sure." Per palmed the twenty. "I'm a bit worried about you, dude. Take care, okay."

"Yeah, yeah. Talk with you soon."

7

The next day, Wednesday, an early afternoon email from Sara Fields, the librarian at Chicago Public Library Jack had talked with, arrived in his mailbox. That little paperclip next to it, so Jack knew it contained attachments. He opened it and read the short note.

> *Jack, good talking to you the other day. Here's what I found. I even searched a few months out, but as you can see not much. Short articles in two papers. Let me know if you need further assistance.*
>
> *Sara*

He opened the first attachment. It was a short, single paragraph write-up in the *Chicago Tribune*, one of the four newspapers operating at the time.

> "Around 7 PM last night a woman's body was found in an apartment lobby at 1767 South Wabash Avenue by a resident couple on their way out to dinner. Police responded to the call, but offered no identification of the woman. The couple told police the woman didn't live in their building, and they'd never seen her in the neighborhood. One of the responding officers, Officer Howard Black, told this reporter that the woman had been shot and knifed. An investigation is underway."

The next day article, also from *The Chicago Tribune*, said about the same thing, however there was an obviously retouched photograph of the woman, with a request for information from anyone who might recognize her.

Chicago was two hours ahead, thought Jack, so it would be around 4:30. He looked up the Chicago Police Department, suffered through a near-endless number of transfers, and finally talked with a desk sergeant who proved moderately helpful.

"Yeah, we got cold cases that go back that far but they ain't computerized. To tell you the truth they're in shoe-boxes in the cellar of the archives, and I got no one that's got time to even go near that morass."

When Jack got home from work, he called Per and filled him in.

"So it really happened."

"Seems so."

"Could it be coincidence?"

"No. The address matched the street, and the photograph was poor quality, but definitely her. It happened, and somehow I relived it."

"Maybe she chose you to find who killed her."

"You know, Per, I had the same weird thought. What do you think I should do?"

"Go to Chicago?"

"Can't. Work's too crazy right now."

"Work's always crazy, Jack."

"I know."

"Damn, this is one of the weirdest things I've ever heard. I don't know what to think."

"Well, she existed, and she was murdered and thrown out of a car. And I know the make and license number of the car."

"Call the FBI. They have a Seattle office, don't they?"

"Already thought of that. They have an office on Third. I'm going to be in Seattle Friday. I should stop in, right?"

"You should definitely stop in."

8

The FBI office in Seattle was a newer twelve story on 3rd Street near the Public Library, buff-white cement with vertical rectangular windows, hundreds of slatted eyes staring out at the world.

Jack walked up to the reception desk feeling anxious, and the abrupt manner of the desk officer, Dahlgren according to his name tag, gave him no reassurances.

Jack explained that he had possible information on a cold case murder in Chicago.

"Did you call the Chicago police?"

Jack explained that they'd essentially blown him off.

"Why do you think this would be of any interest to the FBI?" Dahlgren's voice was flat, cold as polished stone.

"I think there might be mob involvement."

"Mob?"

"Organized crime."

"And you think this why?"

"I'd like to explain it to an agent if possible."

Dahlgren gave him an icy stare and picked up the phone. Jack was both surprised and heartened to see it was a land-line. He watched as Dahlgren spoke into the phone, then replaced it on its cradle.

"Have a seat. An agent will be out shortly."

The waiting room was comfortable, airy, not too much different than his doctor's office, although there were always a lot more people there. Landscape and abstract color-field art hung on a few walls, along with plaques featuring official-looking accolades, awards, diplomas and the like. The array of magazines gravitated towards outdoor sports. Sailing, climbing, biking, skiing. Jack picked up *SKI* and began thumbing through it, settling on an article about urban skiing. Cities with accessible ski areas, including a few paragraphs on

Seattle and Snoqualmie. Jack had skied Snoqualmie when he was in high school, but not since. He preferred snow-shoeing anymore to downhill skiing, but truthfully had no time to do either.

He was reading about Salt Lake City, which was trying hard to shed its Mormon image by metastatic growth of brew-pubs, boutique distilleries and the like, when he heard a woman call his name.

He looked up and watched as a lithe dark-haired woman called his name again. She could have been a lovely doctor at a medical center except for the large pistol attached to her belt.

Jack stood up, realizing that she only shorted his 6-2 frame by an inch.

"I'm Jack Toyokata," he said.

"I'm Juanita Hernandez. Please come with me."

Jack followed her through a doorway, up an elevator, where they did not speak, to floor 7, and down a long hallway lined with doors, many of them wide open. She was very pleasant to walk behind, Jack thought, her hips swaying as the muscular cheeks of her ass lifted side-to-side, and her hair listed slightly. Jack caught the scent of a Hawaiian flower, pikake or plumeria, and thought Juanita would have looked just fine with a flower in her hair.

The offices they passed were staffed by people who sat at computers, and in this way were similar to most white-collar work environments. Again, with the exception of large guns worn in various customs. Shoulders, small of the back, waist. Some just lay on the desk like a threat.

Juanita opened a closed door bearing her name on a small rectangular gold plate, and ushered him in. There were two office chairs in front of a partial desk, and Jack chose the nearest one. Juanita walked behind the desk and sat down. Her office had one of the vertical rectangular windows, and she made use of its light to stimulate photosynthesis in two hanging pothos, and a raphis palm in an elaborately decorated Mexican pot.

"Do you have a problem if I record this?"

"Nope."

Jack studied a photograph on her desk of two handsome boys in baseball uniforms and gloves smiling for the photographer.

Juanita placed a digital recorder on the desk midway between them, clicked a button on. Jack saw the red light change to green.

"This is agent Juanita Hernandez interviewing Mr. Jack Toyokata. The time is 10:16 am, the date is June 7th."

Then Juanita looked up suddenly, fixing Jack with a gaze that was equally intimidating and seductive.

"What's on your mind, Mr. Toyokata?"

"Call me Jack. Please."

"Jack." She said it as if tasting the word in her mouth, and Jack could see her soft brown eyes glitter momentarily.

Jack had rehearsed what he was going to say, but anticipated he was going to tell his story to some macho officer like Dahlgren. Juanita disarmed him completely.

"I witnessed a murder."

"Okay. Did you report it to the police?"

"Well, sort of. And I didn't really witness it. Well I did. Sort of." Her eyes were twinkling again, her voice calm but firm.

"And you reported it to the police?"

"Sort of."

"Why don't you start at the beginning, Mr. Toyokata." Juanita sat back in her chair.

So he did.

Jack realized he'd stopped talking a few minutes ago and Juanita was staring at him with a combination of patience, disbelief, mirth and what? Sympathy?

"You're finished?"

"I am."

"So...." Juanita paused a moment. "So, the desk agent told me you told him there was a mob connection. You didn't say anything about the mob."

"Sorry. I said that so he'd let me talk with someone."

Juanita's eyes twinkled again.

"What do you think? Can you help me?"

"I'm going to surprise myself with this one, Jack, and probably you as well. But I think I can." Juanita ran a hand through her thick hair and leaned forward. "I'm going to Chicago in a week for a set of meetings. I'll make some inquiries while I'm there. I'll give you a call if and when I find anything out. Don't get your hopes up."

"Wow. Thanks. Thanks so much. That's it, then?"

"For now, that's it."

Jack stood and Juanita followed suit.

"I have to walk you down."

They shook hands in the lobby in front of Dahlgren's desk.

"Thank you, Mr. Toyokata. You've most certainly made my day much more interesting."

9

Over the next week Per called several times.

Jack told him about his meeting with the FBI agent. Per peppered him with questions, but seemed pleased.

"She believed your half-assed story. I can't believe it myself, even with those newspaper articles you sent me."

"I don't think she believed it exactly. I think it piqued her curiosity. She's going to Chicago in a few days, said she'd check out the story in more detail. If she finds something, she might buy in."

"God Jack, how do you feel about all this?"

"Freaked out. The whole "why me?" thing. But I'm trying to stay grounded. Deal with the immediate content and events. This could turn out to be nothing."

"Nothing but a dream," Per added.

"I'm too damn busy with work to let this get under my skin in a big way. Two new contracts starting this week."

"That company works you hard, Jack."

"All tech companies are like that now. The field is way too competitive. Everybody's underbidding, rushing projects. But if the work is shabby, bye-bye. There's another company just across the road. Clients can be *super* picky."

"I understand the situation, Jack. I just think these companies have the workers over a barrel. Sure, you make a lot of money, but at what cost to the quality of your life?"

Per called again Thursday to invite Jack to dinner at his condo Friday evening.

"They're letting you take Friday evening off, aren't they?"

"Far as I know." Jack laughed. "Who's coming?"

"Just Marla, and one other woman. I think you might like her. And vice versa."

"God, Per, I can meet women on my own."

"Yeah, you do such a marvelous job at that don't you?"

"Sarcasm doesn't become you."

"Sarcasm is my world-view, Jack. That and cynicism. And pessimism." He laughed. Per had a great laugh. Very Nordic. Cool and warm at the same time.

"Okay, okay, I'll come. What shall I bring?"

"Shall. A future-looking modal verb. Archaic, though well-used by lawyers. But I digress. Bring Prosecco. Two bottles. Good stuff. Santa Margherita. It's on sale at D'Laurrenti's. I'm making Bellinis."

"Oh."

"Don't sound so thrilled. You'll like them."

"I thought it was just Marla and another woman?"

"Huh?"

"You said 'them'."

"I was referring to the Bellinis. You'll like them."

"I've had Bellinis before."

"They go down way too easy and loosen the spirit. That's what we're after here, Jack. A loosening of spirit."

"Go ahead, say it."

"You're too uptight Jack."

"Thanks, now tell me about the woman."

"No way. That takes all the fun out of it. You have to ask her yourself."

Jack could see Per smile.

"She's very attractive. Hot, even. Her name is Rachael."

Jack was thinking about Samantha, the last woman Per had introduced him to. How she'd told him to "fuck off," metaphorically of course, less than two weeks ago. The whole thing suddenly wearied him. He didn't have the energy to start another relationship just now.

"You're going to the reading, right?"

"You have me for two nights, Per."

"Good, good. See you Friday."

"Cheers."

Jack threw on some shorts, a Seahawks T-shirt, and ran the stairs to the condo's lobby, out the front doors onto the Burke-Gilman.

Jack had started running again, something he'd done for much of his life, but an activity that had lost its place over the past three years. But now he was back, largely thanks to his doctor's suggestion, and serious about maintaining it.

The wind was brisk, the sky leaden, whitecaps dancing on the lake. A bicycle swerved by him, but there were few other people out. Jack ran south, exiting at Ballinger Way, trotting across Bothell Way, the parking lot and entering Third Place Books. There was the sudden rush of warmth, the scent of pastries and fresh-brewed coffee, and crossed the lobby to the coffee bar, walking past a display featuring Per's newest novel, *Quaint Toys, Sjarmerende Leker* in Norwegian, surrounded by kid's wooden toys from a by-gone era. A sudden poignant nostalgia for simpler times came over Jack. The poster announced that local writer Per Morten would be reading from his new novel Saturday evening at 7:00. Wine and hors d'oeuvres would be served. Jack had already planned to attend.

Jack ordered a cup of Seattle's Best coffee, grabbed a *Seattle Times* and sat down at one of the small tables in the courtyard. For the next ten minutes he perused the news, Amazon dominating new building projects, the homeless situation drawing fire from the mayor, who accused city council of stonewalling. There was a section D story about elephants that caught his eye. Their intelligence and social structure.

He tipped the cup to drain it when his phone buzzed.

A text from Riordan asking Jack to call him, which he did immediately.

"Hey," Riordan said, "Have you thought about my offer?"

"You're offer?"

"At the party. I asked if you'd be willing to work with me on software related to my art."

"Oh. Sorry man. Sorry. I didn't really take it seriously. I'm way too busy with work to consider taking anything else on now."

"Quit your job. Come to work for me."

"Quit my job."

"Yeah. I talked to another friend of mine, a fabric artist. She'd be interested, and I think I could get a few more people on board. Doing art with computers is big right now. We'd pay you well, of course."

"Do you have any idea how much I make now?"

"More than we'd pay you. But this would be cool-cool work, my friend. And you'd work with artists, not a bunch of Cheeto -eating nerds."

"I like nerds. Come to think of it, I like Cheetos."

"That's a problem, Jack." Riordan paused momentarily. "Why don't you think about it?" Let me know if you're even a little interested and we'll talk details."

"Okay, I'll do that. Ah, thanks, I guess."

"You'd have a lot more freedom than you have now. You

wouldn't be tethered or on call all the time."

"How did you know I was on call."

"Per told me. He says you're a slave to that fucking company. What's their name? Unicode? Sounds Nazi."

Jack sighed. "Okay, I'll let you know. But don't count on it."

10

FBI agent Juanita Hernandez called Jack mid-morning Tuesday of the following week. There was copious background noise and Jack pictured her somewhere extremely public: the lobby of a large government building, a crowded department store, a convention center.

"Mr. Toyokata, can you hear me okay?"

"I can hear you. Lots of background noise though."

"Sorry, I'm downtown at the State of Illinois building. It's crowded. Here, wait." A few moments later, "Is that better?"

"Much."

"Okay. I verified your story and found out a few things. Do you have a minute?"

A couple of his team members were looking at him curiously. "Just a minute," he said. He stood abruptly, and walked out into a wide airy hallway holding the phone too tightly, his heart racing.

"Yes, what did you find out?"

"I found out the owner of the car, found the cold case file, and found a cop involved with the case. Only problem is he's 94, in a retirement home, and has Alzheimer's."

"Holy shit! That's awesome."

"No, Mr. Toyokata, the Grand Canyon is awesome. This is standard police work."

"I'm still awed."

"It's a beginning. Look, I can't talk now. Can we meet again Friday? I'll be back in Seattle."

"Definitely."

"Good. I've scheduled you for a 10:25 appointment. I hope that's okay."

"10:25. That works."

"See you then Mr. Toyokata."

"Call me Jack."

But she'd already clicked off.

11

It turned out to be another rabid work week.

At Tuesday's managerial meeting, Jack was told the new contract with Prosipio Data had been attenuated. The deadline, which his team was already struggling to meet, had been trimmed by three days. The deadline was now this Friday.

"We can't do it. We're stretched already. There's the Boeing trajectory study."

"Thought you said Roger's all over that?" Ken Billetts, Jack's supervisor asked.

"He is."

"Cut him and put him on this," Billetts said.

"I need another body."

"I can't spare anyone."

"I need Emily."

"Especially not her."

"Then it's impossible."

"Even with Roger on it?"

"Yes." Jack was getting sick of being wedged between a rock and a hard place. He was sick of eating cups of tepid noodles morning, noon, and night.

"How long are your days?"

"Tens. A few longer."

"Jump it to twelves and I'll give you Emily."

"Damn, Ken. The team needs a break after this. We've been burning since late February. We're running out of fuel."

Ken Billetts gave Jack a hard look. And Jack knew exactly what it meant. *If you can't do it someone else can.*

"You can have Emily until Friday when the project's done. Three o'clock. That's what we promised Prosipio."

"You know, Ken, just once it would be nice if I could be part of these negotiations."

"Ain't gonna happen Jack. Your team can have the weekend off.

That's the best I can do. Now get to work."

"We can have the weekend off," Jack told his crew at an impromptu meeting he called later that day, "can you fucking believe that?"

He glanced at the four people, his crackerjack crew, waiting to hear what he had to say.

"We are working our asses off people, and the only reward we get is to work harder."

"And the weekend off," chipped Curry, brushing his frizzy blond hair out of his eyes for the thousandth time.

"At least I can get wasted Saturday night, and worship the god of my choice Sunday morning," said Miguel.

"Praise the lord," chanted Roger. "What about the Boeing thing?"

"Shelve it. For now."

"People, Emily Station. Emily, … Roger, Curry, Miguel. You've worked with Miguel before. Everyone's top shelf. Miguel, brief Emily and Roger up to speed on this Prospiro thing. Then we need to tighten up and work late. When we walk out of here tonight, I want to be able to see daylight Friday afternoon. Emily, I want you on the front-end. We've identified several pages of user issues, so start with those. Curry and Miguel are working on the core. Roger, you're on the Oracle interface. We need to be able to interface with all the usual suspects. SQL, Access, Mongo, Redis, Apache. I'll be helping as needed, as well as cloud interfacing. Questions?"

Roger was already heading off, and Emily and Miguel had their heads together.

"Okay. Off to work. Emily, let me borrow Miguel for a minute."

Miguel followed Jack into the hallway.

"I've got an important meeting mid-morning Friday in Seattle. I may need you to package this for me. I should be back out here by noon."

"What's the real drop-dead on this?"

"Three o'clock." Jack, like most team leaders, cut the real deadlines by a few hours in order to have a little wiggle room.

"No problem."

"What do you think of this 'weekend off' shit?"

"Well, we've worked the last two weekends, and my paychecks are swollen, but a day off now and then is a nice touch. I mean, none of us have a life, right?"

"Ken's a bitch, man."

"You know it's from further upstairs."
"Maybe I've been doing this too long."
Miguel gave Jack an appraising look.
"Maybe you have."

12

When Jack walked into the FBI building in downtown Seattle Friday morning he was feeling conflicted. Anxious because the Prospero project wasn't rounding into shape as quickly as they'd anticipated, and excited because Juanita had come through for him. And he had no idea why.

Desk agent Dahlgren had been replaced with a short no-neck whose goofy grin negated any sense of threat. His nametag read Ted Farrell, and Jack bet that Farrell used that goofy grin to his advantage.

Jack told him he had a 10:25 meeting with Juanita and was told to take a seat. Three or four minutes later, partway into the same article on Salt Lake City, Juanita materialized. Today she wore a long magenta cotton dress and a white blouse. The effect was stunning, her luxuriant black hair falling over the blouse, her service revolver on her hip. Needless to say, Jack didn't travel in the circles that brought him in contact with women such as Juanita.

"How's work at UniCode?"

"Okay," Jack answered, wondering how Juanita knew he worked at UniCode, then realizing she probably knew more about him than he did.

Juanita led Jack down the hallway to the elevator where they waited in silence, then more silence, a bit more uncomfortable, inside, then out into the busy, well-lit hallway, and into her office, where Jack took the same chair he had previously.

"Well," Juanita said, steepling her fingers on the desk. "Let's be candid, Mr. Toyokata.

How did you really find out about this murder?"

"I told you."

"I know you told me, but I don't believe you."

"Well, I don't know what to say. I barely believe it myself."

"Well let's let it ride for a bit. As I said on the phone, I did find a few things out."

Juanita slid a manila folder over and opened the cover.

"The car was registered to a Mr. Cameron Phelps. Phelps had ties to the Irish mob in Chicago. He'd come over from Boston, and established quite a reputation before he was shot-gunned down in a diner on Kedzie. So, you were right. The mob was involved.

"I also drove by the apartment you claim to have seen, on south Wabash, but it's been torn down. There's a new apartment complex with retail on the ground floor. So that's a dead end.

"The cold case report is meager. There is little information on the victim, other than obvious physical characteristics. No name, a guess at age. She was Irish as well, by-the-way, which may mean something, or nothing. And, very odd for that time period, she had a tattoo on her lower back. Some Celtic symbol. I'll give you a photo of it. I tried to track it down but couldn't find much.

"Two officers worked the case. John McNeely and Rudy Pearson. Pearson is dead, and McNeeley resides in the Spring Gulch retirement community in Elgin, in the memory care unit. To give you an idea how spry he is, he's been referred to hospice twice. Pulled out of it both times. So, he's a possible. I talked with one of his nurses who told me he was in and out of lucidity. Mostly out."

"Did you talk with him?"

"No. They told me he couldn't handle phone calls, and I didn't have time to drive out."

"Hmm."

"The only semi-encouraging piece of information is the police write-up. There were apparently several similar murders. Women thrown from cars, suffering similar wounds. McNeely and Pearson traced two of them to a gentlemen's club, and conjectured that the other two women, including your Jane Doe, were also hookers or dancers. They questioned people at several clubs but no one identified her. I don't know how far McNeeley and Pearson went with the two identified women, but it doesn't look like there was further development in this file."

"Damn." Jack slapped the table. "A lot of dead ends."

"That's the way it goes sometimes, especially with cold cases. The particulars end up erased. But I do have a theory."

"What's that?"

"I think the mob was using these girls up, then dumping them. Probably had them into some really kinky stuff. The Irish mob was known for heavy S&M. A lot of the guys got off on it. Particularly playing with strangulation. It's a known fact that women died."

"Sick."

"Yeah. Real sick. And based on the lack of write-up in the Jane Doe's file, I think McNeeley and Pearson were pressured to drop the case. That's something McNeeley could clarify if you decide to visit him."

"I wasn't planning on going to Chicago. Hell, I could barely escape long enough to meet you today."

"So?"

"So what do we do now?"

Her eyes twinkled. "The real question is what are you going to do now?" She flipped a lock of hair off her forehead. "I pulled a favor, but there's no case here for me. Everyone is dead, and there's no sense tracking down next of kin or descendants of the mobsters. This was tragic, but it all happened long ago. I'm going to have to put the ball back in your court, Mr. Toyokata. And I wish you all the luck."

"Damn. It's so frustrating."

"Welcome to my world." Juanita stretched, and Jack watched the fabric of her white cotton blouse tighten across her breasts.

"Say, uh, I'm in Seattle a lot. You want to catch coffee or lunch sometime?"

Juanita stared at Jack, a smile playing her lips.

"You do have one of the most original come-ons I've encountered. The whole dead woman in Chicago story."

"Thanks. I worked on that one a long time." He pointed. "Those your kids?"

Juanita's expression became more serious.

"Yeah. Gabriel, he's the oldest. And little Angel. The angel of my eye. They love that game of baseball."

"They play, obviously."

"Little League, rec league, school ball. They go to Bishop Blanchet High School. It's north of Green Lake. Angel's only a freshman, but he's on the varsity team already."

"That's great." Jack realized he was stretching it. "You live by Green Lake?"

Juanita laughed. "You're in the wrong line of work, Mr. Toyokata. You should be a cop."

"No thanks. I've got as much pressure as I can stand."

"I live in Ballard. My sons spend weeks with me, and weekends with their dad in Leschi." Juanita shuffled some papers on her desk then looked up at him. "Does that provide you with the information you sought?"

She was smiling, so Jack pushed it.

"Yes. I think it does. Quite nicely put. So, coffee sometime?"

Juanita hesitated, but Jack knew what she would say.

"Sure. You have my card. Send me an email or text next time you're going to be in the area."

"I'd really like that."

"And if you get any other ideas or information." She waved the file. "I'll keep it open."

13

Sunday morning, and Jack woke early. Five forty. He poured granola into a bowl, some almond milk, took his pills, turned the stereo on, told it to play Lara St. John, Bach's Sonata #2 in A minor, settled onto the couch, and spooned the cereal into his mouth as Ms. St. John's violin ripped into his heart. Insight was now a part of his morning supplement regime, and while the initial clarity he'd experienced had faded, his memory had definitely improved. He hadn't forgotten anything lately. Whether it was InSight or coincidence, he didn't know. Maybe he'd get scientific, stop the InSight, and see what happened. But not today.

The dinner get-together at Per's the night before was relaxed. There was no chemistry between him and Rachael, and neither wanted to manufacture something. That aside, the Bellinis went down like air, and conversation ranged wildly from European socialized medicine, to population dynamics in the local orca pods, to the Seattle Sounders losing their star mid-fielder. In other words, a fairly typical Seattle dinner tete-a-tete. And Per's girlfriend, Marla, had created from scratch scrumptious crab cakes, whiskey crab soup, and a divine Caesar salad, with, of course, chunks of Alaskan king crab meat on top. Despite the failed match-up, Jack had a marvelous time, leaving late, happy, stuffed and slightly tipsy.

And now, spooning cereal, listening to Ms. St. John, he thought about Juanita. He enjoyed thinking about her. He'd been working non-stop for over twenty days, and having the weekend off, was lethargic. And guilty. Like he should be doing something.

He laughed and threw a pillow across the room.

"Screw that. No guilt!"

He turned on the TV, watched pieces of a couple news shows then decided to go for a run. He pulled on shorts, running shoes, a T-shirt advertising Bumbershoot, and headed out the door. It wasn't yet seven o'clock.

Jack had been running around two weeks now, and was

increasing his distance by a quarter mile or so each run, feeling better and better the further he ran. He was finally reaching those "effortless" experiences that used to visit him when he ran long distance in high school and college.

He sprinted across Bothell Way and turned north onto the Burke-Gilman, immediately passing a high school cross-country group running the opposite direction.

The air was crisp, around fifty-five, and the sun hadn't yet crested the ridge across Lake Washington. Several boats broke the glassy surface trolling for kokanee salmon. As he ran, he again experienced the myriad cadences of sound and rhythm around him, and his running became an effortless blend of music and dance. He came out of his runner's trance around Sammamish Park, and realized he'd just run nearly three miles. The run back would jump his previous distance by over two miles. He thought briefly of getting an Uber, but after a few minutes sucking water from the fountain, he turned around and headed back.

The run back was difficult at first, totally mental, but once Jack hit a stride, it opened up for him and everything clicked into place. And then he suddenly knew the dead woman's name was Cathy. It just came to him out of nowhere, but he knew with all certainty it was true.

When he got home, he texted Juanita and let her know. He doubted it would make any difference, but now he was thinking of taking a trip to Chicago. He wanted to visit the crime scene and see if anything else shook out. He wanted to talk with McNeeley, or at least try. And he wanted to find out more about the Irish mob, which he'd maybe heard of in a movie once, but that was it. And he wanted to visit his cousin Kaito he hadn't seen in years. He'd been due a vacation for over a year, but the calendar never cleared. This time he'd clear it. A great weight was slowly lifted from him.

14

Monday saw the arrival of three new projects, all with short turn-arounds. And Emily had been pulled from his team after the Prospero project was completed last Friday. Jack knew this was unsustainable. He called a short meeting with the team and triaged the projects. Roger was back on the Boeing thing, which he'd wrap up in a couple of days, but until then, it was Jack, Miguel and Curry. Curry took the smallest project, an app for renting electric bikes that some of the northern suburbs were looking at rolling out, and Jack and Miguel settled into the other two, beginning with a video game program that needed a security patch. After he dismissed the team, he went to hunt down his supervisor Ken Billetts, but Ken was out for the day. He made an appointment to see him Tuesday morning at nine, then rejoined Miguel and got to work.

Mid-morning Jack got a brief text from Juanita thanking him for the name Cathy, telling him she'd add it to the file. He was again amazed she hadn't tossed him out on his ear. He knew she didn't believe his story of the dream, if that's what it was, and wondered what her motive was? He assumed she'd found his story intriguing, and knew that if she kept him around, he might leak how he'd come onto the information he'd shared with her. That had to be it. Jack texted back that he would be in Seattle Friday and did she want to meet for lunch.

By mid-afternoon he and Miguel had stolen a pot of coffee from the break room, and were holed up in a small conference room pounding away on keyboards. He still hadn't heard back from Juanita, despite picking up his phone every few minutes.

He got home from work around nine and went for a quick twilight run. He and Miguel were making good progress, and they'd be able to jump on the next project, a security camera flaw, by the end of tomorrow. Tuesday.

Returning from his run, still nothing from Juanita, he poured himself two inches of Dewar's and settled onto the couch with the new Scientific American. An article on micro-particles that "inhabit" our bodies and form complex communication systems caught his interest. As he was reading, his body began to tingle, and a warm flush come over him. His senses became heightened, and he heard sounds normally outside his awareness. The ticking of a clock in the bedroom, a faucet in the kitchen, the hum of the refrigerator, and these sounds became an intertwining fugue of melodies. The mind is a funny thing, he thought, and mine is becoming stranger by the day.

15

Jack woke the next morning still on the sofa, the glass of Scotch on the coffee table nearly full, and the potent memory of another murder.

In this dream, Jack inhabited the body of a man. The man was in an apartment, and Jack knew it was the man's home. The apartment was older, oak molding around the doorways, curved arches between the rooms, off-white walls. Several of the rooms were jammed with books, journals, magazines, all with environmental titles and themes, piled haphazardly wherever there was a semi-flat surface. There were also erratic piles of news clippings, manila folders, notebooks and miscellaneous papers. At least four computers perched on tables and another on a desk, and an iPad crowded stacked plates on a neglected kitchen counter.

The man wandered slowly through the apartment, apparently looking for something, lifting piles of papers, opening folders, but Jack did not have access to the man's thoughts. He was a captive in the man's physical pilot house only. Jack's mind was blank, a purely neutral observer.

Catching the man's reflection in a window, Jack saw the he was tall and supple, wore his long black hair in a ponytail, had pronounced acne scars on his face, and heavy black stubble that attempted to hide the scars. The man wore a red and black wool shirt, black jeans. The man was barefoot.

Suddenly, the ponytailed man cocked his head and turned and walked toward the front door. He stood in front of it for a moment, talking, then after a moment, he reached over and opened it. Two men crowded in, pushing him back, one man closing the door. The first man wore black loafers with tassels, khakis, and a brown leather coat. The second man, much larger, wore gym shoes, blue jeans, and a black leather jacket. The first man, hard looking, hair buzz cut, blond going grey, began talking to the ponytailed man. And although Jack could not hear what he said, Jack knew he was angry. His lips chewed the air sharply, his face tightening, yet his pale blue eyes eerily vacant.

Jack knew the ponytailed man was talking back, but again had no clue as to what he said. Then the second man, ginger hair worn shaggy, a linebacker gone partially to seed, stepped in close and slapped him across the face with the flat of his hand. The ponytailed man stumbled back, tripping over a small table, spilling a pile of papers, and falling to the faded ruby carpet. He managed an awkward roll, and clamored to his feet. Blood ran down his cheek where the big guy's ring had cut him. The smaller man grinned wickedly, said something else to the ponytailed man, but the ponytailed man shook his head vehemently. Slowly, the two intruders slipped on latex gloves, blue for the smaller man, pink for the linebacker. The ponytailed man backed up until a larger table blocked him.

Then suddenly, Jack was aware the two men were looking for something, asking the man where it was. They needed something he had.

Over the next indefinite period of time, which returned to Jack that morning in achingly clear fragments, the two men bound the ponytailed man arms behind back, tied him to a wooden chair, then began to beat him, initially with their fists, then with small saps that they swung at various parts of his body. At times, Jack experienced the man losing consciousness, and pain so consuming he felt himself almost black out. In retrospect he was amazed he hadn't wakened.

The two intruders interrupted their beatings to question the ponytailed man. Jack could not hear the man's answers, but knew they were unsatisfactory. The intruders continued to work him over.

Then suddenly as it began, the beating stopped. Jack could see blood spattered on the man's legs, the floor, the nearby piles of papers and books. The intruder with the buzz cut stood looking down at the man's battered body, then slowly pulled a pistol from under his coat, screwed something Jack figured later was a silencer onto the end of the barrel, raised the gun and asked one final question. The ponytailed man could not lift his head and said nothing.

There was a soft pop, then darkness.

As the memory flowed through him, Jack sat up nails shattered his head, and he vomited abruptly onto the carpet. He sat there for ages, head bent, staring at his vomit soaking into the carpet. At some point he stood up and managed to stumble to the shower, where he vomited again. He forced himself to turn the faucet to the right, and stood under its biting cold sting until he could no longer stand it. Then he turned the water scalding and stood another minute, then turned it off and stepped out.

After toweling off, he made a cup of strong coffee, poured it into his to-go cup, left the condo, took the elevator to the garage, got into his car, started it, and drove to UniCode Redmond campus. It was 6:18 a.m.

16

They met Friday at *Soy Haus* on Capitol Hill, a German-Asian fusion restaurant that was all the current rage. The restaurant didn't take reservations and a line wiggled out the door halfway down the block, but Juanita knew the owner, and Jack found her sitting in a choice corner table on the second floor, overlooking a rainy Broadway. The walls were decorated with landscape scrolls, gilded panels, paintings of castles, articles of antique Asian and German clothing, and of course, shelves of beer steins alternating with saki cups.

Juanita seemed pleased to see him.

After brief chatter they ordered a pair of Heinekens.

"I don't usually drink during the day," Juanita said.

"Me neither, but what the hell."

She held up her beer. "To not drinking during the day."

"Amen," Jack said, clicking glasses. "I had another dream."

"Whoa! You are nothing if not entertaining," Juanita said, that familiar twinkle in her eye. "Let's figure out what we're going to order before we dive into your dream. If it's anything like your Chicago story it might be hard to put aside."

They studied the menu, both deciding on spicy beef spaetzle with root vegetables. Juanita asked if he wanted to split a beet salad.

"Sure."

"Food has gotten interesting, hasn't it?"

"Some would say weird," Jack replied.

"I'm from Oaxaca, Mexico, and a traditionalist at heart, but there are some adventurous chefs out there. Do you know Jose Pina's restaurant? *Dos Casas*?"

"Nope."

"I'll have to take you there. Duck, gingered orange peel and pine nut street tacos. All tortillas and tamales fresh made. And their mole. Absolutely delish! *And*, they have the largest tequila selection in town. But enough about my favorite topic. Tell me what happened."

Her eyes came to rest on him.

They were interrupted by a waitress who took their order.

After the waitress had left, Juanita again said, "Tell me what happened."

Jack reiterated the dream, fielding her questions as they came.

They were both silent at the end of Jack's soliloquy. He'd forced the dream to the periphery of his consciousness all week, and the retelling was cathartic. He worried now he'd been overly dramatic.

"Was there anything to indicate the date, the location?"

"I could see the Space Needle out the living room window."

"Could you tell what direction you were looking?"

"It had to be lower Queen Anne. I could see the Seattle skyline beyond the Needle. So I was looking south, or possibly southwest."

"Good. How about a when?"

Jack closed his eyes and replayed the dream, like a film, rewinding, casting about for a glimmer of memory. Juanita gave him time.

"I know," he said abruptly. "There was a calendar in the kitchen. It hung on the wall behind where they beat him. October, 2008."

"Okay then. It should be easy to check the murder log for that month and see what turns up."

Jack caught Juanita's eyes. They didn't look quite so humorous now.

"Do you believe me?"

"No." She fidgeted with her spoon. "Maybe."

The waitress arrived with their lunch, spaetzle with side dishes of colorful root vegetables. Carrots, radishes, turnips. Another side of beet salad. The waitress set them down carefully then asked, "Anything else? Another beer?"

"No, thanks," said Juanita. Then she turned to Jack. "You don't want another beer, do you?"

"No, one's enough."

The waitress glided away.

"So, do you believe me?" he asked Juanita again.

"I'll check it out." She sipped her beer. "Maybe you're a psychic."

"I doubt it. To tell you the truth, I've never had dreams like this. Ever. And they are not at all fun to experience."

"I bet not. You felt the actual pain, right?"

"Yes. Extreme pain. Like nothing ever. Not that I'm a pain expert or anything."

They shifted gears, talking instead about past relationships,

Juanita's children, politics and work.

"How did you escape marriage, anyway? A good looking fellow like you." Juanita's twinkle had returned, her eyes sparkled with a warm, chestnut light.

"No time. Had some close calls, but I've been literally married to my job since I was twenty-two."

"You look about twenty-two now."

"Hah. My baby face."

Juanita gazed at him for a moment too long. "So, Unicode keeps you hopping?"

"It's rather insane. I shouldn't say this, but Unicode's employees are totally expendable. Everyone works crazy hours, juggling contracts, knowing that if they slack, or err, they are out the door and some new hotshot walks in."

"No job security?"

"None. We work contract to contract. Even me. And I'm a team leader. A manager."

"Wow, had no idea. Are all the tech companies like that?"

"Most of them. Some are a bit better. But it's a totally cutthroat world."

After lunch, Jack walked Juanita back to her car, a BMW X5, parked in a loading zone with an FBI sticker loud on the dash.

"Job comes with benefits," Jack said, nodding towards the sticker.

"A few." She laughed. "Let's do this again."

"Definitely."

"I'll call you as soon as I find anything out."

"Deal."

Juanita slipped into her car and Jack shut the door softly. She gave him a small wave and peeled sharply away from the curb into Broadway traffic.

Jack walked another two blocks, found his Subaru Outback, and drove to Unicode's Lake Union office suite. He nodded at Joy, the entry guard, then walked the main hallway to his favorite workroom. It was deserted, and he breathed a sigh of relief, settling into the customized ergonomic Miller chair, logged in, and got to work.

Juanita called around 4:30, her voice crackling with excitement.

"I found it."

"Seriously?" He had no idea if the dream would prove true. But now there were two of them. That meant something tangible.

"His name was Bill McCandless. He was an independent researcher and activist for environmental causes. Big non-profits, like the Sierra Club and the Wilderness Society hired him, as well as local concerns like Conservation Northwest and Greenways Seattle. But dig this. He was slated to appear in a closed hearing three days after he was killed. He and his lawyer were going to present evidence that Lightfoot Air and Marine, a giant shipping conglomerate, had been capturing baby Orca whales and selling them to sea parks. Strictly illegal."

"Orcas are endangered, right?"

"Damn right they are."

"So, he never got to testify."

"Never."

"So those guys were sent to find what he had, steal it, and kill him."

"Looks that way."

"Wow."

"Yeah, wow."

"So what now?"

"I'd like to set up a meeting next week with the two detectives assigned to the case. Of course it's a cold case by now. But I want to see what they have, see what we can fill in. Can you make time for it?"

"Of course."

"With your work and all?"

"I'm taking some time off."

"Okay, then. I'll make this for Tuesday or Wednesday. It will be at my place. My office," she corrected.

"Sounds good."

"You remember this dream vividly, right?"

"That's right."

"I want you to continue to mine it. Look for things you might have missed. You said you couldn't hear anything, right?

Right."

"Try and read their lips. See if you can't make out anything they said."

"I'll try."

"Good. I'll see you."

17

Jack's Monday meeting with Ken Billetts did not go as planned.

Jack had worked for UniCode for twenty-two years. During that time the company name had changed four times, ownership twice, and management and staff reformed almost constantly. Jack's previous director, Marv Taylor, had treated him well, and while they weren't friends outside work, they were solid work buddies, and had conversationally shared personal lives as well as the usual workplace gossip. But Marv had moved to California a little over a year ago, and Ken Billetts was hired to replace him.

One of Ken's promises to the CEO, Tyler Ryder, who ultimately hired him, was to up production by at least twenty percent without increasing the labor force. This was something he'd achieved at his two previous places of employment. At least on record.

But Jack had talked with people who'd worked for Ken at his previous positions, and the stories weren't pretty. Longer hours, less holidays, fewer breaks, competitive bonuses, and in a couple cases, financial penalties. While pay cuts hadn't surfaced as an option at UniCode, yet anyway, the additional hours and slashed time off were following Ken's historical trajectory.

So when Jack sat down across from Ken to ask for two weeks off he was met with a curt refusal.

"I can give you two days but that's it. We're taking on too much new business to spare you."

Jack had started to argue, then bit his tongue and said "Sure. I understand. Thanks for the two days."

But Ken was already absorbed into his computer screen and tuned out.

Jack got up, and after scanning the numerous productivity awards and golf trophies that adorned Ken's walnut walls, walked away. He was already texting Riordan asking to meet. Maybe working for artists was the way to go. God knows he needed something to change.

The Tuesday meeting with Juanita went much differently.

Jack arrived at the Seattle FBI building a bit late. The desk agent said Juanita was expecting him, and asked if Jack knew how to get to her office.

Jack nodded.

"Okay. 7th floor. If you get lost just ask. Everyone knows Juanita."

The two Seattle Police detectives, Neil Robbins and Ned Brown, were already seated when Jack arrived. Neither bothered to stand, simply extended their arms to shake hands as Juanita introduced them. She reiterated that Jack possibly had information relevant to the Bill McCandless murder. Jack took a seat, noticing there was a new photo on her desk. Her oldest boy Gabriel with his arm around her waist. They were both lit up like LED headlamps.

Ned had a manila folder open on Juanita's desk in front of him. Jack could see there were several crime scene photos mixed in with the reports.

"So, Mr. Toyokata, Ms. Hernandez tells us that you saw the murderers. Just how did you do that?"

"I dreamt it."

Brown began laughing. "That's what she said, but I wanted to hear it from your own mouth."

The other cop, Robbins, didn't seem amused in the slightest. He looked like this was a waste of his time.

"Tell us something we don't know," he said.

"Well I'm not sure of what you know and what you don't, but here goes. There were two of them. One linebacker sized, the other, more a fighter, solid, six feet, ex-military maybe. A hard guy. He had grey-blond hair in a buzz cut." Jack could see Brown shuffling through papers in the folder. "He had a small scar on his face. Here." Jack touched his face below his nose. "On his lip. The scar twisted as he talked."

Robbins exhaled loudly.

"The other guy was large, six-three, maybe two-fifty. He had longish red hair, a diamond stud in his ear."

"How long was his hair?"

"Not super long. It came over his ears. He was wearing a cap. One of those flat caps. Reddish-brown."

"Are these the men you saw, Mr. Toyokata?" Brown laid two photographs in front of Jack. In the photographs, both of the men were younger, dressed differently, and the linebacker's red hair hung down around his shoulders.

"That guy, yes." He pointed to the linebacker. "Not the other one." Then, "Are they suspects?"

"They were suspects, along with several other guys."

"They're hit men. It was a professional hit." Robbins coughed into his hand. "But we could never prove it was them."

"They both had stone cold alibis," Brown added.

"What kind of gun was McCandless shot with?"

"A pistol. I don't know guns. It was skinny, grey and silver, had a long barrel. The buzz cut guy, that's who shot him, screwed a silencer onto the barrel."

"Was it a .22?"

"No idea. I'm not a gun guy."

"You said he was beaten. What did they beat him with?" Brown asked.

"They used their fists at first, then switched to saps. I guess that's what they're called. Small leather bags filled with lead or coins. They seemed methodical, not angry. And where they hit him, well…"

"Well what?"

"They didn't seem to be normal places to hit someone. But I'm guessing they were pressure points or something."

"Go on."

"They worked on him for what seemed like a long time."

"Did you see them find anything?"

"No. The dream ended when they shot him."

"And they still hadn't found anything? At the point the dream ended?"

"No."

Juanita jumped in for the first time.

"What do you think? Did they find what they were looking for?" Robbins took it.

"We surmised they did, since McCandless' lawyers and his girlfriend searched the place after the CSI was completed and didn't find what they were looking for. We're assuming the criminal case would have continued if they had. McCandless was a key witness and had the packet of evidence. He was working for a non-profit called *ORCAfirst*. They had seen some of what McCandless had turned up, but he wanted to retain possession until the hearing."

"Didn't he even give copies to his lawyers?" asked Juanita.

"Nope. That was how he rolled, I guess."

"Judge threw the case out at Lightfoot's request. No evidence."

"Has Lightfoot surfaced before?" Juanita asked.

"Oh yeah," said Robbins. "Remember that container full of refugees from Taiwan? That was a Lightfoot ship."

"They denied knowledge as I recall."

"Yeah, it was all dumped on the captain. Corporate said they didn't know anything about it. Fired the captain and most of the crew."

"Cutting their losses."

"What about smuggling?" Juanita asked.

"There've been a few accusations. Nothing that stuck."

"Think they're mobbed up?" Juanita asked.

"That'd be my guess," Robbins said.

"They're a huge company. Offices here, New Jersey, Southampton, Marseilles, Amsterdam, Mumbai." Brown palmed his face. "Out of our league."

"They've got a fleet of at least 200 ships. Sixty-some planes." Robbin added.

"Jesus! I had no idea. I'll ask around. Somebody here has heard of them, I'm sure." Juanita said.

"Baby Orcas," Brown said chuckling. "Hit men for baby Orcas."

"Somebody must have made money off it."

"Every year at least a dozen baby Orcas go missing, here in Puget Sound and off Vancouver Island," Juanita said. "Most of those are assigned to natural causes."

"What's a baby Orca sell for anyway?"

"We looked into that. Around fifty grand, now that they're endangered."

"Who would buy one?"

"Sea parks, zoos, animal parks. Probably foreign. If a U.S. park bought one, they'd have to forge certification proving the Orca was born in captivity."

"Not impossible."

"Certainly not, but more risky. A lot of environmental watch-dogs here."

"They raise orcas in Sweden, Norway. Places like that," said Robbins. "Sell them to these sea world places."

"You guys know an impressive amount about baby Orcas," Juanita commented, laughing.

Brown laughed. "More than we want to know."

"So, we done here?" Robbins tipped his chair forward.

"Can we get a copy of that file?" Juanita asked.

"Sure. I'll get it to you." Robbins stood abruptly. "Let us know if you have any more dreams." He was chuckling as he shook Jack's hand.

"Mr. Toyokata." Brown shook Jack's hand. "Let us know if you think of anything else."

"What do you think?" Jack asked after the detectives had left.

"They were playing along, trying to feel you out." Juanita paused, inhaled loudly. "See, Jack," her voice was patient now, a mother explaining something to a child, "no one knows what to make of this dream stuff, but we know that you know things about a couple of murders, so we're intrigued. We have to ask ourselves, if it's not the dreams, how does he know this stuff? And conversely, if it is the dreams, well, how weird is that?"

"Look, I didn't ask for these dreams, and they haven't been easy to deal with."

"I know, I know. And there's probably a logical explanation for them."

"My friend Per thinks there is a universal memory bank where all memories reside."

"You're telling you friends about these dreams?" Concern crossed Juanita's face.

"That's okay, isn't it?"

"No. Probably not a good idea. At least until we have a handle on what's going on here."

"Okay. I'll keep mum. Makes for interesting conversation though."

Jack slid his chair closer to Juanita.

"I like the new photo. You two look pretty happy."

"He's a sweety." Juanita picked up the oak frame and studied it for a minute, then set it down.

"So," she said, "I learned a few more things. McCandless was shot with a .22, but the computers were blown apart by something heavier. It will be in the report."

"Computers?"

"Yeah. They took out the computers. Too much risk of hidden files, etc." Juanita swept her lustrous hair back.

"The silencer. It's the choice of hitmen, right? And no one in the building heard anything."

"Right."

"My only experience with silencers in in movies and cop shows.

This is blowing a hole in my life."

"In other lives, too."

"Right."

"And it's weird to think of hitmen. I mean, that they really exist?"

"Oh yeah, they exist. There's always business that needs taking care of." She tilted her head. "That's what the mob likes to call it. Business. Keep it above board. Proper."

"Are the two I picked out local?"

"They're from Toronto. And they had alibis in Toronto."

"I wasn't mistaken about the one guy. The redhead."

"Alibis can be bought."

"Anything else?"

"The cops aren't one hundred percent sure this had to do with Orcas. McCandless had pissed-off a number of powerful concerns over the years."

"It was definitely about the Orcas." Jack bent forward. "I've been over the dream a number of times, trying to read lips like you said. Buzz-cut was the talker. He definitely asked about whales. Several times."

"Whales, huh." Juanita still seemed skeptical, but conceded. "Okay then, let's assume it was about Orcas, and that Lightfoot was harvesting and selling them. Or had been. They've probably stopped for now because of the scrutiny."

"What can you do?" Jack asked.

"Nothing, really. Since McCandless was killed in 2008, scientists have really tuned in to the resident Orca populations. They track them electronically. They know where most of them are every second. And sea parks have become leery of owning them. Even overseas. There's too much government scrutiny. Dolphins are so much easier."

"Well, that's a good thing."

"Yes, it is. But let's assume this whale kidnapping happened back in those dark days. And let's assume Lightfoot was involved. It meant enough to them to hire two hitmen to kill a scientific researcher. That tells me this is one nasty corporation." She paused and took a drink from a blue water bottle. "A mobbed-up international corporation with a fleet of over 200 ships and sixty airplanes and offices in nearly every major seaport around the world. Just imagine what they could be into."

Juanita set the water bottle down and stared at Jack, and he saw her eyes twinkle.

"Keep dreaming Mr. Toyokata."

"Jack."

"Jack."

18

Jack drove from his meeting with the two cops and Juanita to the Seattle UniCode offices on Dexter and pulled into the lot. It had rained earlier but was clearing, and the air was fresh, fragrant with the scent of salt air and early summer nectar. Out on Lake Union three sailboats skied in tight formation.

Jack greeted the man, Darrell, at the front desk, then found an empty "pod" as they were called, a small room suited for solo or small group work, settled in, and logged into the desk Mac.

He'd dipped back into the horror of his dream, but pushed it out of this head. It didn't go easily. He called Miguel, who caught him up. They'd finish the game security patch by late afternoon, and there were two other contracts waiting in the wings.

"I might be taking some time off," Jack said, holding the phone loosely.

"No shit. You gonna leave me hanging?"

"I doubt it. Ken is probably already viewing this as an opportunity to remove a thorn in his side."

"You're not kidding, are you. You're serious." He heard silence, and knew from habit that Miguel had tipped back in his chair and was staring out his window into a maze of conifer branches. Last time Jack had been in Miguel's office, Miguel had excitedly pointed out a robin's nest, the mother robin balanced on the lip, a wriggling worm in her beak.

"I'm thinking about some options."

"Sick of the bastards owning your soul, eh?"

"Something like that."

"Google come to you with a seven-figure number?"

"Hardly. I'll be scraping by."

"Shit, dude. You just bought that place with the lake view. That must cost a pretty penny."

"$3200 a month."

He heard Miguel whistle.

"Well let's get this patch taken care of. I'm not leaving in the middle of that."

Jack spent the next three hours coding, adding on to what Miguel was doing, the symbols appearing out of the ether on both their monitors simultaneously. Jack compared it to writing music together, and he'd miss that. But he was getting more certain about leaving by the minute.

At three o'clock he walked across the street and ordered a gyros. By now the sun had burned through the clouds and relegated them to the periphery. The picnic table outside Sido's was still damp, but Jack wiped the bench with his hand and sat. Taking a large bite, he texted Riordan.

Let's talk. Can you meet tonight?

He was crumpling the paper to toss into the trash when his phone beeped.

Late dinner? 8:00?

Where?

Ziggy's. I'm bringing a friend.

C U then.

Jack finished up a few things, called Miguel to make sure all the I's were dotted, then stopped by home, showered, and dressed in black jeans and a white Uniqlo sweatshirt featuring Hokusai's *Wave*. At the last minute he decided to bike, and retrieved his Trek from the storage container, then hit the Burke Gilman.

Ziggy's was a noisy, ultra-casual Italian place in Bothell that boasted excellent and unpretentious Tuscan fare. A few minutes late, he searched the room and saw Riordan giving a large wave. A woman with striking g purple hair sat next to him. Jack wound his way through the crowded tables.

"Hey, Jack!" Riordan said in his quiet roar, "so glad you could come."

Riordan stood and gave Jack a bear hug. Pointing to the seated woman, "This is Monique Rave, or Raven, depending on the show."

He gave a hearty laugh. "She's the fabric artist I was talking about. We're both interested in what you could do for us with computer technology. Have a seat, have a seat. Dinner's on me, by the way, so order heartily."

"Hi," said Monique, her voice quiet, calm compared to Riordan's, extending a hand as Jack sat down. "I hear great things about you."

"Thank you." Monique's hand was small, dry and very warm.

She wore a black cotton blouse that left room for generous cleavage. "We'll see."

Jack sat, thinking he was going to dine with a dialectic.

"First, drinks!" Riordan was already waving the waitress over. "What'll you have?"

"I was thinking of my fist gin and tonic of the year. It's warming up, after all."

"Splendid, splendid." Then to the waitress, "A gin and tonic, Bombay Sapphire okay Jack? Bombay Sapphire, and a refill for me, McCallan's 10, and Monique?"

Monique held up her glass, still full of a yellowish liquid.

"Hah! She's a lightweight. Nothing for Monique yet." Then to Jack, "I'll get her bombed one of these times."

"You won't, Riordan. I'm stronger than you." Monique was smiling a Cheshire smile.

"She's stronger than me, Jack, no doubt about it."

Over the next hour and a half, the three of them ate huge bowls of Cacciucco with fresh rosemary bread, and Jack and Riordan drank several more cocktails. Monique nursed her first drink for a good two hours. God bless her, thought Jack. Discipline.

"What is that stuff?" Jack had finally asked, intrigued.

"Ouzo. It's Greek. Licorice. You want to try it?"

"Ah, no. Thanks though."

They also nailed out an imaginary contract that they'd sleep on, then formalize over the next few days. The contract would hire Jack at the initial rate of two hundred dollars an hour to work in the capacity of an advisor, planner, designer, and coder for both Riordan and Monique, on what Riordan called "Artistic Endeavors." They would meet at least weekly for check-in, but other than that Jack would have utter freedom to schedule his time how he chose.

After the business talk was finished, the conversation drifted to Seattle and Washington State politics. Both Monique and Riordan were far more knowledgeable than Jack as to the mechanizations, personalities, and intrigues. Jack listened somewhat awestruck. He'd always assumed artists to be in their own ether, out of touch with the 'realities' of the day-to-day, but these two were carrying on like an old married couple, sparring and parrying over policy.

They shared an espresso to close the meeting then Jack took off.

As Jack biked home, he ran some numbers in his head. Three and half ten-hour days would give him rent, food and some extra. And if rent was roughly one third of the equation then another seven days would fill in the rest. Except for taxes. He better double it. That meant 14 or 15 ten-hour days a month, and he could make ends meet. Okay, he forgot medical. And a big question mark, those "out of left field" situations. So, another two days. That meant seventeen ten-hour days a month. Which would give him thirteen off. Which was ten more than he currently had. And flexibility, which he currently had none of.

He passed a young man walking slowly, smoking a joint, and took a big inhale as he passed. Scary! No doubt. But he didn't feel scared. Jack was elated. He still hadn't told Billetts, but that could wait until after his two-day holiday.

Jack had a cousin in Chicago he'd never visited, despite a few invites over the years.

His cousin, Kaito, was a huge blues and folk fan. He knew Jack was a music buff, and had invited him back now and then for concerts. But Jack had always been too busy to accept.

He gave Kaito a call when he got home, caught his message machine, and left a message.

"Hey cuz, this is Jack in Seattle. I'm coming to Chicago and would love to see you. And check out some music. Dates haven't been solidified yet, so give me a call and let me know what works for you. I want to check out that club, *Space*, you were talking about in you email. See you."

Jack commanded his stereo to play Jah Wobble's *Japanese Dub*, and settled into the couch with a nightcap and his Mac Air. As the sub-woofer began pulsing, he searched Google for "coding for artists," and started reading a website called *Coding in the Wild*. He also researched LED light boxes, which Riordan had hinted he wanted to use. There were a ton of them but they all functioned the same. They stood on tables or hung on walls and projected visual images. Most of them worked with USB or wifi. Jack was getting intrigued by the possibilities this new line of inquiry offered. And the thought of kicking Billetts in the proverbial balls was extremely gratifying.

Jack awoke with a start. The stereo clock read 3:14 in luminescent green. He realized immediately he was shivering wildly and covered in sweat. His laptop toppled next to where he'd passed out, the remnants of another dream stuttering through his fogged brain like clouds blowing through dark mountains. But the boy's face was abrupt and forceful. It was not a vision that could be erased.

As soon as it was light, Jack was on the phone to Juanita, her private line. She'd called him back shortly after he'd left the message.

He was nursing a cup of coffee. It was morning, the first of two days he'd been given off by Billetts. The boy's face floated in front of him where ever he turned, impossible to evade. In that way the dream had been different, the way he'd floated out of the boy's body just before he died.

"Tell me," Juanita said, not exactly irritation, but something similar in her voice.

"I was in a boy's body, walking, at night."

"Where?"

"Up Pine St. Seattle. I watched the street signs. He crossed 30th, 31st, 32nd. Halfway down the block he stopped in front of a house and whistled. A few minutes later two guys came out from between the houses. On had a bandana across his face, the other wore a black hoodie. I could read Black hoodie's lips, some of it anyway. He asked the boy 'Did you bring it.' The boy shook his head. The hoodie guy asked 'why not?' I'm getting better at reading lips, so I'm sure that's what he said, but I couldn't see or hear the boy's response. Then the guy wearing the bandana said something, but I couldn't see his lips. The boy followed the two guys back between the houses into an alley. It was dark. There were security lights on several of the garages, but lots of dark areas as well. The alley was littered with broken glass and lots of trash.

"The three of them stopped next to a garage door and had another conversation. It was dimly lit. I couldn't catch much. Just some gesticulating, swearing, and the hoodie guy agitated, asking again why the boy hadn't brought it. Then they walked again, further up the alley. I really had no idea what was going on, but the kid didn't seem particularly afraid. The guys didn't wave a gun or other weapon.

"They stopped again, and again I saw the hoodie guy ask where the something, couldn't get the word, was. 'Where is it?' he said, several times, getting more agitated. Then he pulled out a gun. The barrel was shorter than the other gun, the one that killed McCandless. It caught light and flashed silver. Some other words were exchanged then the hoodie guy shot him in the chest. But here's what's different. The lights didn't go out in the dream, it didn't end. Just before the hoodie guy fired, I was surging, that's the best description I can give, out of the kid's body and rising above him. I could see him clearly then, even in the weak light. His face was like that of a Renaissance painting. Angelic, beatific, beautiful. There's no other way to put it.

Not just a handsome kid, but beautiful."

"How old was he?"

"I'd say twelve, thirteen. Somewhere around there. I don't really hang out with kids so I might be a bit off. And his angelic face might have caused him to appear younger than he was."

"You think he was meeting these two?"

"Had to be. I had the sense it was a business transaction of some sort."

"Maybe drugs?"

"Could have been. Nothing was exchanged."

"It sounds like he was supposed to bring something. Probably money."

"Could be."

"Hmmm. Anything else?"

"Just that there wasn't any overt violence before he was shot. Some threatening, words, but no big argument, nothing of that sort. The boy appeared calm."

"What can you tell me about the perpetrators?"

"Two of them, like I said. Dressed in black, except for the bandana, that was red-checked."

"What ethnicity were they?"

"Both black guys."

"Tall, short? What else?"

"Average height. Taller than the kid by six inches or so. The guy wearing the bandana seemed stockier than the hoodie guy, the shooter. The shooter had a thinner face."

"How about the victim? What was he wearing?"

"Jeans, a sweater. Blue, I think."

"Angelic, you said."

"Like a sculpture you'd see in church. It was as if light radiated out from him."

"Fucking weird, Jack, you know that, right?"

"I do not dispute this, Juanita."

"I'll let you know what I find out. Shouldn't be too difficult to track a dead white kid on 32nd off Pine. Text me if you remember anything else." It was not a question, and again Jack heard something like irritation in Juanita's voice.

"Certainly." And then he added, "I'm not making this up Juanita."

After a brief silence she said, "I know. But I sure as hell wished you were." Then the phone clicked dead.

19

The rest of the day swam by.

Jack's cousin, Kaito, called back sounding thrilled.

"I gotta warn you, Jack, that things have changed radically in my life though."

"How's that?"

"I've got a kid." Kaito gave a half-laugh.

"A kid? Wow. I didn't even know you were married."

"Yeah, I'm not too good at conveying details. I've been married over four years."

"No way!"

"Way."

"How old is your kid."

"A girl. Juliette. She's nineteen months." Kaito paused as if he'd said too much. "Reason I'm telling you this is that I'm not foot-loose and fancy-free anymore. I could probably get out a couple of times, but not more than that. And I'm working full time at Allstate Insurance."

"You've been hobbled."

"Yeah. Hobbled. But it's all good." Another pause. "How bout you? Hitched yet?"

"Nope. Work is God. All-consuming. Hardly time to blow my nose."

"Must be clogged bad," Kaito laughed.

"Yeah, no shit. This is the first vacation I've had in nearly three years. I'm been lucky to get weekends off."

"Jesus Jack, that sounds like slave labor."

"I doubt they paid slaves what I'm getting, but still. It's too much. Something's about to change. What's a good time for me to come?"

"Anytime. I could take a day off. We could check out a museum. Maybe the Art Institute. Then go catch a show. Do you know The Birds of Chicago?"

"Never heard of them."

"Check them out. They're playing at Space Saturday night. If you came for the weekend, we could make their show."

"That sounds great, Kaito. I can get there by Saturday. I'll shop tickets and get back to you. It'll be soon though. And you don't need to host me."

"Of course you'll stay here! I insist. No sense me and my wife being the only ones kept up all night."

"Hah. Okay. I've got errands to run."

"Okay."

"Work stuff."

"You still the computer man?"

"That's me. We'll catch up over a beer. You still drink beer, don't you?"

"More wine now, but yeah. I'm not a teetotaler."

"Hey Kaito, what do you know about the Irish mob?"

Kaito laughed. His laugh hadn't changed from when they were kid cousins messing around. "Not a thing."

After he hung up, Jack scored a non-stop ticket on Delta for 9:15 Friday morning, with an arrival time of 3:40. Jack was starting to get excited. The only time he'd traveled in the past few years was to attend workshops and conferences. Seeing Kaito, and going to a show would be excellent fun. A kid? How the world had changed. And he wanted to track down the cop with Alzheimer's. McNeeley. See if he could add anything to 'Cathy's' file.

He texted Kaito, told him when he'd get in, and that he'd rent a car at O'Hare. "Text me your address."

Riordan called a bit later. Jack was heating a cup of ramen with tofu and dried veggies in the microwave.

"Can you meet me at my lawyer's office tomorrow? In Seattle? He's drawn up a contract and we can go over it, sign it if you're agreeable."

"Sounds great. What time?"

"2:30?"

"Sure. Where?"

"600 Stewart. Suite 801. His name is Lawrence Dougherty."

"I'll see you then."

Jack sat on the couch spooning noodles and plugged in his phone to his system, clicking through the screens of Apple Music to his new find, Elephant Revival, a band he'd discovered in a Pandora mix. He selected their cover of Pink Floyd's *Have a Cigar*. He finished the ramen, ate an apple, and absorbed the music. Good stuff. Life was moving too fast, yet in a different way. Life at UniCode was stressful, but predictable. One input level, as his friend Stan liked to say. Suddenly he had numerous inputs. It was all a little overwhelming. Not to mention the dreams, and Juanita. He'd never met anyone like her. A female cop. Tough as nails. Living a dangerous life. 'What the fuck, Jack,' he said to himself. 'Where do I fit into *that* equation?'

Then Juanita called back.

"Got it," she said without any preamble. "The kid's name is Michael Daly. He's 15. 9th grade at the Bush School in Madrona. Which is, by the way, about a mile and a half from where he was found dead, and about a mile from where he lived in Madrona."

"Huh. When did it happen?"

"Two years ago. September. A few weeks after school began."

"And?"

"Cops never arrested anyone, never even caught a lead. There was a videocam on a garage at the end of the alley that caught two guys walking by fast, but it was dark, and one of the guys wore a hoodie, tight, the other guy a bandana. Your guys, but the detectives couldn't get much off it. High-end gym shoes, but all bangers wear those.

"The detectives found no prints, and this is a bit strange for dopers, they didn't find a cartridge. Sometimes they get lucky and can pull a print off a cartridge."

"Why's that strange for dopers? What you said?"

"Pros pick up their brass. Dopers don't give a shit."

"So you're saying this was a professional hit?"

"I'm not closing the door on it."

"Weird."

"Yeah it is. Hold on." Jack heard her cover the phone, say something to someone else. Then she was back on.

"Neighbors didn't admit to seeing or hearing anything. Gun shots are not common in the area, but fireworks might be."

Juanita paused.

"Parents said that Michael told them he was going over to a friend's house to study for an exam. The friend said he never showed up."

"What else?"

"The cops questioned the parents about drugs. They said it wasn't an issue, that Michael had never done them."

"They all say that. Parents are generally clueless, aren't they?"

Juanita laughed. "I hope not. The parents seemed savvy. They claimed Michael was a straight A student. Involved in theatre and debate. Cops checked it out and it held"

"What else?"

"Nothing. You think of anything else that could narrow this down?"

"No. Did you want me to meet with the detectives?"

Juanita laughed.

"Not this time. I've got the case file, what there is of it. We don't need to advertise these dreams of yours to any more cops. Let's keep it between us for now."

"Okay."

"And you were right."

"About what?"

"There's something strange about this kid. Even in the crime scene photos. He looks almost ghostly. You used the word beatific. I can see that."

"Hmm. Hey, I'm going to be in Seattle tomorrow. You want to catch lunch?"

There was a slight hesitation, as if Jack had caught her off-guard. Then she came on all radiant. "I'd love that. You like Wild Ginger?"

"Love it. Pricey though."

"That a problem?" Her voice laughing a little, lilting.

"No, I guess not. I have an announcement to make."

"An announcement. Wow. This sounds special. Can't wait. 11:30 so we duck the noon rush?"

"That would be great Juanita. I'll see you then."

20

The morning of Jack's second day off, he got up early and went for a run uphill into Kenmore Heights. The morning was engulfed in fog which would burn off by late morning. Returning home, he showered then broke three eggs into a frying pan with black olives, mushrooms, and goat cheese. "Play the Birds of Chicago," he told his system. His female-voiced bot, which he'd dubbed Erica, lilted back to him in a Swedish accent, "The Birds of Chicago. I've found the following albums. *Live from Space*, *Self-Titled*, *Real Midnight* and *American Flowers*."

"Play *American Flowers*."

Upbeat soulful acoustic music filled the air, mixing with the steam and aromas from the frying pan.

"Nice stuff," Jack said to himself. He was beginning to relax, a sensation that had been a foreign guest for the past few years. In fact, Jack thought, anxiety took over his life shortly after Billetts was hired.

After breakfast he tracked down Ken Billetts at the Redmond office.

"He going to be around awhile?" Jack asked Jeff, the admin assistant, realizing as he was asking that he was gripping his phone like a vise.

"All morning," came the curt reply.

"Could you schedule fifteen with him? Nine to nine-thirtyish?"

There was a pause while Jeff checked the schedule. "How about nine forty-five? I can give you ten."

"That will work." Jack clicked off.

He made good time to Redmond, going against traffic. He found a parking spot and entered the building from the rear with his key card. Jeff had him wait a few minutes then told him Ken would see him now.

"He's in his office. Typical bad mood." Jack wondered when he'd last seen Jeff smile. Or anyone at UniCode. Billetts was toxic.

"His golf game yesterday must have been off."

Jeff cocked his finger at Jack "I'm sure that's it."

Jack walked around the corner and a few yards down the hall to Ken's office. The door was partially open, and Jack eased his way in, coughing to alert Ken.

Ken was staring at a couple of monitors when Jack entered and sat across from him. He didn't look up. It was a typical Ken move, radiating that 'I'm too busy so make it fast' aura.

Finally he did.

"It must be my lucky week. Here it is Wednesday and it's my second meeting with you. What do you need that I can't get you?"

"I was going to phone, but figured I should have the courtesy of doing it in person."

"Doing what? You going to beat me up?" Ken brayed a laugh.

"Quitting. I'm out."

"Well, that's convenient, knowing you have three major projects on your plate."

"You yourself have said numerous times that I'm expendable. So, I'm expending myself."

Ken gave him a hard stare which Jack let roll off him.

"Okay then. Clear out your stuff by four o'clock."

"You can keep anything there is. Consider it a gift."

"This sudden, there won't be a severance package."

"That's the last thing I'd expect from you, Ken, even if I did this by the book."

Jack wheeled and walked out the door. As he did, he heard Ken say "Jesus fucking Christ," but he was in the hallway, feeling his emotional state hovering between elation and horror. He'd just said goodbye to the only job he'd had since graduating from UW twenty-two years ago.

21

Jack got to Wild Ginger early, took a quiet booth, and ordered a pot of Oolong tea. It had been raining lightly, and he stripped off his raincoat and placed it next to him. The restaurant was relatively uncrowded, but would swell after noon. Juanita entered a few minutes later, her ebony hair glistening with rain. Jack waved her over, standing to give her a hug.

"What was that about?" She asked as they separated.

"Just glad to see you, I guess."

She laughed and her chestnut eyes twinkled.

"You didn't strike me as the hugging type."

"Cause I'm Asian?"

"That. And, I don't know. You seem too cool. Rational."

"Yeah, rational. Except for the dreams, right."

"Ah, those. I guess they throw a wrench into that theory."

The waitress brought another pot of tea and set it on the table.

"Before that however, I have an announcement to make. I quit my job."

"Really?" Juanita slid into the banquette across from him. "Well I guess congratulations are in order. You worked at UniCode for how long?"

"Twenty-two years. Ever since I got my degree from UW."

"Wow. Big changes in store." She started to pour tea into her cup. "You going to pursue criminals full-time?"

"Can you get me on with the agency?" Jack loved flirting, and could tell Juanita was in the mood as well.

"Actually, they may need a coder. I could see."

"No, no," Jack said laughing. "I'm going to work for some artists. I'm meeting a lawyer and signing a contract this afternoon."

"You move fast, don't you? So, tell me about this art job."

"There are a couple of local artists that want to create computerized art installations. I'm going to do the coding. Have you heard of Riordan Quinn?"

Juanita shook her head. "Nope."

"Photographer. Does coffee table books on orcas and salmon. PNW themes. Does quite well apparently."

"There's a market for them, I guess. I'd probably buy some if I had the room. Or a coffee table. Or the time to page through them. Anyway, sounds like a neat job. Creative. Are they paying you anything?"

"Not what I'm used to, but I think I can make ends meet."

They took some time with the menu, both ordering a green curry lunch special, Jack with prawns, Juanita with pork.

"So, any new developments?"

"As a matter a fact there are. We retrieved the slug that killed Michael Daley and it matched two other shootings."

"Seriously?"

"Yeah. Both hits were professional. .22 slug, single shot, no cartridges, deserted locations, bodies left where they lay."

"Who were the victims?"

"Here's the funny thing. They both worked for Lightfoot Air and Marine. Both single men in their thirties. Laborers."

"No shit!"

"Shit, dude."

"But what's the connection to a thirteen-year-old kid?"

"I thought you'd never ask. Michael's father is high up the ladder at Lightfoot."

"Son of a bitch. This is coming together."

"Lightfoot is starting to look interesting." She steepled her fingers in mock suspense. "Very interesting."

Lunch arrived, and they talked of other things, largely kid's baseball. Largely Juanita talked and Jack listened. He delighted in her voice, and her pride in her boys made Jack jealous. He wished he had someone he cared about like that. He realized yet again that his work-focused life had shut the door on many things.

He told Juanita about his trip to Chicago Friday, that he'd be gone four days.

"I want to talk with that cop with dementia. Can you get me contact information?"

"I'll text it to you." She seemed suddenly shy. "Would you like to see my kids play baseball when you get back?"

"I'd love that! Thank you."

"Great!" Then her voice turned serious. "This is uncharted terrain for me. I haven't dated since I left my husband."

"Is this a date?" Jack joked.

"Well, maybe. Is that alright? To call it that? You can come over for dinner after. I make a mean pozole."

"Sure. I'd love to. And I'll find out what pozole is."

"You don't know?" she laughed.

"Ha, I bet I eat a few things you don't know about."

"Touché." She turned serious again. "I need to tell you a few things. That might change your mind."

"You have strange tactics for seduction," Jack laughed.

She swatted at him playfully. "No, this is serious. I haven't been with anyone since I left my husband. It's been over a year."

"You told me that."

"What I'm trying to say, is that my kids, they're not used to seeing me with another man. I don't know what their reaction will be."

"I'm not worried."

"There's something else. My husband."

"You're still married?"

"Well…yes, legally. He's Catholic and doesn't believe in divorce. In his mind we're still married."

Jack stared at her, not comprehending.

"He won't sign the fucking papers, okay?"

"Oh."

"But we're history. I haven't been with him in over a year."

"To history." Jack laughed and raised his tea cup.

She gave him the finger, smiling.

"Does he live around you?"

"No, I moved after I left him."

"Why did you leave him?"

"He was cheating on me."

"Ahhh. So you think he might take this wrong?"

"He's extremely jealous. Extremely. I'm sure the boys will tell him about you. They see him every week. I don't know what he'll do when he finds out." She was giving him an odd stare.

"I guess we'll find that out as well, won't we?"

Juanita hesitated. She looked conflicted.

"You know any martial arts? Boxing? Self-defense?"

Jack laughed. "You're asking if I'm tough? If I can defend myself?"

"Yeah."

"I'm not a fighter if that's what you mean, but I can usually talk myself out of tense situations." Jack took a last bite of curry. "Your ex-husband, you think he might be prone to violence?"

Juanita gave a barking laugh. "I know he is. He's a Seattle cop with a history of anger issues."

After lunch, outside in the light rain, Juanita made the move first and hugged Jack. They stood on the sidewalk, light rain dusting them, neither wanting to let go. But they did, Juanita promising to text Jack about the baseball game. The she headed back to her Third Avenue headquarters, and Jack drove off to meet Riordan and Monique at Riordan's lawyer's office on Stewart.

Lawrence Dougherty's office was in one of the newer russet cement and blue-glass structures that were popping up like mushrooms in downtown Seattle. Jack took the elevator to the 8th floor and stepped into a plushly carpeted hallway, the door to Dougherty's office the only door, his name the only one listed. Jack told the pert blonde woman at the front desk he had an appointment with Lawrence Dougherty at 2:30, and she told him he was expected.

Suite 801 took up most, if not the entire floor, and Jack was directed down another hallway. He heard Riordan's laugh before he got to the office. The door was wide open and Riordan was bent over the lawyer's desk examining something, still chuckling, Monique sitting, mini-skirted, legs crossed, on her phone. He knocked for effect, then entered.

"Hey, the man." Riordan did the intros, they shook hands, then they sat.

Dougherty went through the contract, which was basic, and stripped to a minimum of legalistic bullshit. Even Jack could understand it, but Riordan insisted Jack go over it again and make certain everything was square. So Jack sat, re-read, and asked questions, while Riordan and Dougherty talked cars, Monique fiddled with her phone. Finally Jack was satisfied that he understood everything he needed to understand. The contract defined the scope of work, but left ample room for improvisation. It loosely defined Jack's obligations, and set up a salary schedule and definitions, as well as some miscellany. Riordan and Monique had already signed, and Jack added his signature at the bottom, using the Montblanc fountain pen Dougherty provided. As he watched the ink glisten, then dull as it dried, it was like he'd leapt into the void.

Riordan proposed he, Jack, and Monique have their initial

meeting next Wednesday, the day after Jack returned from Chicago. He offered to host. Both he and Monique had projects in the hopper and were ready to roll.

The meeting broke up, and they left the building together. Outside, the rain had stopped, and patches of blue were showing. Riordan offering to buy them all a drink to celebrate the contract, and Jack's "take this job and shove it" moment. Jack took him up on it, Monique deferred, saying she had another engagement. Jack watched her walk down the hill, looking seductive as hell in her red miniskirt. And immediately thought of Juanita. What ther hell was he getting into?

With Riordan leading the way, they walked to Quinn's Pub on Capitol Hill. During the walk they discussed some ideas Riordan had, local politics, the Mariner's prospects, and a bit about their mutual upbringings.

Riordan was originally from New York City. He'd come to Seattle thirty plus years ago to participate in a series of workshops with glass artist Dale Chihuly. He fell in love with a fellow student, with Seattle, with Queen Anne Hill, and never left. Originally a painter, he'd drifted into photography, started making serious money, and photography took over. But he had copious ideas, and was excited about working with adding code to photographs and seeing where that took him.

They ended up getting fairly drunk on shots of Irish whiskey, Riordan leading him like a novitiate through the pallet tour of whiskies Jack had never encountered. Redbreast, Powers, Teeling, Tullamore, Slane, and Dead Rabbit which Riordan saved for last. Piling into the Uber, Jack brought up the Irish mafia, and Riordan responded by pontificating, which Jack had discovered was Riordan's primary mode of communication. Repartee didn't serve him.

"The Irish Mob rose out of Irish gangs in New York City early nineteenth century."

And Riordan went on to regal Jack with stories of the White Hand Gang, Richard Lonergan, Big Bill Dwyer, The Westies, and Kevin Weeks before the Uber dropped Jack at his car.

"See you next Wednesday Jack. Safe travels."

"Thanks. Hey one last question. Do you think the Irish mob has moved into Seattle?"

"Don't know, but maybe. They moved into smuggling drugs in a big way. Began buying out legitimate shipping companies, moving into port cities. Seattle's a port, so the odds are…"

He mocked a salute then began animatedly talking to the Uber driver as they pulled away. Jack had no doubt the Irish Mob was still his topic. As he started his car, he realized he was too drunk to drive safely. He pulled out his phone and called another Uber. He'd pick up his car tomorrow.

22

Friday morning, nursing a stunning headache he'd bombarded with Tylenol and Ibuprofen, Jack boarded a 747 bound for O'Hare Airport. As soon as he was able, he ordered two Bloody Marys, drank them down with no delay, and promptly fell asleep. Waking three hours later as the jet touched down, he was surprised to be clear-headed and headache free.

He texted Kaito, then took a cab to his house to Schiller Park on the north side of the city. While in the cab, he got two texts, one from Juanita and one from Kaito

Loved lunch. Ball game is at 4:30 on Wednesday. Know that's the day after you get back, but dinner will be worth it.

Jack responded *I'll be there. text me where the ballgame is. I'll meet U. loved lunch 2.*

Kaito wrote *still at work Amy's home with toddler Juliette see u soon*

Kaito lived in a brick bungalow in a former German neighborhood that retained its carefully coifed lawns and vibrant flower gardens. The cab dropped Jack, stiff from the trip, in the driveway behind a new silver Toyota Camry. Jack experienced a pang of jealousy when he saw the car seat in the rear seat. Kaito had really done it. A kid. Wow.

He took the cement stairs by twos and rang the bell, hearing voices and scrambling.

A moment later a beautiful heart-faced woman opened the door, her blond hair cascading over sturdy shoulders. "You must be Jack!" She stuck out her hand. "I'm Amy, and this is Juliette," pointing to the equally blond little girl hanging on her leg, hiding behind it.

"She's shy for the first two minutes, then you won't be able to get rid of her. Kaito just phoned and said he'd be home in a half-hour."

"He works in the Loop?"

"No, a branch office. Just a few miles from here. Pretty convenient really. He usually takes the bus."

Jack played hide and seek with Juliette, and was reading her a third book, *My First Winnie the Pooh*, when Kaito crashed through the door, ran over and embraced Jack, then Juliette, talking a blue streak.

"You look tired, man," stepping back, giving Jack the once over.

Jack didn't tell him about the hangover. He knew he was exhausted. "Life," he said, grinning. "Great to see you Kaito!"

Kaito looked good. He'd filled out, wore his hair on the long side, flirted with a moustache. His glasses were blue, Scandinavian or German design, and he wore fashionable but understated slacks and shirt.

"I was trying to think of the last time we saw each other. I think it was right after you graduated from college. You were taking a job with a tech company."

"UniCode."

"Yeah. And you came out and we did crazy city things for a few days."

"Some of them unmentionable in mixed company."

"Hah, nothing so bad. Just good kid times." Kaito gestured around the room strewn with toys, toddler clothes, books. "Now look at me."

"Looks great! I'm jealous. Dad!"

"Yeah, guess I have it pretty good. Hey, remember those family get-togethers? In San Diego?"

"Definitely. Been a long time since I've seen anyone in the Ito clan."

"But every summer back then. They came to a halt after your dad died. He was the force behind them."

"Yeah, that, and everyone getting older, more wrapped up in their own lives."

"Good memories though. That's what we want to provide Juliette with." Kaito walked over and picked her up. "Hey Julie, this is your uncle Jack. Can you say Jack?"

Jack noticed her eyes, chocolate brown, were fixated on him.

"Jack," she said. "Unca Jack."

Wow! Jack was flooded with a warmth he'd never experienced.

Dinner was relaxed and wonderful. Amy had whipped up a giant Caesar's salad with sashimi-grade ahi chunks, and a cream of broccoli soup. The family was kind, funny, and genuine, and Jack was in another world. After dinner they retired to the living room with glasses of chardonnay.

"Birds of Chicago tomorrow."

"I listened to a bit of their stuff. Very nice."

"Want to take in a ball game before that? Cubs are playing the Dodgers, and I can get tickets."

"Can you get away that long?"

"Already cleared it. You're still good with that Amy?"

"Definitely. You guys get away for a bit. It's been months since Kaito got to do anything fun with another guy. Besides, my mom's coming over, and we're taking Juliette to the park. Weather's supposed to be gorgeous tomorrow."

"Excellent! We'll take in a game, then catch dinner in Evanston. There're several places right around the club, Space. I told you about Space, right?"

"A bit. You know the owner?"

"One of them. A bit. He's a blues guitar player. David Specter. I interviewed him once for the *Reader*. Nice guy, great guitarist. And now the club. I'm pecking away at an article about it. It's really making it, and Dave's drawing some big names. Chick Corea in two weeks. Gotta see that." Kaito smiled. "But won't get to. Family first."

Jack was thrilled to see Kaito so jacked, so full of life. He'd been in a real slump a few years ago. They'd talked a lot then. Right before he'd met Amy. She'd really turned his life around.

Lying in his hotel bed that night, the murdered angelic boy drifted into Jack's mind, but this time he was peaceful, holding out his hand for Jack to follow. In the morning he vaguely remembered taking the boy's hand and walking down an alley.

23

Saturday was fun. Overpriced hotdogs and beer, the Cubs winning a nail-biter on pitching. And the concert was fabulous. The Birds were captivating and talented. Kaito's friend David was at another gig, but Kaito introduced Jack to several music-buff friends, and they went out after the show and caught a local up-and-coming troubadour named Kai Tent. He played a lot of minor keys and had the saddest voice. Jack thought of the boy again. He'd said something to Jack last night. If only he could remember...

Jack had called the retirement home in Elgin, but former officer McNeeley was sleeping. He talked with an attendant, telling them he wanted to visit Sunday, and would that be okay?

"Ben loves visitors, and he gets way too few. But you're aware of his condition, right?"

"I've heard he had Alzheimer's."

"He's in and out. Sometimes he's still quite lucid, describing things that happened decades ago in exacting detail. Other times, he can't remember his name, if he's eaten lunch, where he is."

"I look forward to it."

It had taken Jack far longer to get to Elgin than he'd anticipated, and he was starving when he turned down Main Street, spotting a Teriyaki stand and pulling into an empty slot in front. He ordered a plate of Yakisoba with veggies and tofu and wolfed it.

The "retirement home" turned out to be a 1950's mid-class advanced care facility, two turns down a long drive. The grounds and expansive lawns were well-tended, and numerous large oaks lived in relative peace.

The woman at the front desk, a large jolly black woman with a flowery name tag that read Holly, welcomed Jack, and told him that Officer Ben McNeeley was at lunch, and that he always dined with his lady friend, but today, Hazel was sick, so he was dining alone.

"Just walk down the hall and it's the first double doors on your right. You can order lunch if you dare," she said, laughing. "I wouldn't."

"How will I know who Ben McNeeley is?"

"Oh he's the only one in there who looks like a cop." She was laughing harder now, her body shaking with it. Jack thought her lucky. Not everyone was that easily amused. And laughter was the best medicine.

Officer Ben McNeeley did look like a cop, and was easy to find. Ninety -one, he still possessed the stolid square shape of a fullback. His grey hair was buzzcut, and he was dressed neatly in khakis and a worn light-blue cardigan. His large hands engulfed a cheeseburger.

"You're Ben McNeeley?" Jack asked.

"Who're you?"

"I'm doing some legwork for an FBI agent in Seattle."

Jack handed him Juanita's card.

McNeeley glanced at it, shook it, then shook his head.

"Can't see worth a damn. I'll take your word for it."

"Can I sit down?"

"Sure." McNeeley's voice was gruff and wheezy. Probably a life-long smoker. Most cops were in those days.

"Hungry?"

"Just ate, but thanks."

"I can order you a cheeseburger. Only damn thing that's any good." He paused and wiped mayonnaise off his mouth with the back of his hand. Jack noticed his napkin was untouched.

"Except the chicken. That's okay. And the eggs and bacon. Sometimes they have sausages. They're okay. That's it though." He took another large bite of his burger.

"I'll keep that in mind."

"What's on your mind, young fellow?" McNeeley turned his head, and Jack saw his rheumy blue eyes trying to focus.

"There was a woman murdered back in 1951. Left in an apartment vestibule. A dancer. Never solved."

"Her name was Cathy."

"That wasn't in the file."

"Huh."

"What was her last name?"

"Called herself Cathy Peacock. But her real last name was Brennan. Cathy Brennan. She was twenty-three. Robbed of life."

"What can you tell me about that case?"

"One of my first, so's I remember it okay. Some days. Some days I can't remember who I am, why I'm here. They've been trying a new medicine. Maybe it's helping."

Jack thought suddenly of the supplement, InSight, which he took faithfully every morning along with his multi and vitamin D. He realized the memory lapses had ceased. Maybe that's why.

"I was 19. You could get on the force early in those days. Didn't need to go through all that bullshit training you do now. My partner was middle-aged. Jaded and cynical. But he taught me the ropes. Dick Pearson." McNeeley laughed. "He was a prick though."

"Huh."

"There were several of them. Girls. All killed the same way. Shot and dumped out of a car. They'd all been messed up pretty bad. Beat up. Signs of strangulation."

McNeeley paused and looked up, staring into the fluorescent lights. God knows what he saw.

"They were dancers for a couple clubs owned by the mob."

"Do you remember the club names?"

"*Dy No Mite* and *PussyCat*."

"Still around?"

"Nah. When they cleaned up south of the Loop, they razed them. Built condos."

"So the mob you mentioned, was it the mafia?"

"The micks. They had their own mob in those days. Maybe they still do. Anyway, they ran the clubs and the girls danced for them. When the girls were used up, not used up by the dancing mind you, they disposed of them."

"What do you mean 'used up'?"

"The micks, they tortured girls. Rough sex stuff. Abused them till they were near dead. Then they shot 'em and dumped 'em. As I said, I was right out of the womb and wanted to catch these bastards bad. But you couldn't touch 'em. They were well-protected. Lots of politicians used those clubs. The Irish were moving into politics big time in Chicago, and the mob walking along hand-in-hand. Deals went down in those clubs. They didn't want them closed."

"So you struck out?"

"Yeah. Struck out." He laughed then coughed.

"We found her sister though."

"Cathy's?"

"Yeah. Her name was Susan. Susan Flowers. She was a Brennan like Cathy, but married a guy named Flowers. She'd been afraid something like this would happen. Warned Cathy. But Cathy was making money, living a fast life, meeting important people."

"How do you know? Important people?"

"Politicians. See the dancers were whored out to the politicians. And to cops. Big business guys. That's why we got steered away from it. When we started getting too close. My partner, Pearson, he told me, 'Ben, we gotta let this one go. It's too hot.' I remember that. It was a tough lesson to learn. My first. But there were lots of them."

"Interesting. You probably don't know if the sister is still alive?"

"Hell no. Haven't thought about this case in years. Just another corpse. Sad."

"Know anything about Mr. Flowers, that she married?"

"I remember he was in shipping. Worked out of town a lot."

"Huh."

"Lots of them."

"Pardon?"

"Lots of lessons. Being a cop was a good thing, but we weren't good people. We were just people. And we were exposed to the worst of humanity. And it rubbed off."

Jack was silent for a moment.

"Anything else you can think of?"

"Nah. You caught me on a good day. Mostly I can't remember my name. Or why I'm still alive." He coughed into his fist. "I don't want to be alive anymore. But I'm Catholic. So I can't kill myself. Funny, huh?"

"Yeah, funny. I appreciate your help, Ben."

"I don't know if I helped, but it was nice to talk to you. You seem like a decent young man. What are you doing with the FBI? They're a bunch of pussies."

"Just helping out my friend."

"Friends and family, that's all we got." He'd finished the burger and was licking his fingers.

Jack stood up.

"Goodbye Ben."

"Be careful out there."

Jack could see him telling that to his kids years ago. He knew what it was like. Out there.

24

Jack drove back to the Holiday Inn sorting it out.

The biggest lead seemed to be Cathy's sister's husband, Flowers. Both he and the sister were probably dead by now, but there was a chance their kids, if they had any, were still alive.

And the clubs, maybe the FBI had records that could be of use, although it seemed like a labyrinth. The mob, politicians, police, probably businessmen. And seventy years ago. Maybe there were ownership records somewhere. A long shot.

He texted Juanita asking her to check into a Flowers in shipping, see if there was anything there. Then he ducked into the shower, dressed, and drove to Kaito's for dinner. This was the last time he'd see them. Tomorrow, Monday, he was going to visit the location of Cathy's death, then hit the Art Institute and maybe the Museum of Natural History. Tuesday morning he needed to be at O'Hare by eight.

Juliette was waiting with a game in one hand and two books in the other, Kaito was in the shower, and Amy, after a brief kiss on the cheek, returned to the kitchen, where mellifluous scents of cardamom, cumin and the sweetness of butternut squash mingled and escaped.

"Hope you don't mind entertaining Julie. She's been waiting for you. Kaito will be out in a few."

"No, I'd love to."

Jack took her small hand in his and let her lead him over to the sofa, where she climbed up, patted it and said, "You sit here."

Jack sat, and she handed him the books and a game, a push-button sound game called *Number Colors*, then climbed up into his lap.

Kaito showed up ten minutes later, gave him a wink and mouthed the words "Everything okay?" to which Jack nodded, and Kaito ambled off into the kitchen to help Amy.

Dinner was fantastic. They drank a bottle of Chablis that Jack brought, ate pear, walnut and kale salad, butternut and chicken soup, and rosemary bread from the bakery down the street. For dessert, they ate home-made vanilla ice cream drenched with blueberry syrup. Amy served large helpings and had given them large spoons. No sense playing around.

Relaxing afterward in the living room, Kaito playing some Chicago jazz for Jack, calling out the artists, they drank brandy and chatted. Sprawled out on the couch, Julliette leaned into him, asleep, Jack was more relaxed than he could remember.

"You gotta come back," Kaito said as Jack was leaving.

"I'll plan on it."

"And don't wait too long. Julie will be in college before we know it."

"I won't. Sooner than later."

In turn he hugged Amy, who kissed him lightly on the lips, Kaito, and Juliette, now roused, saving the longest hug for her.

"You have to visit," she said simply. It wasn't a question, or a plea, or a demand. Just a simple fact.

As Jack drove back to the hotel, he couldn't help but think, "I could live like this."

25

Jack pulled his rental over to the curb in front of 1767 South Wabash. Low stratocumulus clouds clogged the sky. The forecast was for thunderstorms later that afternoon.

The building that replaced the apartment Cathy died in was newish, red-and-grey brick, lots of tinted glass. Across the street was an extensive gravel parking lot, and several construction projects were evident up and down the street. The neighborhood was gentrifying. Getting better by some people's standards, worse by others.

Jack got out of the car. He'd thought maybe he'd catch a vibe from the location, but it had been washed clean. An elderly black man in a cap, balancing a cane against his leg, sat on the low cement wall directly in front of the building. Jack walked over to him.

"Hello."

The man looked up.

"Do I know you?" he asked in a crisp voice.

"No. I'm just visiting. You live here?"

"Up there." He turned and pointed up toward the top floors.

"Nice place."

"It's okay. New."

"You live here long?"

"Since they opened in 2009. I used to live in the old building but they condemned it and moved us out. Gave us a priority with this place. Gave us a good rate too."

"You lived in the apartment that was here before? The one with the lobby?"

"Yeah. The Royal Arms. Lived there most of my life."

"Huh."

"Yep," the old man said, looking down at his shoes, "that was a long time ago. They tore it down in ninety-two or three."

"Do you remember a woman that died in the lobby."

"She was murdered. Neighborhood was bad then. Lots of crime. Better now."

"Remember anything else about it?"

"Long time ago. In the fifties it must have been. Don't think the police ever found out who killed her."

"Did you see the body?"

"Nah. I remember I was out late. I used to go to clubs. Got home and the lobby was roped off. Crime scene. Had to go in the back way. Found out about it from my neighbor the next day."

"Did the police talk with you?"

"Nah. I would have gone to them if I knew anything. I didn't like the cops, but I respected them. It's a hard job. But I didn't know anything about the girl, or why she'd been shot." He hawked up some mucous and spit it onto the sidewalk. "Lot of people got shot those days. Hell, lots of people get shot now-days too, just not here. Farther south is bad."

"Well, thanks for your time."

He looked at Jack and smiled.

"Hell, time's all I got."

Jack parked five blocks away on south Michigan and walked to the Art Institute. It was hot and muggy, around ninety degrees he figured.

One of the things Jack tried to do in cities he visited was visit an art museum. Given that there were more than several in Chicago, and he only had an afternoon, the Art Institute was a must. He spent the good part of the afternoon wandering the many halls, rotundas and galleries, soaking in the art, studying it, letting it move or not-move him. Jack's knowledge of art was sporadic at best, piece-meal. He read the articles and columns in the Seattle Times, and Peter Schjeldahl's column New Yorker which he loved. His tastes ran from the Impressionists through surrealism to abstraction. He hated pop art, considering it a scam.

He'd come primarily to see a show by Valeria Trasatti and Aliza Razell, two artists who were merging painting and photography. The show was small, maybe thirty pieces, but fascinating, and he photographed most of it. Studying the works gave him several ideas for working with Riordan.

Wandering blindly after that, Jack suffered a minor fit of ecstasy when he stumbled on Joseph Cornell's boxes, of which the museum owned forty-two. The boxes each contained what could only be described as miniature worlds, inviting the viewer to enter and explore. Emerging from the gallery that housed them, Jack realized the museum would be closing in twenty minutes. He'd been swallowed up, spending nearly two hours there.

The drive back to the Holiday Inn, through rush hour traffic was exhausting, made worse by the eruption of a wicked thunderstorm. Suring the drive, he turned the dream of Cathy lying in the lobby of The Royal Arms over and over in his mind, remembering what McNeeley had said about the murder being untouchable. Despite how he'd gotten involved, he owed that woman some justice. Perhaps there was a way to make this not right, but righter. After a quick shower, a bratwurst at a local brewpub, Jack crashed. The wake-up call would come far too soon.

26

It was raining lightly when the plane landed in Seattle, a friendly rain his friend Sam had called it. He retrieved his car and drove north to Kenmore on a freeway clogged with cars leaving the city.

The apartment was stuffy, so he opened the windows and let fresh air off the lake circulate and cool it. Chicago had been hot and muggy. Not his cup of tea at all.

Tomorrow was his first meeting with Riordan and Monique. He had some ideas he wanted to run by them, and he knew that Riordan had several he wanted Jack to start working on. Monique was more of a mystery. She had showed Jack pictures of her work, largely batiked fabric sculptures, but he didn't get a sense of how she wanted to proceed. They'd talked briefly about integrating computer screens into sculptures, which had been done a lot using video footage, but she didn't need a programmer to do that, and besides Jack thought it was boring. He hoped the meeting would clarify some of this.

He texted Juanita and told her he was back, that he'd see her at the Magnolia Playfield around 4:30, warning her that he'd be coming from a meeting and might be a bit late.

She responded with a smiley face followed by an exclamation point.

Then he went for a run up to Sammamish Park and back.

It was weird not to have to go to a "job," and he felt a bit guilty. He could hear his dad telling him the value of an 8-5 job, the structure of it, the sense of place it gave one. His dad had been strict, Japanese. There were rules that needed to be followed, and society would fall apart if they weren't. His dad died of a heart attack three years ago. He was out on his sailboat off San Diego and just keeled over. Jack figured it was a perfect way to go. The crew on another boat had witnessed it and pulled aside, navigating his dad's boat into the marina. After a small memorial service, the family had spread his father's ashes in the ocean.

"Shit," he said out loud, "I should call mom and tell her I have another job."

His dad and he hadn't been close, barely talking over the years since he left home. But he tried to call his mom every month or so, and keep her appraised of the few highlights his life held.

Instead, he began researching face-recognition software. The primary code for writing it was Python, which he knew well. However, he knew next to nothing about face-recognition. It turned out there were several algorithms for the software: Eigenfaces, Local Binary Patterns Histograms (LBPH), Fisherfaces, Scale Invariant Feature Transform (SIFT), and Speed Up Robust Features (SURF). Each method had a different approach to extract information.

Jack quickly read through the algorithms, deciding to focus on LBPH initially. He was thinking of Riordan's initial project of facial collages. He had an idea he wanted to run by him.

He'd been ignoring e-mail, and finally succumbed. There was the usual garbage, along with a packet of documents that needed to be signed and returned to UniCode. And it turned out that despite what Ken Billetts said about severance pay, there was a hefty package, over $90,000. The amount had already been wired to his checking account. Jack was immediately overcome with the desire to buy a Tesla, which he suppressed.

Along with the email detailing severance pay, there was an attachment. When Jack opened it, he found a letter of recommendation from Tyler Ryder, UniCode's CEO. The letter embarrassed Jack with its praise. A third page contained a private note from Tyler, thanking Jack for all he'd contributed to UniCode in his twenty-two years of service, and assuring him that if things did not work out, he had a place there. "Ken Billetts is on his way out," Tyler had written, "but currently, that's between you and me." Jack sat back and let the praise and good wishes flow through him. He never got positive feedback from Billetts, and found he was hungry for it. It was good, and also verified his existence at UniCode. He had been of value; he had made a difference. The severance paperwork took most of an hour, and by the end of it he'd forgotten about the Tesla.

There was also an e-mail from Miguel telling Jack the team was getting together tonight at Cairn Brewery. Cairn was just off the Burke-Gilman, about a mile from Jack's condo, and he decided to run over. He'd catch a ride home from Miguel. Miguel told Jack they'd have a send-off party for him soon. This was a prelude. Jack texted Miguel and told him he'd be there around six.

The get together was warm and low-key. His old team was there, Miguel, Roger, Curry, and Emily and Horatio, who he'd worked with years ago.

"I'm buying," said Jack, hugging everyone then sitting down.

Miguel explained they'd doubled the team for a huge contract with Puget Sound and Energy due at the end of the week.

"Billetts promoted me," Miguel said, hoisting a pint into the air. "Your loss is my gain."

Jack was laughing. "No man, your gain is my gain." And Jack told them about his new job. As much as he knew.

"Sounds fun, dude."

"Yeah, good luck with that."

"Let me know if you need any help."

The crew drank, reminisced, gave each other shit, and Jack knew that however it shook out, he would miss these guys. Their bonds had been forged in the trenches of deadlines and punishing stress.

The night wound down early, as most of the crew would be back at UniCode by seven. Miguel gave Jack a ride home, and they sat in front of his building talking for another fifteen minutes. The sky lightened briefly before its final darkening.

"I'm going to miss you, dude," Miguel said, leaning over to give Jack a hug.

"Ditto. Let's keep in touch."

"Yeah, and let's not just say we're going to keep in touch, let's actually do it."

"Agreed."

Once inside, Jack poured himself a snifter of brandy, selected Dvorak's *New World Symphony*, and turned the volume up. He walked over to the window, sipping brandy, watching the lights of the few night boats, listening to the powerful swells of music, the haunting folk melodies hidden in daring counterpoint.

It had been great to see Kaito, meet his family. And he'd learned a bit more about Cathy's death. Not much, but every little bit helped. And he'd been blessed to work with such a talented and dedicated crew. He would truly miss them, and the camaraderie and support of working with a team. He was a lone wolf now.

And finally, he thought of Juanita, saw her standing before him outside Soy Haus, her long ebony hair in a loose ponytail. As tall as he was, her vivid chestnut eyes met his directly, which thrilled him. He remembered their twinkle, some silent mirth toward him or the entire human condition, and warmth spread through him. They were dancing around the edges now, but dancing closer all the time. It was getting late but he texted her.

Hey, just thinking of you. Missing you.

His phone dinged almost immediately. It was a simple *Me too. C U tomorrow* that made his heart leap.

Jack finished the brandy and lay down on the couch immersed in an unfamiliar euphoria. He woke three hours later.

The boy had visited him.

In his dream, Jack was running a stretch of the Burke-Gilman he didn't recognize when the boy stepped out from a clump of snowberry and wild rose. He was radiant, glowing white light. "Like an angel," Jack thought, stopping suddenly.

"The backpack," the boy said. "You need to find the backpack."

Jack couldn't speak. He was paralyzed.

"You need to find the backpack."

Then the boy was gone, and Jack was bent over staring at his shoes, his breath heaving. Then he woke.

27

The meeting with Riordan and Monique went long, but was productive, and was a preview of what Jack's work life would be like into the foreseeable future.

Riordan had a show in November at the Seattle Art Museum, which locals called SAM. Two rooms, enough wall space for twenty to thirty framed photographs, depending on size.

"But I'm envisioning screens, all screens. Each with a different display. Let's talk ideas."

"We already talked about photo-collages. I think we should start with those and see where it goes," Jack said.

"Okay. Run with it."

"First screen, a basic grid with thirty squares, each with a photograph, each holding the photo for a certain amount of time, say five seconds."

"Two seconds," Riordan interrupted, "no more."

"We use the database of three hundred portraits you gave me. And to make it more interesting, we could vary the speed, randomly or deliberately, on select grids, or all of them. Make it more interesting."

"Cool. Like it."

"Then we move out from there in several ways. Break down the grid structure into a screen where size and location of the photos is fluid. Whole faces or partial. For partial, I'm thinking of isolating certain prominent areas, eyes for instance, mouths, ears. Again, mix and match randomly or with structure. Then pulling from undifferentiated areas of the face, patches of skin, or partial shots that leave the origin vague, unrecognizable."

"Pure abstracts."

"Yeah, and again, random or not, or vary it."

"Okay, but what about something simpler as well. Take two photographs, a man and a woman, or fuck that, two people, and merge them in an interesting way. Not that freaky web shit, but let the photos really integrate."

"Hmm. I could do that. That might be cool. Let the images merge."

Riordan was nodding his head. "Think liquids flowing into each other, mixing, but slowly."

"I like it."

"How long would it take you to work up some prototypes of these examples?" Riordan asked.

"I could have, say nine or ten in a couple weeks. They'd be rough but would give you an idea of potential; the possibilities of where we could go."

Jack glanced over at Monique who seemed absorbed in drawing something on a sketch pad.

"I've been taking a look at facial recognition software. I think we could do something sweet with that, mapping similarities for symmetries, or the reverse. Disparities. That's going to take longer. I haven't played with the algorithms before."

"Nice! That sounds cooler than hell! How soon before I could see something like that?"

"Don't know. I'll keep you posted."

Jack and Riordan talked details awhile, then Jack addressed Monique, who'd been quietly absorbed in jotting and drawing on a sketch pad.

"What do you think Monique? Where are you with all this?"

Monique flashed him a wan smile, and Jack realized how beautiful she was. Winsome, her blond hair now frosted with silver, cool in a Nordic way.

"I have a show in Portland and another in Los Angeles. I was hoping for something new, especially for the LA show. I'm bored with what I've been doing."

"Bored, hah!" Riordan broke in. "She's fucking brilliant! Bored, my ass."

"I think the two are intertwined," she said coolly. "If I'm not bored, I do nothing new. I go nowhere."

"I've seen the series of batiked fabric sculpture. You're thinking of something working with those, or something entirely new?" Riordan asked.

"New." She glanced at Riordan then fixed her gaze on Jack. "Is there a way to have fabric project, the way a computer screen projects?"

"Good question," Jack answered. "I don't know, but I'll find out.

There's certainly a way of projecting the contents of a screen through or onto fabric…"

"I've seen that. Both ways. I'm thinking of something a little different."

"The fabric would be the computer."

"Something like that. One thing I'm thinking of is a large language piece. That could be done with projection I suppose."

"Language piece. Could you expand on that?"

"I'm thinking of text on fabric that is continually altered by projected light, so that different words or areas of text are highlighted, and these shift constantly. I want to play with the transience of meaning."

"That's so cliché, Monique. The transience of meaning. Good Lord." Riordan snorted.

"Ignore him. He sold out years ago," Monique laughed.

"Let me think about it," said Jack. "Do you have any photos or sketches of the text piece?"

Monique deftly tore off the top page of her sketch pad and handed it across the table to Jack.

"Start with this, but keep going. I'm new at this. I'm not really sure how technology can assist me in expressing my visions, but I'm excited about it."

"I've heard of something called network fabric," Jack said. "Let me check into it."

"Neat. Please do check it out. Text me if you think it's promising."

28

Jack arrived late to the ballgame, second inning, and immediately saw Juanita sitting in the bleachers next to another woman. A few other spectators, parents he assumed, sat staggered throughout. He skipped up the bleachers and slid in next to her. She was wearing jeans and a short-sleeved white cotton top. The white accentuated the luxurious brown of her arms. A thin silver bracelet adorned one wrist. He noticed again there was no ring on her left ring finger.

"Jack, you made it!" She leaned over and gave him an awkward hug.

"Sorry I'm late. Did I miss much?"

"Gabriel hit a double. Their team, the Goldies, short for Elite 14U Gold, are up two-zip."

"Great! Where are the boys?"

She pointed. "Angel's playing second base, Gabe's in center field."

"Alright! This is my first ballgame since seeing the Cubs last weekend."

"You saw the Cubs?" the woman next to Juanita exclaimed.

"With Kaito, my cousin, in Chicago."

"Well, this is going to blow that away," said Juanita laughing.

Just then the batter hit a ground ball that skipped between Angel and the shortstop. Gabriel ran in, scooped it, and bombed it on the fly to Angel. Jack could see they'd worked this combination until it was effortless.

"That's Denton, one of their best hitters."

"Held him to first."

"You ever play?"

"Little league for one year." He laughed. "I sucked."

"Jack, I want you to meet Felice." Juanita sat back and the woman next to her extended her hand. "Felice, Jack."

"Nice to meet you." She had a wide smile and perfect teeth. "My star is pitching," she said laughing.

"Jason. He's a great pitcher. We always win when he pitches."

Just then man in a golf shirt sat next to Felice, and they kissed and began talking.

Jack looked around, then asked Juanita quietly if her ex-husband ever came to the games.

"When he can. But I knew he was busy today. So you can relax." Juanita laughed. Jack realized he was feeling apprehensive.

The rest of the game went well for the Goldies. They won 6-2 and held a lead the entire game. Juanita was passionate fan, screaming support, waving her arms, leaping to her feet to dispute a call.

After the game, she introduced Jack to the boys, who seemed nonplussed until she told them he programmed computers. Then Angel lit up.

"You program games?" he asked excitedly.

"Yeah, I've worked on a lot of games."

"Wow. Like *Earth Defense Force?*"

"Not that one, but we just did a fix on *Whispers of the Machine*, and a few months ago, some patches for *Mulaka*."

"Holy shit!" Angel exclaimed. "Mulaka! I LOVE that game."

"Language, young man!" Juanita snapped, but again Jack saw bemusement in her eyes.

"Sorry. Holy shirt. Is it hard?"

"Yeah, but it gets easier the more you learn."

"I'm taking computers in high school. We're learning Java."

"My turn to be impressed! Keep it up. They'll always need programmers. And it pays well."

Jack followed Juanita, only mildly surprised she drove a black Ram pickup, to her house in Green Lake, an older bungalow with sagging gutters and peeling paint. Her yard was a carnage of rhododendrons, dogwood and azaleas reclaiming turf from a lawn comprised largely of dandelions. Clearly appearances were not priorities.

"Excuse the mess," Juanita said, opening the front door. "I have no time for house-cleaning these days."

The delirious scent of Mexican food hit Jack. He hadn't realized he was starving.

Despite the warning, the house was clean and almost tidy, except for the "boy" areas – a rec room off the living room, and two bedrooms upstairs.

"I don't venture in," Juanita said, pointing to two closed doors. "Biohazards, for starters."

"At least they're old enough to do laundry," Jack said. "Right?"

She laughed and gave him a light punch in the arm. "You don't know much about kids, do you?"

Jack laughed awkwardly. "Not really."

"They're good kids. They've really stepped up since I left Aldous."

"Aldous?"

"My ex."

"Interesting name." Juanita laughed. "Interesting, it is. He hates it. Goes by Alex."

"Good to know."

She looked at him strangely. "Let's eat."

Dinner was delicious.

Juanita had prepared green chili pozole, served with homemade tortillas, rice, and refried black beans. There were bottles of Dos Equis for the adults and apple juice for the boys.

Gabe remained aloof, saying little, acting bored, eating quickly, and excusing himself for

homework before anyone else finished.

Angel was a different story. He milked Jack for information on computing, arguing with Juanita on the side for a new MacBook. Jack and Juanita got a few words in edgewise, and Jack agreed to take a look at Angel's homework assignment.

"Leave cleanup to me," said Juanita. "Why don't you take a look at Angel's work, then we'll take a walk. Green Lake's only two blocks away."

"Sounds good," Jack said, "Okay Angel, show me what you got."

Angel bounded up the stairs and Jack followed him into his room, which smelled mildly of sneakers and teen spirit. Books were splayed open on a small desk next to a well-worn Dell PC.

"Here, check this out." He handed Jack a piece of paper covered in code. "We have to print everything out. Old school proof."

As Jack scanned the code, which was for a web database interface, Angel fired up the Dell which ground and hissed its way to life. Angel really did need a better computer. Jack had a few extras at home. He'd talk to Juanita about it.

"I'm working with two other guys on a game. It's based on the board game GO."

For the next twenty minutes Jack pointed out a few redundancies in Angel's code, suggested a couple of rewrites, insisting that

Angel understand the rationale behind them, and gave him a few suggestions on the game code, which was written in rudimentary C++. Angel thanked him profusely, still in awe of his mom's friend's prowess, and Jack took his leave.

"Angel's sharp," Jack said as they walked toward the lake. "Really, really smart."

"He is if the subject interests him. He bombs on history, social studies, English. Couldn't care less about them. But math and science, and now computers, really light his fire. The trick is getting him to try hard enough in the other subjects so he can get a passing grade. I want him to go to college. A good school."

"Where did you go?"

"UW. I was the first person in my family to get there. We didn't have money, but I was able to get a minority scholarship."

"What did you major in?"

"History and political science. But I was always interested in law enforcement. My dad was a cop in Oakland before we moved up here."

"Oakland. Whew. Tough place for a cop. For anyone, in those days."

"Yeah. It took a lot out of him. He got into private security up here and did well. Lots of paranoid rich people around Seattle." She laughed.

Jack loved the way her infectious laugh bubbled up from her core.

"My dad just retired last year, but he's still consulting, much to mom's chagrin. She wants them to travel. Has a list a mile long of places to go. Dad's always been a homebody. Give him a beer, a newspaper or ball game on TV, and he's fine."

"How did you get into the FBI?"

"After I graduated, I started surveying the field. The Seattle office was hiring, and I knew from an inside connection, that all things being equal, I stood a good chance. They were trying to put a more diverse face on things, and I filled two slots," she laughed again, "a woman, and a Hispanic."

"How long have you been there?"

She laughed and slapped him lightly on the arm.

"Are you asking my age?"

"Heavens no," Jack said laughing. "But you probably know mine. Hell, you probably know what kind of gum I chew."

"I peeked at a few things." They were both laughing now. "You don't chew gum."

A mild breeze blew as they turned onto the looping path around the lake. Juanita slid her hand into Jack's, and it was the most natural thing in the world. They waded through a gaggle of Canadian Geese choking the path, and Jack pointed out several mergansers clumped just offshore.

"Birds. They'll be here after we're gone."

"Hope so," Juanita said. "Something's got to be."

"Did you find out anything about Flowers? The husband of Cathy's sister?" Jack asked.

"I did. He was a captain for American Steamship Company. Worked there until retirement. He's since passed, as has his wife, Cathy's sister Susan. But they had two kids. A daughter, Katie who lives outside Portland, and a son who works in New York City as a hedge fund manager. Neither kid was alive when Cathy was murdered, so I doubt they'd know anything, but it might be worth checking."

"Sounds like a dead end."

"How about you? Anything else you didn't tell me?"

"Oh, I have a club foot."

Juanita smacked him on the shoulder. "Silly. I mean from your visit to Chicago, with the cop McNeeley?"

"Cathy Flowers was a dancer and prostitute at one or more clubs owned by the Irish mob, and apparently frequented by a lot of politicos and business types. The cop I talked to, McNeeley, said they, the politicos, were into heavy S&M with some of the dancers. He said when they were "used up" they killed them and dumped them. Anonymous Jane Does. He also said the mob was protected, and they got chased off the case. I could tell that bothered him a lot. It was one of his first cases."

"He was still an idealist."

"Weren't we all."

"So that's what happened to Cathy Flowers some seventy years ago."

"Yeah."

"I'd like to say we've come a long way since then, but we haven't. I remember my first commander telling me that I would lose cases, a lot of cases, but not to dwell on them. Think about the ones you get."

They walked without talking then Juanita pointed to a wooden bench and said, "Let's sit."

The wooden bench was warm in the evening sun.

"Beautiful, isn't it?" Juanita asked.

"Definitely."

They sat quietly watching the breeze riffle the sky's reflection, lost in their own thoughts.

"I live with a view of Lake Washington. Something about having water nearby."

"Soothing. I run this lake trail almost every morning."

"No way!"

"Way!"

"I just got back into running. The doctor I went to for memory problems recommended exercise, so I fell back on what I knew. I ran a bit of track in high school, and running damn near got me through college."

"Why'd you quit?"

"Got too busy with work. I'm come off those long days and just collapse. Feels good to be back at it."

"You run the BG?"

"Yeah. It's right out my door."

"Sweet. I used to run it more when I lived closer. I always enjoyed the people watching."

A group of teenagers passed by laughing, throwing each other shit.

"That kid, the beatific one, visited me again last night," Jack told her.

"Really? Tell me more."

"He wanted me to find the backpack."

"Not *a* backpack, *the* backpack?"

"Yeah."

"The parents didn't mention a backpack. Be worth checking to see if he left home with one."

"The two guys who killed him wanted something he didn't have. Maybe it was in the
backpack. Maybe he stashed it somewhere, figuring he'd bargain with them."

"Huh. I'll make a call tomorrow."

"Let me know?"

"Of course."

Jack had forgotten they were still holding hands until she gave a slight squeeze. "What's his dad do at Lightfoot, by the way?"

"He's in some middle management position. Vice president of

bullshit something-or-other. I talked with him. He appeared shattered. Which would be normal if your child was murdered. But he could be lying as well. Lightfoot probably has him over a barrel."

"You guys look into him?"

"Nothing there that we could find. Boring. Undergrad at Gonzaga. Played some ball. Then to Columbia for his MBA. Not even a misdemeanor. Went to work for Lightfoot the summer he graduated."

"What if he was additionally upset about what happened to that backpack?"

She turned and faced him, mirth dancing in her eyes again.

"I thought I was supposed to be the cynic, and you were the bright-eyed programmer."

"Just trying it on for size. After what McNeeley told me, I realize I've got a window into some very bad people."

"There are some of those around to be sure. Should we head back? I've got to be up early. Meeting at 7:30."

They rose and began retracing their steps.

"I think it's weird the way Lightfoot keeps popping up."

"Could be coincidence."

"Could be."

"Probably not."

"Probably not."

29

Jack was up early, threw on his Asics, shorts, a light sweatshirt proclaiming *Yang for President*, and headed to the Burke-Gilman.

It was evolving into a perfect end-of-June day, already in the high fifties, a time of year that loved to defy the expectations of Seattleites, who'd barely made it through five months of extreme gloom without committing suicide or devolving into raving alcoholics.

He ran south past Lake Forest Park to Sheridan Beach, then back, swinging by Safeway to grab some onion bagels and cream cheese, then home, where he turned the coffee maker on, put on a vinyl of Glenn Gould's Goldberg Variations which filled the room with baroque wonder. Then he fired up his laptop.

For the next three hours he ate bagels, drank coffee, and worked on the first two prototypes for Riordan, who'd given him a database of 300 plus portraits to play with.

Jack did some quick sorts by gender, age, ethnicity to see what came up, then began writing software for shifting grids. He created software that identified certain facial areas and isolated them, also categorized basic face shapes. The work was fun, challenging, and absorbed Jack's concentration. When he came out of his zone, he realized the room was silent and it was nearly noon.

Checking his cell, there was a text from Juanita to call him.

She picked up after two rings.

"Can I call you back? Meeting."

"Sure."

She called back twenty-three minutes later.

"Gotta be quick. Two things." Juanita sounded breathless.

"Michael Daly definitely had a backpack when he left home. His mother remembered that he turned sideways in the doorway to say goodbye, and she saw it then for sure. It was his usual backpack. Dark blue or navy. She thought a Jansport, but couldn't remember for sure.

"Secondly, Bill McCandless' girlfriend called. We'd talked to her once, but she said she remembered something that might be important. I set up a meeting in my office for 1:30. Can you make it?"

"I think so. I'm just wrapping up some work. What is it?"

"Didn't say. Seemed reluctant to talk over the phone." Jack heard loud voices. "Gotta go. See you later."

Jack wondered why, whenever he talked with Juanita, the click of the phone sounded so final, her words floating in the air, then gone.

The FBI desk guard was a guy Jack hadn't encountered before, but after calling Juanita, he asked, "Do you know the way?"

"Yes."

The guy gave him a bemused look, then said "You're expected."

Jack nodded.

There were three other people in the office, a brunette woman in studded jeans and a Seahawks T-shirt, a mid-thirties crew-cut male wearing Khakis and a blue Arrow shirt, no tie, and a lanky outdoorsy woman with a hatchet face wearing a black and red squared Woolrich shirt. Jack guessed her around forty but her age was indefinite. She looked as tough as beef jerky.

Juanita introduced them as agents Michel Faber and Christine Magic who were also working the case, and Penny Wakes, Bill McCandless' girlfriend.

Faber and Magic were accommodating, but Jack knew they silently questioned his presence. Juanita seemed neither to notice nor care. Once Jack was seated, Faber got down to business.

"Mind if I record this, Ms. Statmore?"

The outdoorsy woman shook her head.

"Ms. Statmore, you told agent Hernandez that you had further information you didn't share with us when we interviewed you on June 11th. Can you clarify?"

"It's something I didn't remember at the time. Billy had a safe deposit box."

"Oh?" Jack could see Juanita's interest sharpen. "What bank?"

"It's not a local bank. Billy was paranoid. The bank was in Wenatchee."

"Wenatchee?" Faber expressed surprise. "Why Wenatchee?"

"It's where Billy grew up."

"Go on."

"I think the bank's name was Washington something. National, federal. Something like that. Something officious."

"How did you come to know this?"

"Billy told me. He was paranoid someone was going to break into his apartment and steal his research."

"Did he tell you who would do that?" Magic asked.

"He only told me it was regarding the Lightfoot trial."

"I know we've asked you this before Ms. Statmore, but can you remember if Bill told you he was directly threatened by Lightfoot?"

"He didn't. He was just really paranoid about this trial. I think he knew the implications of taking on a company of their size. And he loved the whales. He wanted to help them."

"Yes," Magic said, "but think hard Ms. Statmore. Just because a company is large doesn't mean they will cause you harm. Thousands of people sue Comcast every day, and these people don't worry about being killed."

Faber chuckled.

Penny Statmore was staring at the table but her voice focused the room.

"Billy knew he'd discovered criminal activities involving the shipment of Orcas. That's a bit different than suing Comcast for being a Stalinist organization."

"I grant you that, Ms. Statmore, but still, is there anything you can think of? Phone calls he might have received? Emails, texts? Anything at all that constituted an actual threat?"

"No. I'm sorry."

"It's okay," Juanita said. "What you've told us is valuable."

"Yes, thank you," said Juanita.

Penny stood up.

"Could you let me know if you find anything?"

"Certainly," Faber said. "Thanks for coming in, helping us out."

Penny Statmore was walking toward the door when Jack said, "Wait, please. One more question."

She pivoted and stared at Jack, questioning. "Yes?"

"Had Billy ever mentioned Lightfoot with regard to any other issues, environmental or otherwise?"

She didn't hesitate.

"He told me once they were smugglers."

"Smugglers?"

"Yeah. The Orcas were the thing he was most concerned about, but he said they had their talons in other smuggling as well."

"Was he specific?"

"He mentioned wildlife once, but nothing more specific than

that. I'm sorry."

"Endangered species? That type of wildlife?"

"I'm sorry."

"Thank you for coming in, Ms. Statmore. You've been a great help." Juanita placed her pen on the legal pad.

Penny stood poised, expectant.

"We'll call you if we need anything else," Juanita said. "Thank you."

"I'll escort you down Ms. Statmore." Magic stood and walked her out, closing the door behind her.

"We need to get into that account," Faber said when Penny was gone.

"No shit," said Juanita. "Give Hendricks a call and get him over there."

"Washington Federal, I'm thinking."

"Me too. Start there."

"On it." Faber gave a mock salute and wheeled out.

"You need to be anywhere quick?" Juanita asked Jack after the door clicked shut.

"I need to get back to work. I'm in a zone coding for Riordan."

"Got time for a quick cup?"

"Sure," Jack said. "I'm getting damn weary of being a conduit for these murders, not just weary though. Spooked."

"I'm sure it sucks. Tell me about it over a cup of joe. Starbucks okay?"

"Classic bitter," Jack laughed. "I was just thinking."

"Don't get me started."

They walked down Third past Seneca and entered Starbucks, Jack glancing around for a seat. The place was jammed, but luck was with them, and a couple of suits were clearing their small table.

"I'll grab it," he told Juanita. "Get me a 12-ounce drip, lots of cream." He smiled at her,

then added, "Thanks."

"God, I'm already your bitch."

"I act fast."

She flashed him a smile. Half sexy, half sweet, then laughed and walked over to the counter.

Jack studied his phone. A text from Kaito, which he answered.

Juanita joined him a few minutes later. She immediately asked, "What did you think of Penny Statmore?"

Jack stretched up, then placed his hands behind his head, leaned back. "She didn't seem as angry as I thought she'd be. Her beau murdered. All that."

"Eleven years ago. Dead end."

"True, true."

"She remarried, then divorced, quickly. I think they made it a month. It's been four years since that. She's numb, Jack, numb and weary."

"You checked her out." Not a question. Jack already knew, mildly spooked by the near-infinite data mine Juanita had at her disposal. But thankful, maybe, as well.

"We check everything out."

"Okay." He picked up his coffee and took a sip, shaking his head and setting it down. "Whew. Hot."

"Not enough cream?"

"No," Jack laughed, "but we're still getting to know each other."

"True, dat."

"So what did you think?"

"I thought your follow-up question was good. Opened the door on Lightfoot further. We would have missed it. The wildlife smuggling."

Jack took a mock bow. "Thank you, thank you. It's gotta be exotics though. Ivory, tiger gall bladders. That sort of thing. That's where the money is."

"We need to put a bigger microscope on Lightfoot."

I agree."

"I'm glad you do."

Silence for several long moments. An alto sax whirled, trembled out of control, then mellowed into a melodic rendition of Sentimental Mood. Voices buzzed, sometimes sharply, rose and fell, a random backdrop cadence.

"So where do I fit in anyway?" Jack asked. "I mean, I saw the look those two agents gave me. They didn't exactly say I shouldn't be there, or that I was a.) an impediment; b) a nutcase; or c) a suspect. But they thought it. I have no official capacity here Juanita. No credibility. I'm a witness, an informant. I know stuff. That's all."

"Let's give you some." She smiled that Cheshire smile.

"What?"

"I can hire you as a researcher." The twinkle was there. Flirty now, he realized.

"Is that legal?"

"If you fill out the necessary paperwork. Get fingerprinted, interviewed. Necessary bullshit."

"You're kidding me, right?"

"Not at all." She stretched her hand across the small table and touched his arm.

He stared at her for a long moment then gutted a laugh.

"Okay, I'll do it. Supplemental income is good, but I hate the thought of working for another organization. There's something in the name organization that I cringe at."

"You're not working for another organization."

"I'm not?"

"No. You're volunteering." The twinkle was back.

"Volunteering?"

"No money changes hands. But the minute you stop having those dreams, I drop you."

"But only as a researcher, right?"

"Do I have to answer that now?"

"Hah. Too cool." Then, "I like you."

"I like you too. But you'd be atmosférica if you spoke Spanish."

"What's that mean?"

"You'd be my guy."

"I'll learn. Spanish. Fast." Jack saw her smile just above the horizon, getting hotter. "I could do that." He picked up a packet of fake sugar, shook it, set it down. "What else? You said there were two things."

She held his eyes. Jack noticed the twinkle had gone.

"The backpack."

"Yeah, that."

"I've been thinking we should walk from his house to where he was killed, look for places he might have stashed it. I checked Google Maps. There are three more or less direct routes, and I'm starting with assumption he would have used one of those, and wouldn't have gone too far astray. One of the routes crosses a narrow green-belt. I want to start there."

"When's good?"

"How about this afternoon? Threeish?"

"Can't. I've got to get some prototypes in line for Riordan to prove I'm earning my keep."

"But now you're my researcher'?"

"Uh-oh, conflicts already."

"Life's messy. Tomorrow afternoon, then. Same time."

"Let me check." Jack pulled out his phone and checked his

calendar. "Looks good. Meet you at his house?"

"No, silly. We're spies. We park a block away from each other. Walk slowly towards each other. Ignore each other when we pass."

"Text me a location." Jack grinned.

"Deal."

"You have lots of other cases?" Genuinely interested.

"You don't know the third of it," she replied, suddenly subdued. "That, and kids to raise, and I'm going for an advanced degree, a PhD I think. In Criminology. I think."

"PhD! Seriously! That's fantastic!"

"I haven't made the decision yet, but I'm leaning that way."

"I could help, maybe?"

She picked up her mug and set it down.

"Can you hack into Linus systems?"

Jack snorted. "Linux, not Linus."

Juanita ignored him. "Can you?"

"Easy peasy. I did my first Linux hack when I was ten."

"Ten? Seriously? Think Angel's doing it?

"Which 'it'?"

"The Linux thing. What did you think?"

Jack smiled.

"Not Angel," Juanita answered.

"Hah. Got you."

"Baaaad! What do you think? The Linux thing."

Jack laughed. "I think he is."

"Hacking?"

"Yeah. He's smart enough. And that's the fun stuff. Hacking. Before life gets serious. They're kids. They're just playing around. Of course, sometimes the stakes get too high for kids. A dare to break into a government system."

"Wow!" Juanita sucked her bottom lip. "Never would have thought that. Maybe I should ask him to hack this system."

"I *like* you."

"Me gustas." The twinkle was back.

"What system, by the way?"

"I'll keep you posted. Just wanted to see if you could."

30

They met at 3:30 the next afternoon a block from Michael Daly's house, the neighborhood full of old Tudors, bulging Queen Anne's, stately Beaux-Arts; sky-high hedges and immaculately manicured yards.

Juanita had suggested walking the green-belt route first. The day was mild, mid-seventies, the sky hazy with cloud. They walked slowly, carefully, for three blocks, and they saw nothing. They even glanced into several convenient trash containers. They examined shrubbery and the large hedges, but there were few hiding places and they found nothing.

Jack threw a few jokes at Juanita, but she was all business now, and slowly the sadness of what they were doing sink in. He saw the boy's angelic face, the fear and twitching grimace just before the .22 slug ended his too-short life.

A narrow path cut into the green belt, used by walkers, runners, mountain bikers, bird-watchers, kids getting into mischief. The tall cottonwoods and fir choked with English ivy immediately engulfed them in dark forest, and the tony neighborhood they'd just passed through seemed shadows away.

"You think Michael would have walked through here that night? It was dark. No moon. Would have been scary to a kid," Jack asked.

"Yeah, but this was *his* woods. He grew up three blocks away. He would have known this greenbelt like his backyard. Probably better."

They walked in silence, glancing around, looking for places Michael could have stashed a backpack, following a few side-trails.

"I don't think he would have gone too far off this path. He'd want quick access."

"You still think he was bargaining with his killers?"

"Nothing else makes sense to me right now."

A thrush's liquid song flooded the air, then faded. The woods seemed suddenly peaceful, sun-dappled.

"Over there."

Juanita pointed to a mammoth cottonwood that had crashed to earth years ago. Along the length of the log, and underneath it, were any number of troughs, caves, and hollows, any of which could have concealed a day pack. Jack and Juanita spent the next fifteen minutes searching each of them, finding some empty bottles, a plastic bag stuffed with dirty clothes, and a sodden Penthouse magazine.

"Damn. I was pretty sold on this being the place."

"As well. Seems ideal. A few blocks from where Michael met the two men."

"He could have easily run back and gotten it."

"Let's walk it out."

They walked another half-block, checked-out a couple of other possibilities to no avail, then were out of the green belt and back onto the street.

"Damn," repeated Juanita. "That cottonwood seemed like the spot."

They walked slowly on to the murder site, seeing nothing that seemed a likely possibility. Then they walked off the other two routes, again finding a few possibilities, but nothing that hid a backpack.

They were standing in the alley where the murder had gone down.

"You think he might have shoved it into one of these garbage cans?" Juanita asked

"No. He was with the murderers then. He wouldn't have had the backpack on. They would have grabbed it."

"Hey, we weren't there. Maybe they did take it."

"I was there. They didn't get the backpack." Jack was irritated. I've told you all this already."

"Okay, Okay. Back off!" Then after a pause, a breath. "You up for searching the greenbelt again?"

Jack glanced at his watch. "It's almost five. I've got to go write code. Sorry."

"Well, I'm going back in there. It's the only logical place. Maybe he ventured further off the path than we thought."

"Maybe he stuck it in a tree."

"I thought of that. I'll keep an eye out for easy climbs."

Juanita jogged off towards the greenbelt, Jack following. Despite the view of her lovely rear, Jack wondered if this was metaphoric, him following, her leading. Not that he was necessarily opposed to that. But he'd learned in the short time he'd known her.

Juanita was not a follower.

Once in the ribbon of urban forest, Juanita stopped.

"Look, you head out. I'm going to go over this place more carefully. If the backpack exists, it's got to be here."

"Text me later?"

"Sure."

"Kiss?"

Juanita glanced around.

"You worried we'll be seen?"

She seemed embarrassed.

"I don't like to mix personal with professional."

"One little kiss Juanita. One. Little. Kiss."

She stepped into him and gave him a peck on the lips, letting her tongue tease as she pulled back.

"Whew! Bye," Jack said.

"Take care."

"You too."

Then Juanita headed off the path toward a thicket of currant and wild rose.

31

Jack worked Riordan's project until after midnight, lost in the rush, part caffeine, part the pure joy of creating art with code. Juanita had texted him around nine o'clock. The text had consisted of one word.

"Nada."

At one-ten, he clicked off the Mac, poured himself a healthy two inches of Scotch, and turned on the stereo, selecting an old album of Catherine Russell's called *Cat*. The Dewars blended perfectly with Russell's smoky voice, the timeless standards like "Can't We Be Friends?" And he thought of Juanita. That he didn't want to be "just friends."

Around one-thirty his phone rang, jarring him awake.

"Jack speaking."

A gruff, Hispanic voice said, "You the guy who's fucking my wife?"

It took Jack a minute to reconnoiter, then he remembered Juanita's husband, the Seattle cop, Alex Rubio.

"You got the wrong guy, buddy. I know her, but I'm sure not having sex with her."

There was a lengthy pause.

"Stay away from her or I'll kill you. That clear?"

"That's recorded dude."

The phone clicked dead.

32

Two days flew by, Jack consumed with code. He, Riordan, and Monique had met Wednesday. Jack had demonstrated what he'd come up with. They were both impressed, and Riordan went on a tear, brainstorming other possibilities with the speed of light until Jack put on the brakes.

"Look, we've got to identify the pieces you want. I can play with this stuff endlessly, but we've got a deadline."

"Such a buzz-kill," Riordan roared, laughing, slapping him on the shoulder as he stood up to leave. "I'll leave it to you. Get me thirty prototypes by next month and I'm good."

"Now that's a deadline I can handle," laughed Jack in return.

"I aim to please, you aim too, please."

"And always hit the bullseye," he yelled to the disappearing Riordan.

Monique was quiet, but remained after Riordan left.

Jack filled her in on the little he'd learned.

"Network fabric was a bust. Fabric is used metaphorically."

"Dead end?"

"Yeah. But," he drew the word out, "I did find some information on smart fabric."

"I've heard of that." She was getting animated. "Tell me more."

"Also called smart wear, electronic textiles, smart textiles, e-textiles. Basically, clothing that has sensors or circuitry woven into it, enhancing the functionality."

"Interesting. Give me an example."

"Clothes that communicate with an app, like smart socks. They record the exact areas of the foot that receive the most force. Useful for podiatry, not art, or maybe it is. You'd be a better judge than I. Under Armour's got something they call *Athlete Recovery Sleepwear*. It absorbs body heat and releases infrared light to supposedly increase sleep quality and improve muscle recovery."

"Interesting, interesting." She paused, stared at him with a curious smile. "I never think about clothing any more. Funny, because that's how I got into art in the first place. Fabric, I think about all the time. Clothing, never. But now, maybe, no?"

She ran a hand through her hair. Jack noticed how coarse it was, how blond. There was a sexy, raw quality to it. Earthy, organic. Monique, whom he'd dismissed as relatively uninteresting, was not. Riordan simply overshadowed her. But then Riordan overshadowed everyone, and Jack had misjudged someone again.

"But I like the interactivity aspect. Fabric that interacts with viewers. That could be tres cool. An installation, obviously. Maybe coats they put on, gloves. Gloves would be cool. Can they measure emotions? Like those mood rings used to?"

"Don't know. Want me to look into it further?"

"Definitely!"

"Okay, I should have something by next Wednesday. I think I'm on top of Riordan's project. It's just a matter of deciding which models to use."

Monique flashed him an intriguing smile.

"You work awfully fast, don't you?"

"I guess." He smiled back. "I'm used to having crazy impossible deadlines. Haven't shaken off that mind-set. If there's something that needs doing, I just work straight-through until it's finished. Then onto the next project."

"Hmmm. You ever do anything fun?" Her very attractive lips, perfectly painted with coral lipstick, bloomed into a sexy smile.

"Never."

Her smile was contagious.

"Well, if you change your mind, let me know. I can be pretty fun at times."

"I'll keep that in mind."

Jack stopped by World Market on the way home to purchase some water glasses, and wandering the aisles, he stopped in front of a small carving of an elephant sitting cross-legged. The elephant possessed four arms, and was painted gold and wore an indigo tunic. The sign next to it stated "Ganesha" in block letters. Under that was a short block of fine print that read: *Ganesha is an elephant-headed Hindu god of beginnings. He is a remover of obstacles.*

Jack picked the statue up turned it in his hand, and immediately experienced a penetrating intimacy, as if encountering a dear long-lost friend. "I could use some obstacles removed," he said out loud.

Ten minutes later he walked out of the store with a box of four water glasses and the Ganesha statue.

That evening, as he was shoveling noodles into his mouth and putting the finishing touches on several Riordan prototypes, Juanita called.

"Hey, cowboy. Want to come run with me tomorrow morning? Green Lake?"

"Love to. What time?"

"Meet me where we walked into the park at 6:30 sharp. Don't be late or I'll start without you. Being late was one of my ex's traits, and I hate it."

"I'm never late. But speaking of your ex he called me last night."

"Oh shit! Sorry. The boys must have told him. What did he want?"

"He told me that if I didn't stop fucking you, he'd kill me."

"Seriously? That was it?"

"He was brief. Didn't seem interested in complex repartee."

"What did you say to him?"

"That I'd just recorded him."

"Did you?"

"No. But he doesn't know that."

"Hah. What a hoot." She paused for several seconds. "Maybe we should start then."

"Start what?" Jack asked, knowing full well what she'd say.

"Having sex."

"Let's just see what happens. I'm a bit spooked by the guy."

Her voice turned soft, concerned.

"I don't know what to say. It's a healthy reaction. Maybe you should report it to the cops."

"Yeah, right. We'll talk more about it tomorrow."

"Okay."

"See you then."

There was a momentary pause.

"Can you talk and run?"

"Trick question?"

"No, serious. I need to discuss something else with you, and thought we could do it while we ran. But not everyone can...do that."

"Not a problem, as long as we're not sprinting."

"Good! See you then."

"Miss you," Jack said, but he said it to an empty line.

33

Jack was sitting on a bench tightening his shoelace when Juanita put her arm around his shoulders, whispered something in his ear, then let go.

"Come on, tough guy, let's run." There was an edge to her voice Jack hadn't heard before.

"Tough guy? Don't think I've ever been called that."

"You're going to have to step up if we're going to hang out," she laughed quickly, sharply, taking off with a sprint.

Jack struggled to catch her. What the hell was going on?

"Hey, slow down," he yelled. Juanita backed off her sprint.

When Jack caught up, he was panting.

"What's a matter tough guy, I thought you could run and talk?" Almost a taunt.

"Cut the shit Juanita. What's going on?"

"I didn't sleep last night, analyzing this thing we've got, where we're headed. Then in

the midst of it Alex called, and we talked for an hour. And now I'm a bitch. An unapologetic one at that."

"Okay."

"I just want us to be honest with each other. I'm having real doubts about this."

"You seemed fine with us last night. Even joked about starting to have sex."

"I think that's what started it. I began analyzing how far, how deep I wanted to get with you."

"Okay. So do I. I think about it a lot."

"It's different for you. You're unmarried, unattached, have no kids, and your job is flexible."

"What's that supposed to mean anyway?"

"I have a lot more to lose."

Jack could think of no retort.

"These dreams of yours. I've been thinking about them. A lot.

Sometimes I think you have to be involved somehow. That's the simplest solution."

"Occam's razor."

"It's a guiding light of ours." Juanita slowed to a jog. "I've been an agent for twenty years, and I've never ever heard of anything approaching what you tell me. Dreaming you're in a victim's head, seeing through their eyes their last moments on earth."

"Oh Christ, Juanita, why would I make this up? You think I'm a criminal? Some kind of psycho?"

"I certainly don't know."

"Oh, come on. I don't know how to explain the dreams either."

Juanita slowed to a walk. "Okay, I don't *really* believe you're involved criminally. But Christ, Jack, your nightmares are freaking me out."

"Okay. Let's sit down. Talk this out."

"No. Keep running. I trust that more."

They picked up the pace and ran awhile in uncomfortable silence. Two kayakers passed them out in the lake, which lay under the emergent dawn sky like a mirror.

"You dreamt that Michael told you to find the backpack, right?"

"Yes."

She glanced over. They were side-to-side now. She ventured a quick smile.

"I remember him telling me I had to find the backpack. He told me several times."

"How reliable do you think that was?" She turned toward him again, harder, catching his eyes, hooking them.

"Everything's played out so far. I guess I've come to accept what's in the dreams as true."

"Why *do* you trust these dreams?"

He didn't answer immediately.

"They're different from other dreams. They are dreams, but they feel real. There's nothing exotic about them. They don't have time/place shifts, surreality, intense emotions, or altered consciousness like normal dreams. They're as simple as seeing through another person's eyes."

"A person who's about to be murdered."

"Yeah, there is that. But they've proven themselves, haven't they? Haven't I given you valuable information?"

"Yes. Yes, you have. You've been a valuable informant. But then I return to Occam's Razor. My head is spinning! And it's not like I need it. I have enough cases already. I have two sons I'm barely there for. And now I have you."

"Don't make it sound so joyous."

"Joyous, yeah. That's what it is. You're an enigma, Jack Toyokata, a conundrum. Why can't you just be a simple likeable guy that I can fall heads-over-heels in love with and have no regrets?"

"I do not have an answer for that." After a few yards. "I'll leave you alone if that's what you want."

"I don't know what I want, dammit."

She threw him a quick smile. "I'm a mixed-up chick and you're not helping."

They ran in silence now, Juanita picking up the pace again.

"I guess it scares me. Only someone privy to these events could know the details the way you do. How is that possible?"

"I really don't know Juanita. The only thing that makes sense is what Riordan said. That in some parallel dimension there's a universal memory bank and for some reason I'm tapping in."

"Bullshit and crazy talk."

"You have a better guess?"

"No."

Another ten yards passed. They were half-way around the lake, and Jack was feeling it in his calves and thighs. He wasn't accustomed to this pace.

"Have you talked to a therapist about them?"

"No. You think I should?"

"Don't they worry you? I mean, do you think they're symptomatic of a mental disorder?"

"Absolutely not. I feel great. For the first time in over twenty years, I might add. And I've given up analyzing the dream's cause. I just accept them. And I hope that I can help some of the victims. That's why I came to the FBI in the first place. The drams are like a strange gift. If I can help some of these people…"

"The people you dream about are beyond help, Jack. They're fucking dead!"

They passed a tall blond woman leashed to a black German Shepherd that tried to take a piece out of Jack's thigh.

"So is that what you wanted to talk to me about?"

"All of it. I don't know if I should trust you. And trust is huge with me, Jack. Huge. I trusted Alex and he fucked me over. I couldn't take another one of those."

"I can't force you to trust me, Juanita. You have to arrive there on your own."

"I know that."

"Give it more time?"

"Sure." It sounded to Jack like a tired concession. "But I'm hung up on the backpack. It's the first thing that hasn't been accurate."

"Just because we didn't find it, doesn't mean the dream isn't accurate."

"If it doesn't exist, we're not going to find it."

"Can we drop this?"

"Sure." Juanita began to accelerate into a long turn, and Jack dropped behind. They passed a couple jogging, another woman with a terrier walking towards them.

At the terminus of the turn Juanita slowed again and Jack pulled alongside. He was sweating heavily, and feeling angry.

"Did my ex's phone call bother you?"

"Hell yeah. What if someone called threatening to kill you?"

"Feeling the way I do, I'd probably go after them."

"Yeah, well we're different that way. I'm not a fighter."

"You need to become one."

"Come on, be serious."

Juanita stopped abruptly and pivoted to face Jack. He could see conflicting emotions, anger, frustration, and affection, playing out on her face, in her eyes, which were suddenly honey in the new morning sun.

"Okay, since you're not a proactive guy, I'd wait and see what happens. Maybe he'll kill you, maybe he won't."

"Jesus!" Jack took a huge gulp of air. "I didn't say I wasn't proactive; I'm just not going after him with a gun."

"Alex Rubio. He loves being a cop. I don't think he'd do anything to jeopardize that. If he

thinks you have a recording of that call, he'll probably back down. But like lots of cops, he's a hothead. And he still cares about me. A lot. And he's jealous."

"He ever hit you?"

"Came close a few times, but he knows I'd file charges, and he'd be out on the street without a uniform."

She began to jog.

"Let me know if he contacts you again?"

"Sure."

Jack spotted the parking lot ahead.

"I think I just broke a speed record."

"Arguing can do that. Adrenaline and all that. So, you Okay?"

"I'm Okay."

"Good."

They slowed to a walk, and Jack reached for her hand.

"Was this our first fight?"

She stopped abruptly, faced him and blurted a laugh.

"Are you kidding? You should hear me yell and break dishes. Neighbors have been known to call the cops. This was a spat. A disagreement."

"I do not love being yelled at." He was smiling.

"Part of the deal if you choose me. You get the whole ball of wax."

They'd arrived at her car.

"Oh, you're much more than a ball of wax."

"And I can be nice too. And sexy. Take care, Jack." Then she kissed him. And he wore that kiss most of the morning.

34

The next afternoon she texted him.

We found the backpack. Call me.

He did, immediately. And she picked up as quickly.

"Son of a bitch, I knew it!" Jack said, "Where?"

"A friend of his had it. Tommy Shields. Says Michael gave it to him the night he was murdered and told him not to tell anyone."

"Okay. So how?"

"Since you revealed the backpack dream, we started leaning on two of his friends. They both lived between Michael's house and where he'd been murdered. Both boys originally said they hadn't seen him that night. We went back and questioned them, their parents. Mentioned the backpack. Tommy caved. The other kid's in the clear. But Michael stopped by Tommy's house an hour before he was murdered, and left him the backpack for safe keeping. Want to know what's in it?"

"What?"

"Five 8 ½ by 12 glossy photographs."

"Of?"

"You're not even going to guess something cliché like child porn?"

"Just tell me."

"You would not guess this in a billion years."

"I believe you. So, what's on the photos?"

"Elephant tusks. Hundreds, maybe thousands of them."

"Damn!"

"Someone's smuggling elephant tusks. Tons of illegal ivory. Highly illegal ivory. And extremely profitable."

"And Michael found out."

"Michael found out, and now he's dead."

"Lightfoot?"

"You think?"

Juanita texted him as soon as she hung up.

Find out everything you can on illegal ivory.

So Jack hit the web, Wikipedia first, *Ivory Trade*, then spread out. He emailed Juanita twenty minutes later.

I'll keep digging but: ivory illegal in the US, unless older than 1947 (some law or treaty); **billions of dollars** *a year in illegal sales; decimating African elephants (90% illegal from elephants); estimates of 40,000 elephants a year or more killed for their tusks; international criminal organizations; Singapore, Hong Kong, Taiwan common ports; busts in Manhattan, La Jolla; US market increasing.*

A few minutes later she texted back.

More news. Can you meet for lunch?

Where?

Soy Haus?

What time?

12:45?

See you.

Any hopes Jack had for a romantic interlude disappeared when he entered Soy Haus and saw Juanita sitting with agents Michel Faber and Christine Magic.

Magic pushed out a chair for Jack.

"Sit, researcher."

"Yeah," Faber said, "Juanita tells us you're her researcher? Sure you're not her boy-toy?" Magic and Faber laughed; Juanita looked irritated.

"Settle people, we've got developments. Jack, we're going to pull Michael's dad in for questioning, show him the photos, see if we can shake something loose. I talked with him before. He's cordial, but cold. Ex-military, marines. Has a short history with Blackwater in Iraq which we missed the first time through. He's obviously not a cliché MBA middle manager guy we first assumed."

"A middle manager paper shuffler?" Faber scoffed. "My ass."

"Do you think he had his own son killed?"

"For a billion-dollar industry that probably has screws in him deeper than his heart and soul, yeah, I do." Juanita's eyes shone cold. "Anyway, my bet is that he'll lawyer up."

"Yeah, we won't get a thing from him," Faber quipped.

"Fuck, I'm tired," Magic said. "How long does it take this tea to work?"

"Get a fucking espresso if that's not making it," Faber told her.

"We got into McCandless' safety deposit box,. The contents are being couriered over and we should have them later this afternoon. The rudimentary inventory says lots of paper, most of it about Lightfoot. Some of it's just press reprints, but there's detailed corporate structure, locations, key players, financial information. Probably a lot more. But here's something interesting," Juanita leaned forward and pointed across the table, "there's a photo similar to the one Michael had. We don't know if it's a duplicate or not."

"Speaking of which," Faber pushed a folder at Jack.

He picked it up, flipped it open, and feigned surprise, flipping through the five photographs.

Hundreds of elephant tusks were leaning or stacked against walls, laying in piles on a concrete floor. In one photo, three dark-skinned men were carrying tusks out of a badly-lit room. The photos were taken at three locations. The first location was a steel Quonset hut, dimly lit by clear weak light bulbs strung over rafters. The second location was shot from above, and could have been the same Quonset building, as the walls were not visible. The photograph focused on at least ten haphazard piles of elephant tusks. The third location, however, was distinct, the vertical corrugated walls and plywood floor of a shipping container. The photograph was an interior pan shot from the door. The ambient light was faint, but someone held a strong flashlight pointing into the interior past the camera, and in its beam hundreds of tusks were stacked to the ceiling, bound with tie-downs, and roped to the walls.

"This is a travesty. How much are these worth?" Jack asked. But he was also thinking about the slaughter behind the money. All these animals shot and left to rot after their tusks were sawn off. He'd read somewhere that elephants possessed highly developed emotions. That meant there were others, companions, family members, that had grieved for the deceased.

"Ten million, maybe twenty. We need to bring in some people with specialized knowledge."

"U.S. Fish and Wildlife, World Wildlife Federation, Wildlife Justice Commission. The UN must have some branch that deals with this type of crime. Interpol. Haven't identified all the players yet, but this is way out of our league." Magic looked and sounded fatigued.

Just then, the pert waitress arrived with a pot of green jasmine tea and four glasses, telling them to let it steep for another two-to-three minutes then taking their orders.

"Definitely international in scope. We've got to bring in Interpol," said Michel Faber, after the waitress left.

"Still figuring out the players," said Magic again, pouring a cup of tea before its time and lifting it to her lips. "Damn, hot." She blew across it and took another sip.

"Any ideas on the geographical locations in the photos?"

"We've got lab people combing them for clues."

"The fact that Michael had these led me to think originally they were local, but now I'm thinking at least the Quonset was somewhere far away. The three guys carrying tusks look Filipino, and the way they're dressed indicates it's hotter than hell."

"Filipino or Malay is my guess," Juanita said. "Could be Malaysia, Singapore, Manila. Most likely a major port." She took a chance on the tea.

"As you probably guessed, we think there's a connection to Lightfoot. Otherwise, why would they be in a lockbox with a bunch of Lightfoot documentation. Michael was the son of a Lightfoot guy. Two other Lightfoot guys were shot, or should I say executed, by the same gun that took Michael's life. Lightfoot has already been tied to Orca kidnapping and transport."

"That's not proven."

"Yeah, but it's out there. Ain't going back in the box." Magic drained her tea and poured a second cup.

"Sorry to be the bad guy here Jack, but you won't be on the task force. Hope you understand. I'll still keep you involved, and definitely welcome any input."

"Hell, we probably won't be on it, except her," Faber pointed to Juanita, "and maybe not even. International heavies, lots of classified information."

"Big money, big crime."

"We'll probably have to hand the whole thing off."

"Which is fine with me. I'm plenty busy without this shit, and it's way above my pay grade." Magic was pouring a third cup of tea, shaking the pot for a few last drops.

"No problem," said Jack. "I'm happy to help in any way I can. And I'm plenty busy as well."

The waitress came back balancing three plates and one bowl of pho, setting them down with an artfulness that Jack admired. "Thank you," he said, the only one who thanked her.

"Good. Let's eat," Juanita said.

"We have miles to go before we sleep," Faber said.

Jack had to double-take. An FBI agent quoting Frost.

Juanita was staring at him as if she was reading his mind.

"At least he's not quoting Rimbaud," she said, tossing noodles around her fork.

Jack thought she looked like a goddess. Pick the religion.

35

That night Jack woke sporadically, startled by dream images, voices he couldn't quite hear. At 4:30 he finally got up, fired his computer, heated a cup of day-old coffee in the microwave, and began working on Riordan's project. It was the beauty of work that it could take him out of any "life" issue and transport him to a world of total immersion.

After a banana and yogurt smoothie, he shook supplements into his hand, opening bottles, upending them, dropping pills into his palm. Vitamin D, Vitamin B12, Niacin, Magnesium, COC12. But when he tipped the white plastic InSight bottle, one pill rattled around then dropped into his hand. That was it. No more. He hadn't even been thinking about it, what to do when he ran out. Some things were knee-jerk. Vitamin D. His doctor had told him that everyone in the Pacific Northwest should be taking a minimum of 2000 ICU of Vitamin D a day, no exceptions. So some things were mandated, and not thought about. But others? Like InSight? A supplement that might be helping, but was costing him over $100 a month? What to do? he thought for a brief moment. His stress had obviously been caused largely by UniCode, and Unicode was no more, so that probably solved it. Not worth spending another hundred on. And that easily it passed from his consciousness.

He worked for a couple hours on Riordan's project, then switched to researching information on the illicit ivory trade. For all he knew, the group had already learned all this, but he was a researcher now, so doing a bit of work should keep him in Juanita's good graces.

He sent her seven pages total with a short introduction.

The Convention on International Trade in Endangered Species of Wild Fauna and Flora (CITES) brought together 179 nations to combat the illegal wildlife trade on a global scale. The U.S. Fish & Wildlife Service's Division of Management Authority and Division of

Scientific Authority, as well as the Office of Law Enforcement, are responsible for implementing and enforcing CITES in the United States. (Partners?)

Recently, CITES founded the International Consortium on Combatting Wildlife Crime (ICCWC), a collaborative effort between the CITES Secretariat, INTERPOL, the United Nations Office on Drugs and Crime (UNODC), the World Bank and the World Customs Organization (WCO). ICCWC was formed to increase prosecution and punishment for caught smugglers and poachers as well as increase law enforcement in developing nations. The U.S. Wildlife Service stations inspectors at ports across the country and provides enforcement training around the world.

Elephant poaching is increasing throughout Africa, and the amount of illegal ivory shipments destined for markets in Southeast Asia has surged dramatically over the last few years. U.S. Fish and Wildlife Service's Wildlife Without Borders, and the African Elephant Conservation Fund, are working together with the FREELAND Foundation to fund a cooperative training and poaching investigation by the Kenya Wildlife Service and Royal Thai Police officials. They are accompanied by the Lusaka Agreement Task Force. As a result of this law enforcement training and investigation effort, several large shipments of ivory have been located and seized at Kenya's Jomo Kenyatta Airport prior to leaving the country. This project has enabled the coordination of Kenyan, Tanzanian, and Thai law enforcement authorities to trace ivory shipments recently seized in Bangkok back to the country of origin to identify international smuggling routes.

And he learned Juanita had been right. This was far too large an operation for the FBI. They needed global partners. Still, if Lightwood was involved, and some of these activities occurred in their Seattle operation, the FBI should have the authority to investigate. It may just be a small piece of the puzzle, but it was a piece.

He was sleeping when the Eno riff of his phone woke him.

"Jack here," he rasped, throat dry.

"Hey, I want got to apologize for the other day. When we went running. I was a bitch."

"Yeah. It was weird. All that 'tough-guy' stuff, your tone. I had no idea where it came from."

"Sorry. There's a lot going on. The kids, the psychotic ex, an overwhelming job, you and your weird dreams. Especially that. And my own neurotic sensibilities."

"At least we're both minorities."

Laughter, followed by, "I needed that."

"Keep talking."

"You don't mind?"

"I love it."

"Are you naked?"

"Naked and hard."

"Really?" She giggled.

"Kidding."

"Darn." She was quiet for a moment.

"Go on."

"You love it when I call and bitch at 3:13 in the morning? You're quite a find, you know?"

"I love the sound of your voice. I can imagine what you'll sound like after we've made fantastic love. Lying back, making small talk. Nothing else to achieve." He was whispering now.

Juanita was quiet.

"I like you. A lot. I want to get to know you. I know it's messy, but you're a terrific woman. Unlike anyone I've ever met. And I say that sincerely. And I know I'm not a *tough guy*. But I'd like a chance."

Juanita was silent a moment, then whispering, her voice husky.

"Thank you for saying this, Jack. It's the nicest thing anyone has said to me in a long time. And yes, I'll give you a chance. You're the best thing that's happened to me lately."

He could hear her breathe, in, out. Rolling waves.

"You just have to give me some space, Jack. I'm sorry, but that's the way it has to be. I get weird. I can't breathe. I have panic attacks."

"Okay."

"Rubio crowded me. He was in my face constantly."

It sounded like someone was humming.

"I can't be with someone like that."

"I'm not like that."

"I want this to work, Jack. I want to move slowly."

"So do I." The moment was unbearably fragile.

"So where are we?" He asked after a moment.

"Here?" she responded. The phone went silent.

Jack got up, pissed, then poured himself a glass of water from the tap. Straight from the lake outside his window. You couldn't get more local than that. Juanita's voice still in his head, the words like birds, swirling around.

There were few lights, and Lake Washington seemed a huge hole in the night. Standing there, staring out, he was off-balance, pulled into its darkness. The phrase "black water" drifted into his mind. It was from a poem he'd written for a class in college. Creative writing. One of the few deviations from computer science he'd allowed himself. *God, we are not the worthy. We, the recipients of the lie of faith, of black water.* He couldn't remember what he'd meant then. If he'd meant anything at all. How far he'd come from that questioning, idealistic kid he'd once been.

And he said a silent prayer, to the black water. *Don't let me screw this up. Please, don't let me screw this up.*

36

He knew he wouldn't be able to sleep again. Juanita's words were tying him in knots. He needed to see her, hold her, inhale her scent. Instead he had an empty apartment, an empty bed, a lonely night.

Jack fired up his laptop.

It took him over an hour, but he finally hacked into the Seattle Police's personnel files. He wanted to know more about Alex Rubio, his apparent opponent in love.

Rubio was described as Hispanic, 5-10, two hundred pounds, forty-one years of age. His religion was listed as Catholic, with the directive that if he were severely wounded, to call a priest.

He'd worked for the department sixteen years, joining the force after a stint in the army. Promoted several times, from patrol officer to detective to corporal, including a promotion to sergeant three years ago.

His file contained a list of cases he'd solved or helped solve, several letters of accommodation, and copies of his yearly, now biennial reviews. A summation of these, which was apparently completed after each review, included an evaluation of his skill-set -- marksmanship, judo, boxing, karate, and knife fighting. He'd apparently worked undercover in a lot of drug cases, as there were numerous references to this. One supervisor commented that he was a convincing street tough, another that if "he wasn't a cop he'd be a criminal." Jack wasn't quite sure how to take that.

His few weaknesses were listed as "doesn't always play well with others" and "recommended for anger management." There was no mention as to whether he'd attended or completed said training.

One item caught Jack's interest. The Seattle Police Department listed Juanita as Rubio's wife, and two boys, Angel and Gabriel, were listed as offspring. There was no mention of a divorce. Which got Jack thinking. Was there really a divorce? Or was this wishful thinking on Juanita's part?

37

The day after he stopped taking InSight Jack woke to a fog. It continued through two cups of strong coffee, a three-mile run, and Jake Young's online yoga/pilates workout which he'd discovered while surfing the web. Maybe he was coming down with something. He popped two Tylenol. Then an Ibuprofen to be safe.

However, over the next week, and despite not coming down with a cold or flu, Jack felt terrible. Groggy, thick of thought, lethargic. And he left the refrigerator door open for over ten hours, his phone in a restaurant, walked away with his card in the ATM, left his car keys in the ignition, let a stir-fry burn and trigger the smoke alarm, and worse, blanked in front of a page of code, an experience that immediately triggered a terrible sense of déjà vu.

He finally broke down and ordered more InSight. Then he did something he should have done initially. He began researching it.

There was nothing in Medline, but it would have surprised him if there was, and he found only anecdotal information on the web. All of it was positive. One woman from Idaho commented how it had saved her life, which was a terrific product endorsement, life being worth what it was in the first world. However, it seemed like no one could stop taking it without being thrown into the hell of memory loss and mental confusion. Which was disturbing. He hadn't anticipated this was something he'd have to take for the rest of his days.

He checked out all the ingredients, Hericium erinaceus, Ashwagandha, Gotu kola, Kelp, Ginko biloba, and Seakale. They all made claims of enhancing memory or mental health or good karma or chakra cleansing, none of which were scientifically proven. But Jack was nothing if not a man of science.

He checked them all in Medline. Nada.

But there was one ingredient, organic aesther compounds, which he couldn't get a handle on. There was absolutely nothing returned by Google on aesther compounds. It seemed to be bullshit, a made-up phrase. So, either someone had been lucky, and combined a bunch of ingredients that actually sharpened consciousness and improved memory, or there was some other ingredient, an "aesther compound," that was doing the heavy lifting. But Jack had no idea which was true, or what the secret ingredient might be.

He gave up thinking about it. Tylenol worked, and he didn't care what was in it. InSight worked, and that was enough for him. His three-month reorder would be here tomorrow.

The sun had broken through a girdle of clouds and was riffling the bay, when he found a blog post from a user that shocked him. Literally.

A woman identifying herself as "Laura" wrote about dreams she started having after taking InSight. Without getting into details, she indicated they were memories of other people. There were no comments under the post, four months ago.

Jack exhaled loudly, stretched, paced the condo awhile, then shot her an email.

> *I've been having dreams as well. Memories not my own. Can we talk?*
>
> *Jack*

The package of InSight arrived the next morning, thanks to Amazon Prime, and he quickly popped one of the grey/green capsules into his mouth and gulped it down.

That evening he went for a run, and experienced the same sense of exhilaration and harmony as before. The songs of birds, people, cars, all a symphony, an intricate interconnected song. Life was a piece of art, of music one moved through.

Running was effortless, beautiful, like flying. This stuff, InSight, whatever it was, was truly amazing.

To culminate his run, he effortlessly trotted the stairs eight floors to his condo, and now entering, bowed to the Ganesha statue.

A few weeks ago, he'd done something so foreign, he could hardly believe it. He'd built a small shrine for the Ganesha statue, and decorated it with flowers and a bowl of water. When he came in the front door, he typically gave it a small bow. Jack was not Hindu, and had no idea why he was behaving this way, but it felt natural and right.

He drank a glass of water, then sat down and began working on Riordan's prototypes. Diving into these projects was akin to entering into an alternate world where everything else was left behind. He forgot all about InSight, Lightfoot, Juanita. His brain crackled with energy and ideas. He didn't know how bizarre Riordan wanted to get, but as he toyed with the facial recognition software, he figured out how to isolate abnormalities – moles, freckles, sun blotches, scales – and replicate them with randomness and symmetry.

Meeting with Riordan the following day, he showed him eighteen prototypes, and gave him mock-ups of six more.

Riordan was ecstatic.

"These are phenomenal! I knew this was the right move. Knew it. You get co-billing, Jack. You're a fucking artist!"

"That's twenty-four. Six more will give us thirty. What do you think? Is that enough?"

"Should be. Let's meet in downtown next week, get over to SAM and walk the space. I want to take some measurements, discuss the optimal size for the pieces. Twenty might be enough, but we've still got plenty of time. One idea I had was to place four similar pieces, let's say for the sake of discussion that they're pieces that collage one facial feature, say eyes, adjacent to each other. What do you think the effect would be?"

"Not sure. Disconcerting, probably. But how about this? One eye collage on each of four walls, staring at each other."

"Whoo, damn! I like that idea a lot. I thought I had two rooms, but I might have three. One would be small, square. Perfect for the eyes. Paranoids and schizos beware!"

Jack laughed. "Spooky tunes."

"We'll know more when we walk the space. I'll give Tish Tosher a call and set it up. She's the curator extraordinaire."

"Good. Hey, where's Monique anyway. I figured she was late, but now she's a no-show."

"No idea. But I might have another partner, if you want more work."

"Maybe. Let me think about it. I kind of like the pace right now."

"It can't be leisurely. You bust these things out ridiculously fast."

"It's fun. And it is leisurely when I'm not working. I have space between the spates. Before, at UniCode, I had only exhaustion."

"Well, good. I think everyone should be able to make a living doing what they truly love. So many can't." He belly-laughed. "And then there's those that don't have any fucking idea what they want to do."

"I've never belonged to that cult."

"Me neither, thank God! I'm writing 'Never had enough time'

on my tombstone."

They stood up and shook hands, Riordan giving Jack a bear-clap on the shoulder.

"You take care of yourself, hear?"

"You too."

Jack watched Riordan's large head and shaggy mane disappear out the pub door. He was really getting to like the guy. And this was true collaboration. Each had a technical and creative role in the products. Despite all the other shit happening in his life, this was turning into a dream job.

38

Thursday morning, July first, and after he'd run four miles and showered, Jack decided to go camping over the Fourth-of-July weekend. Get away from the city, the noise and the crowds. He had a spot up the Skykomish on a plot of private land his uncle owned. He'd be alone, by the river. The bugs would be bad, but that was camping. No phone, no computer, just time to think, or not think, and fight bugs. He'd bring a novel or two, take some walks, maybe do a little fishing. He still had a bunch of freeze-dry dinners from two summers back. Those things never went bad. His stove, tent, camp chair, sleeping bag were downstairs in storage. Settled. He took the elevator down into the basement and retrieved everything he needed in two trips, spreading it out on living room floor.

His phone pinged as he was walking to the kitchen to get some more matches.

Want to do something this weekend?

Juanita.

What to do? Invite her?

What do you have in mind?

Kids will be on a sleep-over. Maybe a romantic meal. Some Salsa dancing. Some of the other stuff. ☺

Damn. Was planning a camping trip up the Sky.

A few moments later her response.

Want company?

What to say? He started typing.

Let me think about it. I was kind of relishing the thought of being alone.

A few long moments went by, Jack staring at the phone, then those little dots that indicated she was typing. He'd fucked up. Should have been more tactful.

Thanks for being honest. That means a huge huge amount to me. You can't imagine. And I can understand being alone. Doesn't happen very often. I'll be here. Let me know if you want company.

You good with bugs? Flies, mosquitoes?

I'm too tough for bugs ☺
Okay I'll let you know.
Bye.
Bye.

Ten minutes later he got another text.

Call me. Monique

Then immediately his phone rang.

"Hey, Monique. I was just going to call."

"Who's Monique?" It was Per.

"Per, damn, it's been months."

"One anyway." Per laughed. "What's shaking?"

"Quit my job, have a girlfriend, have a new job working with a couple artists, one named Monique, hence the way I answered. What else? Feeling good, relaxed. Went to Chicago to visit my cousin. Having weird dreams."

"Jeez Jack, I can't leave you alone for long, can I?"

"I guess a lot has happened. Kind of a blur. What about you?"

"Just got back from the East Coast. Meeting with publishers, agent, quick book tour. New York, Boston, Providence, Bangor. I was thinking maybe we could get together. I might throw a little shindig Friday evening. You available?"

"Not sure. Thinking of going camping."

"Camping. Huh. Bad time of year. Bugs."

"Yeah, believe me I know. But I want to get out of the July 4th craziness. And noise."

"Comprende. I get really stoned and turn the music up loud. Tool. Sex Pistols. Fucking Praxis, Metallica. How about a drink tonight?"

"Tonight? Did you just invent that, because it works."

"I miss you, you maniac."

"Yeah, me too. Crazy times."

"I'll tell you things."

"And I'll tell you things."

"Cool. You quit your job?? I can't believe that! I thought you were one of these solid dudes. A lifer. Rock my world."

"Yea, yea."

"We could meet at *Cairn*. Grab some dinner, a few beers, catch up."

"Sounds good! Six-thirty?"

"Deal. See you there."

Jack clicked off, retrieved Monique's card off the coffee table, which was now adorned with two of Riordan's photographic books, and punched in the phone number.

Monique answered after four rings.

"Hi." She sounded warm, sunny. Sexy. She was usually cool. But he was being judgmental. He didn't know her well.

"Hey, missed you at the meeting this morning. Got your text."

"Good. Hey, I thought we could have our own meeting. At my studio. It would give you a better idea of what I'm doing."

"Yeah, that sounds like it could work."

"I feel like Riordan runs the show at our group meetings and I can't concentrate. Nor get a word in edgewise. It's awkward."

"I've picked up on that. He's pretty over-bearing."

"We used to be married, you know."

"I had no idea!"

"We debated telling you, but ultimately…. Maybe we should have. There's weird energy sometimes. Between us. When I'm around him."

"Look, it's no problem meeting at your studio. And if you want to make that permanent, we can do that as well. Riordan and I can continue meeting at the *Harrison*."

"That's another thing. We used to go there a lot. Lots of memories."

"I understand. I could come over today."

"That would be awesome."

"What time?"

"Oh, come as soon as you can. I'll make you lunch."

"I could leave in a half hour, forty-five minutes. I'm meeting a friend later for drinks, but I'd have until four or so."

"That would be perfect. Any dietary restrictions?"

"Well, I thought a while ago I was going to become a vegan, but things have transpired against that. So, no. I eat anything."

"Good. I made a delish carrot curry soup yesterday. I'll heat it up. It's vegan."

"Sounds great! Where are you?"

"Capitol Hill. I'm on 11th, just north of Aloha." She gave him the address.

"I should be there in an hourish."

"See you then."

He texted Juanita back.

I'd love it if you came camping with me. God Damn I would love that!

39

931 11th East was a four-story red-brick apartment dating back to the thirties. Neatly tended, it had weathered several face-lifts, and was far classier than Jack had imagined. Either Monique was doing very well with art, or Riordan had cut her a generous largesse.

He entered the lobby and rang the bell of #423, remembering another apartment lobby in Chicago, a woman named Cathy, her finger pointing at the row of mailboxes, copper rectangles, tiny white buttons underneath. It seemed a long time ago.

The buzzer rang, and he entered an atrium heralding an explosion of tropical plants, yellow and black birds flitting from branch to branch. Ficus trees thirty feet high blooming in a glass dome. "Wow," he thought, "Didn't expect this, either." Monique was full of surprises. The elevator was on the left. After watching the birds flit around, Jack entered, and pressed the raised chrome 4. The car smelled faintly of lilacs.

Monique opened the door wearing black panties, a black nylon T-shirt that clung to her light skin. Her hair was no longer purple. It was black to match the other accessories.

"I would have dressed down, if I'd known," Jack said, laughing.

"Sorry. I'm pretty clothes-optional when I'm home and working. If it bothers you, I can throw on some pants. A hoodie."

"I'm cool. As long as you don't mind a few side-long glances."

"Stare all you want. I've never been shy about my body." She mocked a shy bow. "I think it's ok."

"That must be nice, to accept your body." Jack said, thinking of the horrors of high-school body image.

"This way." She turned abruptly and Jack followed.

As Monique led Jack through the small living room, he took in the artwork jammed onto walls, the classy built-in walnut bookcases crammed with art theory and romance novels, and a mix of funky, comfy Goodwill furniture, all edges and blond wood. Several clay and stone sculptures were planted in front of a bank of rectangular windows overlooking the street. A pothos owned the windows, winding through hooks above them, dangling like a skinny, but robust python.

The living room emptied through a low arch into a dining area, which housed a bar-high table with six chairs, and several antique hutches full of antique dishes. An elegant green wainscoting accentuated rich cream walls. The art here was sparser, more calculated. Even some abstracted landscapes depicting the Skagit Valley. Artists Jack had heard of.

Another row of windows looked out over a perpendicular street.

"I didn't realize you were on a corner. Very nice apartment."

"Check out the kitchen," she said, waggling through the dining room arch. Jack was having a difficult time noticing anything but her lovely pert ass. It was exploding ancient genes, and he was getting aroused.

The kitchen was small, extremely tidy, and the scent of carrots and curry wafted from a tall silver soup tureen was delirious.

"Smells incredible. I abandon all will power"

Monique laughed, surprisingly guttural. "Let's eat."

She retrieved two large jade-colored bowls, ladled them full of soup, then carried them to a small triangular table on a tiny back deck overlooking the courtyard. Jack saw several flowerbeds flooded with daylilies, peonies, roses, zinnias, and cosmos. A man with a hose was lost in watering them.

She placed the bowls on blue place mats across from each other. A wooden cutting board with a partial loaf of uncut white bread, and a small porcelain bowl containing butter, tiny silver knives to the side, were center on the small table.

She gestured Jack to sit.

"Bon appetit" she said when they had both settled, lifting a spoon to her lips.

The soup was delicious, and as they ate, Monique gave Jack a sketch of her life. He tried to keep his eyes off the way her nipples teased the fabric of her black T-shirt as she lifted her spoon. A losing battle.

She'd been born in Connecticut, studied art at the Rhode Island School of Design and NYU. She'd worked in New York City for three years until she couldn't take the city any longer.

"But I still needed to live in a city, you know? Just not one so crazy."

"Seattle's getting pretty crazy."

"You ever visited New York?"

"No."

"Seattle is so not-crazy compared to New York. No comparison."

At Rhode Island she studied under Alec Grotten, who'd been Dibenkorn's student and disciple. Her early work was painting, abstracts using color as an emotional tableau. Then she was introduced to fabric and paper by a Japanese artist she met in Vancouver. It changed her life overnight.

"And now I'm looking for that new thing. You know, as the poet Ezra Pound said, 'Keep it new.'"

Artists and FBI agents quoting poetry. "Interesting," thought Jack.

After lunch Monique placed the dishes in the sink and led Jack into one of two bedrooms, this one overflowing with fabric, fabric sculptures, cutting tables, dyeing vats and racks.

"You do all your work here?" The room seemed cramped.

"The smaller work. I'm part of a co-op in Belltown. I have a larger studio there."

"So, what are you working on?"

"I have two big shows coming up. One this Fall in LA and one next Spring in New York. I still have a lot of connections back there, and they have patrons sympathetic to what I do."

"Which is?"

She waved her arm around the room, and the chaotic jumble gradually sorted itself out.

"I specialize in fabric sculptures. These," she pointed at an oak table with maybe twenty pieces on it, "are from the series I'm doing for New York. They are, as you can see, flowers, although somewhat abstract. I use all organic natural dyes, and do most of my own dying. I use epoxy, or various glues to achieve different states of rigidity."

Jack thought the flowers, once identified as such, looked remarkable. Some were in groups, others single, some brilliantly colored, others hesitant, muted. They possessed both strength and fragility.

"These are beautiful."

"Thank you." She did a mock bow. "But for the LA show, I'd like to experiment with what we talked about. Interactive fabric. Smart fabric. I'm thinking of several small installations."

"What's the gallery like?"

"It's classy. *Gallery Strasse*. But what I'm thinking of won't fit there. I talked with the owner, and she's thinking of converting a warehouse a few blocks away. I guess she owns or rents it."

"When is the show exactly?"

"Early October." She gave Jack a delicious smile, and the full effect, a beautiful scantily clad woman standing next to him, suddenly hit Jack in the gut.

"You okay?" she asked still smiling.

"Barely. It's the effect of great art."

"I see," still smiling, now playing with the T-shirt, stretching it away from her neck.

"So, these interactive pieces. What do you want them to do?"

"Ahhh, that's the million-dollar question, isn't it?"

"Apparently." Jack was feeling a bit dizzy, and for a moment wondered if she'd doped his tea. He was in over his head here.

"I was thinking of doing something with colors. Different colors manifesting different reactions. Creating a sense, or at least the illusion of synesthesia. Is there a way to code these fabrics for temperature? Blue might be cold."

"Possibly. I'll need to do more research."

"Another idea would be to, and this is what I'd really l-o-v-e," she stretched the word out, "to do, is create emotional reactions. Could we do that?"

"No idea. Cool idea though."

"Maybe something simple. A tight fabric creates a mild sense of paranoia, a loose-fitting fabric, the sense of freedom. That kind of thing."

"Or it could do the opposite. Temple Grandin's work with autistic people. They seem to relax when constricted."

"I've heard of that. I'm open to whatever."

"Anything else?"

"You have to go?"

"Actually, I do."

"Darn." She was smiling again, started to say something, then stopped. "Okay, get serious Monique. Another idea was something with music. Different fabrics play different music."

"That sounds cool, and doable. I've got a friend who we might get involved. He's a wizard with sound."

"Good, good."

"I'll have more next week, I promise. I've been immersed in Riordan's project, but I'm over the hump."

"Riordan is needy." She gave a sardonic smile.

"Yeah, you're right. Hadn't thought of him that way."

"Oh yeah." She was staring directly at him now, her eyes crystal blue. "I know all there is to know about that man. And he always comes first. Don't ever drive with him. You'll have a heart attack."

Jack was thinking about a heart attack. How close was he?

"This a good time?" She casually ran her tongue over her lips.

"For wha…what?"

"Our next meeting. Next week."

Jack exhaled loudly.

"You need to lie down," her voice soft.

No, I need to get the hell out of here, Jack was thinking. "I'll be okay. Art overload. It happens."

"Sure it does." A Cheshire grin.

"And yes, this time is perfect. Next week. Hey, thanks for lunch!"

"No problem. Maybe a sandwich next week. I could pick up some Tofurken. For your inner thwarted vegan."

"I've actually never had that."

"You'll be in for a treat."

As she led him to the door, he deliberately focused on her mid-back. Her ass in those panties was to die for, but he didn't want to die just yet. She opened the door, and stood wedged in the doorway, so Jack had to brush past her as he exited her apartment.

"Bye Jack. I'm glad we did this."

"Bye, Monique. See you next week."

She blew him a kiss.

Jack walked to the elevator, hit the brushed nickel button, and finally heard her door click shut. He almost collapsed.

When Jack got home, he checked e-mail, hoping, and yes, he had a message from Laura, the woman who wrote she was having weird dreams after taking InSight.

Call me. 234-789-9978.

He walked over to his "bar," five bottles of liquor sitting on a bookshelf, and poured himself a triple shot of tequila.

Jack hated tequila, but the bottle, a rich golden color, was a gift from a friend, and Jack felt obligated to drink it. He never drank tequila for the taste, he drank tequila to get drunk. Maybe tonight would be an exception. Enough said. He opened the freezer, retrieved an ice cube, and plopped it into the glass. Maybe he should toss in some salt. Didn't they always serve tequila with salt?

He took his glass of tequila over to the couch and sat down. Outside, the city glittered.

He punched the number into his phone.

The voice was soft, childish, unguarded. Melanie Griffithish.

"Hello," it said. "Hello."

"Hey," Jack said, "I'm the guy who emailed. About the dreams. My name is Jack Toyokata."

"Oh."

Then nothing.

Then, "I was hoping you'd call."

"Well, I did. So, what's going on?"

Silence for another moment.

"I'm approaching sixty."

Jack heard her inhale deeply.

"I started taking InSight a little over two years ago because I was forgetting everything under the sun. I'd make lists and forget them. I'd hang them on the fridge and there they would hang. Neglected. Little things were adding up, starting to oppress me. I went to doctors, had tests. Possible beginnings of early onset dementia. God, that's what everyone wants to hear. You have a horrific incurable disease that is going to eat you up and make you crazy, and then will kill you. Thank you, science, or God, or whoever gave me this knowledge."

She stopped talking. Jack sensed her grief like a wave of energy, and it struck him like the back of a hand. She wanted to confess, and was trying to phrase it just right. He gave her space.

"I took a bunch of over-the-counter supplements, but nothing worked worth a damn. Then this friend told me about InSight. She said it saved her. So I ordered some, and it improved my life immediately. I became energetic, purposeful, motivated. My memory sharpened so much it was scary. I even stopped making lists because they were easier to keep in my head. Then I began having dreams unlike anything I've ever had."

"Tell me about the dreams," Jack said. Firm, but calm. Not at all how he was feeling.

"I had the first one after taking InSight for about a week. It was like I was in another person's head. But not their mind, I couldn't mind-read or anything like that. Just see what they saw. I couldn't hear anything either. Very weird. Limited in a strange way."

"What was the person doing?" Jack was a mousetrap ready to

snap.

"Shoveling snow of all things. It was a guy, I saw his hands, arms. He, we, shoveled this entire walk, I mean it was long, a hundred yards, more, up to a stately Victorian home. Then he banged the shovel clean of snow against the railing, tipped it against the stone wall, and opened the front door and went inside. He, we, were crossing a poorly-lit parlor when a shadow seemed to leap from a jumble of coats. It came right at us. Then the dream ended."

"That is weird. How did you feel? When you woke up?"

"I was terrified. I'd never had a dream like that, and at the same time I knew it wasn't a dream. It was real. I had tapped into real life but in some other dimension. Things that had happened in another dimension."

"Go on."

"Then I had another one about a week later. I was in the head of a woman, Asian, walking fast. I caught her reflection in store windows as she walked. It was New York, Midtown. I recognized some landmarks. She was walking along and suddenly turned into a deserted alley. I don't know if she was cutting through to another street or what, but part-way down the alley two guys pushed off this brick wall between a couple dumpsters. I saw the flash of a blade, then the dream ended. I've had four more like this. People almost getting killed." She paused again then collapsed. "Oh God, this is terrible." She began sobbing softly.

"I know, I know. Try to relax."

Silence and some rustling, clothes or paper.

"You said these people were almost getting killed. You don't think they actually did?"

"I don't know. I woke up before there was any conclusion. Someone was always 'about' to hurt them, but I never witnessed the consequences."

"Hmmm."

"Are these like the dreams you have, Jack?" She sounded scared, terrified.

"Yes. Very similar." Jack gave her his sketches without mentioning he'd talked to law enforcement, or verified details. He wanted to see where she was going with this.

"So, have you gone to the police about these dreams?"

"No way. I haven't talked to anyone about them. Until now."

"But you mentioned them on the Internet."

"I was scared. I thought people would contact me after the blog post."

"They didn't?"

"Only you."

"So…"

"What do you think is going on?"

"I really don't know. But it seems to be linked to the supplement. Have you stopped taking it?"

"I tried," Jack heard her voice break, "but the memory loss came back, worse than ever, and headaches, and I was beyond fatigued. I could barely drag myself out of bed."

"That happened to me too."

"Weird, huh?"

"I'm thinking of talking to a psychiatrist," she said.

"I think that's a good idea. Look, Laura, I need you to do something for me." Jack stopped, trying to think of how to phrase this. "You told me you've had six of these dreams. I need you to think about them really hard. Are there clues to location and when they occurred? If there are, I need you to check newspapers for that place and time and see if they made the news. Can you do that? A librarian could help you."

"I remember some details that might help on a couple of them. The Midtown one. You think these are real events?"

"I know they are, Laura. Every one of them."

"Oh my God." She began crying harder.

"Laura. Nothing is your fault. We need to keep in touch. You have my cell number now, and email. I'm in the Seattle area. Maybe we could meet."

"I'm in Ohio, so probably not, but I'll let you know if I find out anything from the papers."

"Good. And thanks!"

He realized he hadn't touched the tequila, and the ice had almost melted. He drained the half the cup, grimaced at the disgusting taste, and dialed Riordan, who answered after six rings.

"Got me out of bed, so this better be good Jack."

"I met with Monique today. At her apartment."

"Hah! Did she do her Monique thing?"

"You mean dress provocatively and try to seduce me? Yes, in fact, she did."

"Yeah, she's into that. I remember the first time I went over there she was wearing a pink bra and panties."

"What did you do?"

"I said, 'Hot damn!' and stripped to my skivvies. She appreciated that. We didn't have sex though, just sat around drinking wine and talking about art."

"She says that she gets flustered when you're at the meetings. She'd rather meet alone."

"Yeah, there's weird energy alright. I ignore it. You know me, it's my personality to bull through things, but she's too sensitive. Fucking good artist though. Been written up in all the art rags. *ArtForum Art in America*, et al."

"So you guys were married?"

"Twelve years. Was a bit of a storm at times, a cyclone really, but my relationships tend to be that way."

"I agreed to meet her again next week at her place. What should I do?"

"Hah! You're kidding! Asking me for advice about women." He started to laugh, then cut it. "Okay, tell her right off you're not interested. You have a girlfriend, even if you don't. Tell her you don't appreciate being manipulated that way. Which is what it was. It's how she achieves power over men. It's all about power with Monique. Even her art. She wants to control the public's reaction to her art. Anyway, tell her that if she doesn't stop her shenanigans, you'll need to meet on neutral ground. And if that doesn't do it, tell her you'll drop her as a client. I really don't think you'll have to go that far. She's not stupid."

"Thanks man, I'll go with that. It surprised me though, because she hasn't been at all flirtatious."

"That's because this isn't about sex, it's about power. Flirting is mutual, sexual."

"Right. Anyway, thanks. I'll be frank with her."

"Hah. It's hard, you know, to be Bogart."

40

The day bloomed into a perfect Pacific Northwest summer day, clear sky, mid-seventies, faint breeze, a clarity and crispness from air gusting in from the wide Pacific.

Juanita had to work until ten-thirty, and said she'd need about an hour to "get her shit together," so Jack pulled to the curb in front of her house around noon. The bungalow looked happy today, despite needing a couple coats of paint. A dogwood was covered in white blossoms, and irises from numerous untended beds bloomed valiantly among the weeds.

"Hey," Juanita said, opening the screen door. She was chewing on a bagel sandwich. "Perfect day." She offered Jack a bite, which he took.

"Damn, that's good!"

"Einstein Brothers bagel, organic-cream cheese, and home-made lox. A fisherman friend of mine, Ruben, makes the lox. Twelve-hour cold smoke. Uses Coho and Sockeye exclusively. It's all about the fish."

"It's all about the fish," Jack said, stepping through the screen door into the living room. An overly large pile of camping equipment covered a substantial part of the living room rug.

"Wow. You moving into the woods?" Jack laughed.

"Too much? I haven't been camping in awhile, and I wanted to bring enough. But I've got good gear. I used to get out a lot."

"We'll sort it when we get there. Here, let me help you with it."

Jack and Juanita carried the pile, two trips each, to the Outback, where it dwarfed Jack's gear.

"Oh, the cooler! Almost forgot."

She came through the front door a minute later with a large cooler that they managed to squeeze into the mix.

"That thing's heavy. What do you have in there anyway?"

"Beer," she flashed him a wide smile, "and more beer. Oh, and I made a blueberry pie. Someone brought me all these blueberries from Chelan and I froze some. Seven pounds. And I brought some oranges. Can't get enough fiber or vitamin C. How about you?"

Jack smiled at her enthusiasm, how it lit her up in a way he hadn't seen before. He'd no clue how many personas inhabited her, but was game to find out.

"Four freeze dry dinners, eggs, bacon, coffee, bread, salami, mayo, lettuce. Might catch a fish or two if I'm lucky. Which I never am. At fishing that is."

"Enough to survive till we drive into Gold Bar for dinner," she said laughing. "Where is this place anyway? All you said is that it was up the Skykomish."

"You'll have to wait and see. It's kind of a surprise."

Juanita rubbed her hands together. "Goody! I love surprises. Let me lock up, and we're on the road."

She leaned in and kissed Jack on the lips. A feather kiss. "Thanks for this, Jack."

On the drive up, Juanita filled Jack in on some developments with the Lightfoot case.

"It's gone up the ladder pretty fast. US Fish and Wildlife is now working with Interpol, and we're on advisory status. If anything local breaks we can work it, but they're in the driver's seat all the way. They told us that Lightfoot has a partner shipping company based out of Bangkok. This is global. Big leagues.

"The tusks in the photos belong to African elephants, but poachers are targeting Asian elephants as well, particularly in Thailand.

"We handed over copies of McCandless's papers from the safety deposit. There were some papers in there referring to international organizations. Names, more photos. McCandless was digging, and turning over some rich earth, believe me."

"Enough so they removed him from the planet."

"Not entirely Jack, his memory and papers remain."

The other item of interest referred to Michael's killers.

"We believe they're the Benz Brothers, so named for their penchant for Mercedes cars. They own twelve between them. Two black killers in their thirties. Amos Roper and Slade King. They live in Detroit, and operate out of the Detroit-Toronto area."

"The guys who killed McCandless were from Toronto."

"And the Irish mob is big in that area, so they have plenty of contacts. These two, the Benz Brothers, work for criminal organizations around the country and in Canada. In the few crimes they've been linked to, they evaporate. They always have solid alibis.

"Their MO is that they garb and act like bangers, but they are anything but. Moses is the son of a wealthy Detroit dentist, and Slade's parents are lawyers."

"And the sons are professional hitmen."

"Yeah. Sad professional trajectory, huh? Moses was in dental school following his father's footsteps, when he changed careers."

They chatted more on the drive up, filling in the gaps of childhood, career, love. Touched on politics, music, sports. Seattle government and development, two hot topics for any local.

Juanita was from the Los Angeles area, and migrated up to Seattle for college at UW. She'd married Alex Rubio shortly after she joined the FBI. They'd worked a case together, had similar theories, were physically attracted to each other.

"And there was the Hispanic in law enforcement thing. We're pretty marginalized. So we bonded over that."

"I can imagine."

"And he was tough. I liked that. There are a few exceptions, but our culture values machismo. My dad and brothers were tough. It was something a man did. Pussies didn't make it. So, Alex was comfortable for me. He fit the mold of what a man was. But a man isn't cruel, and I learned the hard way that Alex had meanness in him. A lot of it."

Jack said "I'm sorry," but Juanita ignored him and went on.

"I came from a strong, loving family. I grew up with four siblings, three sisters and two brothers, and a plethora of cousins. We'd get together at the drop of a hat. Alex's family was a mess. His mom left when he was five, and his dad, an alcoholic and drug user, moved different women into the house weekly. Alex lived on the streets a fair amount. Which is why he makes such a good street cop. He's authentic street trash, damaged goods."

"And you thought you could fix him."

"We women don't learn that lesson easily," she laughed.

Jack glanced over and she met his gaze, her laugh receded into a smile.

"I took a look at your husband's personnel file."

"You hacked into the Seattle police computers?" Juanita laughed heartily. "Shit, I shouldn't be hanging around with the likes of you."

He looked over again and saw her shaking her head.

"Probably not. Just keeping my skills honed."

"Can't they backtrack it, follow the hack back?"

"They could, if I were a Dorito-eating teen." Jack's turn to laugh.

She was staring out the window.

"Find anything interesting?" Juanita asked a few minutes later.

"Well, as you said, he's a legitimate tough guy. Let's hope he doesn't feel the need to show me." Jack didn't mention there was no reference to a divorce. He'd save that for another time.

A few miles out of Gold Bar, less a town, than the idea of a town memory forgot, Jack turned down a gravel road without a sign. They drove silently for ten minutes, passing a few farms and houses on lots sliced out of forest thick as dense fur. Jack turned suddenly into a sparsely used drive blocked by a locked gate with a metal sign that read simply "Keep Out." The gate and road were surrounded by forest.

"Makes you feel welcome, doesn't it?" Juanita asked, laughing.

"It does if you own it, or know someone who does." Jack laughed.

Jack got out and unlocked the gate, which swung open easily despite its age, then drove the track through a mixed forest of spruce, alder and Doug fir to a grassy clearing overlooking the river. Jack's uncle Sora liked to mow the clearing, but he hadn't been up yet, and the grass was high and vibrant. Across the river jagged mountains tore at the rich azure sky. Butterflies flitted everywhere, and below the clearing the dancing river braided around several small islands.

"This is gorgeous, Jack!" Juanita exclaimed, getting out, stretching, walking to the overlook where a thin path led down to a cobble beach.

There was a picnic table adjacent to a ragged circle of charred rocks.

"Let's sort this gear out and get set up. Then we can take a walk. There's twenty acres here. My uncle bought it years ago, when they were giving this land away. The plan was that Gold Bar would become another Leavenworth. They'd capitalize on some motif or theme, the way Leavenworth has with Bavarian style. Never even came close to happening."

"Wonder why not?"

Jack laughed. "I think the people who settled here didn't want any development. By and large, they're an anti-social crowd."

Jack and Juanita spent the next half-hour sorting gear. They decided on the large four-person tent, and stashed the other two in the car. They blew up air mattresses, fluffed sleeping bags on top of them. Juanita had brought three pillows to Jack's none, but he wasn't complaining. The tent was large enough to stand in, and Jack hung two LED lanterns from the aluminum cross-beams.

Juanita put Jack to shame in the cooking department. A freestanding Camp Chef Explorer, Sea-to-Summit pots and pans, neat kits of dishes, silverware, and a leather portable spice case containing twenty herbs and spices.

"I brought a surprise for tonight."

Jack rubbed his hands together gleefully. "Oh goody, I love surprises."

"Are you making fun of me? I'll wrestle you to submission. I used to wrestle my brothers. I was merciless."

"Come and get me."

Jack dropped into a wrestler's stance, and Juanita responded, a glint in her eye he'd never seen before.

"You're in trouble now, Jack."

They began circling each other slowly.

"At least you didn't call me tough guy."

She feinted at him, Jack shifting back then leapt across the grass, catching her off-balance, wrapping her and dropping her to the ground.

She grunted as she hit, him on top, then twisted swiftly bringing him over on his side. She was surprisingly strong. She was working to get her legs under her, and he countered by rolling the opposite way, again using her force and movement against her, and she was underneath him again, face down.

"Damn you!" she huffed.

Then she stilled, and Jack could sense her relax, plotting what to do, starting to tense again. He spread his legs fast against her giving him leverage, holding her down, resting quietly on her back. He felt her relax again, her body strong yet supple beneath him. Jack liked the way her feet were touching his own. He'd never dated anyone as tall as her.

"Okay, you win. This time. Now let me up."

Instead, Jack used a move he'd learned in Judo years ago, lifting off then, twisting her roughly. Then she was on top, her face inches from his. For a moment he didn't know if she was going to spit at him or curse him. She surprised him and kissed him hard, slipping her tongue between his lips, licking his teeth, exploring his mouth. Jack responded, his erection hardening against her groin, and she rose to meet him. And kept going, flipping him onto his back. And suddenly he was on top staring into those beautiful eyes.

"Touché." she said then kissed him again, probing. "Where did you learn that stuff anyway?"

"Studied Judo for nine years."

"Why didn't you tell me?"

"It's good to leave a few things in your back pocket."

"What else do you have in that pocket?"

"Maybe you'll find out."

She cooked hamburgers and a packet of freeze-dried macaroni and cheese Jack brought.

They drank some of the beer. Then some more.

As the evening air swept out of the mountains, bringing chill with it, Jack built a fire. They sat snugged tight on a worn log, there for that purpose, talking softly, taking an occasional sip of beer, stealing the occasional kiss. There was a lot of ground to cover, but there didn't seem to be any rush. The symphony of birds ebbed and flowed, then died away, and an owl began to hoot. Coyotes across the river yipped and howled.

They eventually crawled into the tent, coupling the sleeping bags together as best they could, making love again, softer this time, arrhythmic, responding to tiny shifts of tension, movement, making their own language as the night deepened.

In the morning one of the air mattresses was nearly deflated, and Juanita had her leg wrapped around Jack's, her face inches from his, exhaling in tiny rapid puffs. He eased out from under her, dressed and unzipped the tent, greeting the dawn.

The weather had predicted a warm dry weekend, and although the sun was below the mountain crest, the chill air was withdrawing with night. The meadow was still, and covered thickly with dew which would explode into jewels the moment sun crested the eastern ridge. Jack hopped in bare feet, jamming on his jeans, throwing a sweater over his T-shirt. Then he set about making coffee.

By the time Juanita peeked out of the tent, Jack had bacon browning in a cast iron frying pan, six eggs ready to fry, and two oranges and bagels on the side.

"Hey, sleepyhead," he said, "how do you like your eggs?"

"Easy over. Kind of like making love last night."

He heard her giggle.

After breakfast they took a long walk, exploring the trails Jack's uncle had blazed through the thickets and forest. A cow elk exploded from a cove of small alder, and they watched the ungainly calf attempt to keep up with its mother. Thrushes were trilling, and the sun spilling through trees was diced into elaborate polygons that blanketed the forest floor. The damp foliage muffled their footfalls, and out of respect for that silence, they were silent.

One of the trails paralleled the river, and Jack pointed out the swimming hole. A short grassy bluff with an outcrop of granite, the dive spot, and a deep slot below, maybe thirty feet across, a mixed cobble and sand beach across for drying off.

Returning on one of the back trails, they discovered a cluster of morels under two massive cottonwoods. Jack pulled out a pocketknife and cut four of the larger, brain-like fungi.

"I'll fry these up in butter and garlic tonight," Juanita said, folding her sweatshirt up to cradle them.

Jack tried his luck fishing, catching several tiny steelhead smolts and a sixteen-inch Bull Trout, an endangered species that he returned carefully to the water. Juanita stayed in camp reading, swatting at mosquitoes that quieted as the sun slid higher into the flawless blue sky, interrupted only by a dissipating jet contrail.

That afternoon, the temperature in the low eighties, they walked to the bluff overlooking the swimming hole and stripped naked, daring each other to jump in.

Jack guessed the water, largely snowmelt from the high peaks, at forty-some degrees.

"Cold enough to shrivel the testicles," he said, laughing.

"I've been known to resuscitate many a shrunken testicle," Juanita responded, both of them perched on the smooth bare rock edging the bluff, naked to the world. Eight feet below the thin branch of the Skykomish ran cloudy turquoise, visibility around three feet.

"How do we know how deep it is?"

"It's at least eight feet, probably more like ten."

"Let's go together," Juanita said quickly, grabbing Jack's hand.

"Deal. Want to run at it?"

"Sure," but after they'd walked six feet back and turned, Juanita got cold feet.

"You've done this before right?"

"Many times."

"What's it like?"

She dropped Jack's hand and rocked from one foot to the other, a tentative smile on her face.

"To be honest, it will knock the breath out of you. You'll surface and won't be able to breathe. You have to move, immediately. Swim for the far shore. It shallows out fast, and you'll be able to wade after three or four strokes."

"You go first," Juanita said teasingly. "Show me how it's done."

"Promise you'll follow?"

"If you survive I will."

"Okay. Here's looking at you."

Jack sprinted to the edge and leapt, Juanita running over to watch. He hit the water and disappeared, then immediately shot out of the water shrieking, and began pulling hard for the far shore. Fifteen feet and he stood up, roaring like a bull, then began laughing hysterically as he waded into the beach, stretched, and shook like a wet dog. "C'mon scaredy cat!"

Juanita walked ten feet back, turned, and ran directly at the brink, launching herself out over, then into the water.

"AAIIIEEEEHHH!" she screamed, disappearing, then popping out of the water like a screaming cork, trying to skate across it like a skipped stone. Seconds later she was wading out onto the beach.

"My God! I have never felt anything like that before."

"It's like an electric shock, right?"

"Definitely. My senses are brilliant. Everything seems so intense. Colors, sounds."

They did a few basic yoga stretches in the sand, warming.

"We're going to be sandy."

"It will brush off when it dries."

"Damn, we have to swim back, don't we?"

"Nope. There's a cottonwood log forty feet upstream that connects that gets us off the island without getting wet."

"I might swim back. That was a hell-of-a-rush."

Jack punched her lightly in the shoulder.

"You're crazy."

She ran her eyes down his body. "Looks like things are thawing down there."

41

The next day they drove back, realizing something had happened that would be hard to negate. Conversation wove in and out of relevance, detail, emotional depth, history. They were both relaxed around each other now. Giving each other shit had replaced caution at saying the wrong thing, hurting each other's feelings.

As they hit I-5, Juanita was explaining the persona she'd had to adopt as a female cop.

"For all the politically correct talk, guys rule the roost. A woman has to become masculinized, has to become like a guy. The opposite sure isn't going to happen. Which means, she has to swear like a guy, talk tough, act insensitively, ignore the latent and open sexism, the overt hostility. And, do her job better than a guy, cause no matter what they say, the bar is set higher."

"It must piss you off."

"It does piss me off, but there's nothing I can do about it. If I want to be a cop, it's the playing field I'm on."

As they approached Seattle, talk turned to the Lightfoot case.

"Jack, I'm going to tell you something I want you to think about seriously."

"Okay."

"I want to take a close look at Lightfoot's operations down at the Port. McCandless had detailed schematics of that site in the safe deposit box. God knows where he got them, but I want to put them to use."

Jack said nothing.

"I've been thinking about this awhile, Jack."

And he knew she'd already made up her mind.

"Can you get a warrant?"

"Read between the lines, Jack. This would be strictly illegal. Getting caught could mean arrest, even getting shot. But we both know something is going on."

"If you find anything, it will be inadmissible."

"If I find anything, when I find something, I'll get a warrant and go back legally.

Call this exploratory."

"Shit Juanita, are you sure?"

"I'd like you to come with. I'd be more sure then."

Jack was silent for several minutes, and Juanita gave him space.

"If you think it's a good idea, and if I can help, I'll do it."

"Thank you, Jack."

"You're welcome."

"I'm beginning to realize you're far more complex than I thought."

"I'm taking that as a compliment."

"You should."

Jack dropped Juanita off at her house, helping to haul her camping gear back into the living room.

"I don't suppose you want to come up?"

"Tempted, but can't. I promised Monique I'd get a handle on her project this afternoon."

"Oh yeah, the smart fabric gal. Is she attractive?"

"She's an 8 or 9."

"A number rating, and a high one. Like Yelp." Juanita raised her eyebrows.

"I'll Yelp you."

"You do that, mister. Yelp me good. So, what about this Monique gal?"

"She's attractive, but I'm into someone else."

"Someone more attractive, right?"

"Someone more attractive. A ten."

"A perfect ten."

Juanita gave Jack a burning soulful gaze that made him rethink the afternoon of work. But no. He'd promised himself, and a promise was a promise.

"You're disciplined. Don't worry, I respect that. But…"

She grabbed him and pulled him fiercely to her.

"Let's give the neighbors a thrill."

She kissed him hard, forcing her tongue into his mouth. He was wild, unmoored. Then she let go, and he released himself into the unbearable lightness of being. Jack drove home reeling, pulling into the safety of his underground parking garage like a burrowing mammal come home.

Given the lack of cell service up the Sky, Jack hadn't looked at his phone all weekend. Before he'd left, he'd gotten curious again, and texted a friend in the Computer Science Department at UW, asking him to forward it to someone in Chemistry. The text asked about aesther compounds, painted a little background, and gave contact information.

There was a text waiting from a chemistry professor named Henryk Czochralski.

> *Dear Jack Toyokata, I'm sorry to inform you that aesther compounds, unless it is a misspelling of ester compounds, is nonsense. It means nothing.*
>
> *Henryk Czochralski*
> *Associate Professor of Chemistry, University of Washington*

Jack was puzzled. He'd figured a chemistry professor would shed some light on the mysterious InSight ingredient. And ester compounds, what were they? Jack immediately Googled them, and found they were a class of organic compounds that react with water to produce alcohols and organic or inorganic acids. Digging further, he found that esters called parabens are used as food and drug preservatives because they prevent the growth of microorganisms such as molds and yeast. Furthermore, esters have a sweet fruit scent and low molecular mass. He did a bit more digging, but found nothing that had the least bit to do with memory.

Jack turned on his stereo and streamed the Dead's Cornell 77 concert, and with Jerry's soaring riffs, he turned to the work on Monique's project he'd been patently neglecting.

He Googled, then explored results for "smart fabric" and other synonymous phrases, narrowing it finally to artists, and finding a possible break-through. A gay Filipino artist operating out of Los Angeles named Li-Ne Line, was working with shirts that registered a person's temperature and heart-rate, and colored the shirt's fabric to correlate. Interesting. He shot Mr. Line an email, using the link on Line's website.

By the time all this was complete it was almost four. Jack stripped, pulled on his running shorts, shoes, and a worn T-shirt advertising Red Hat Linux, and hit the Burke-Gilman.

He ran out of his thoughts, the entanglements with InSight, Juanita, Monique, and himself, until there was only running, pure and simple. The late afternoon was filled with scents, and Jack honed in on them. The fetid algal and fish smells of the lake, the bursts of blooming perennials planted along the trail, the scent of urine where homeless men sprayed their fluid, various colognes, gels, shampoos and sweat from passersby. A continually altered and interesting landscape that Jack typically ignored, but now saw was an interwoven wonder as complex as a symphony. Once again, he experienced the feeling of flowing with the day, as if time and space were truly one current, and he was surfing it.

42

The next morning, Monday, Jack opened an email from Juanita that contained a schematic map of the Lightfoot operation at the Port of Seattle. It consisted of abundant warehouses and miscellaneous outbuildings, numerous containers, and eight docking ports connected by a warren of small roads and alleyways. In addition to the schematics, there were several aerial photographs. On both the schematics and the aerial photos, two of the small outbuildings, and three containers were circled in red. No additional information clarified the meaning of the red circles. All the circled items were clustered in one area of the docks. Examining the photographs, Jack could see this area was gated off from the rest of the operations.

Juanita's note was brief.

> *Obvious where we need to look. You in? If so, we need to get you some firearm training.* ☺

Was she kidding? No. Jack was thinking, "This is it." I jump or back down. He didn't know exactly what the effect of saying no would be on his budding relationship with Juanita, but guessed this was a test of sorts. By saying yes, he was entering further into her world, which he was discovering wasn't as straight and narrow as he'd initially thought. But maybe he was reading too much into it. Maybe it wasn't a test. Maybe she thought they were in something together now. Something that resonated beyond being lovers. Partners in crime or some cliché like that.

> *Okay, I'm in. You serious about the firearms training?*

A short moment later his phone buzzed.

> *Yes. This afternoon. I'll take you to our range.*

They hooked up after she got off, 4:40, and she drove him to a warehouse off Aurora, north of 85th. Flashing her badge at the door, they entered a large anteroom. Jack could hear the pop of pistols, the staccato ratatatatat of automatic weapons. Agents in various array of official dress were in clusters talking, or walking to and from an entryway that led into the gallery. Juanita led the way, nodding at several colleagues on the way in.

The range was divided into aisles and stations for each shooter, who stood, knelt, or lay prone, all shooting at life-sized human silhouettes that hung from wires.

"I'll grab us some headphones."

After, they walked left toward the end of the aisles.

"We'll stay out of everyone's way," Juanita said over her shoulder. "I don't want you killing anyone on your first day." She winked.

They reached the last aisle, and Juanita lay down the black nylon case she was carrying, unzipped it, and folded the top back. There were two guns. A pistol, Jack learned was a Berretta nine-millimeter, and a short rifle Jack didn't recognize. Black metal, lightweight, it looked like a tiny military fighter plane with a barrel and laser scope.

"What is that?"

"Custom. It's a .222. Small. Holds 300 rounds. Automatic. Very fast."

"What's that?" Jack pointed to a carbon fiber attachment screwed into the end of the barrel.

"It's a silencer. A very high-tech one. This gun doesn't pop, it whispers. You'll see."

Juanita signaled to an unseen man in a booth that she was ready, and immediately a silhouette target slid down the wire and locked itself in.

"You've never had training, have you?"

Jack shook his head.

"Ever even shot a gun?"

"Where we went camping, my uncle would bring up a couple .22 pistols and we'd plink cans. Never shot a rifle or shotgun."

"Okay, let's see what you can do." She handed Jack the pistol.

"It's light."

"A woman's gun. Nazis loved it. I guess they had strong animas."

Jack stood sideways, mimicking an actor in some random movie scene, extended his right arm, straightened it, sighting down the barrel. He heard his uncle's easy voice saying 'squeeze, don't pull,' and he squeezed the trigger.

The pop was far quieter than he'd anticipated, and there was barely any kickback.

Juanita had a pair of small Nikon binoculars raised to her eyes.

"Shoot five more at the chest area. Left side."

Jack squeezed the trigger five more times. He couldn't really see what damage he was doing to the target, thirty feet distant.

"Okay. Set the gun down and take a look."

Jack laid the pistol on the nylon case and took the binoculars.

Four of his shots had hit the target, though somewhat wildly. One just above the left knee, two in the stomach, one near where he imagined a beating heart was located.

"So?"

"Pretty damn good for no training. All four shots would have taken someone down."

Juanita took the gun, popped the clip and slid in another full one. Then she took her stance, feet a bit wider than hip distance, arms in a triangle facing the target, right hand holding the gun, left hand supporting the shooting hand, knees slightly akimbo.

"This is called the fighting stance," she said. "It was developed in the Special Forces as a stable, versatile posture. Since both feet are lined, it allows movement to either side, and well as reverse and forward. We'll practice this. I think you'll find it more comfortable."

She shot six times in quick succession, then handed Jack the binocs.

"Don't you want to look first?"

"No need," she wore her bemused smile.

Jack raised the binoculars. Juanita's shots were clustered within an inch of each other overlaying the heart.

"He's dead," Jack said, a bit of awe in his voice despite himself.

"Damn right he's dead," she said. "Granted, people you shoot at are rarely going to stand and present themselves the way these targets do, and we don't have time to work on moving targets, but still, it's better than nothing." She pointed beyond the range at another large warehouse. "If we had the time, there are some very sophisticated simulations in there."

"Guess I'll just shoot the ones standing still. You can take the movers."

"Okay, come here."

For the next two hours she coached Jack on stance and style, and by the end of it he was feeling comfortable, and his shots were consistently in the mid-chest and belly, areas Juanita told him to concentrate on.

"Only high-end snipers take head shots, and all this bullshit I hear from the public about shooting someone in the knees, give me a fucking break. You get someone sprinting away from you and try to shoot them in the knees you might as well write them a pass. Always shoot at the rectangle between the neck and groin. Always. Remember that."

Then Juanita took out the space-craft weapon, signaled the tower for a new target.

"Now this you hold differently, like a rifle, but you don't have to worry about it, because I'm not letting you near this thing, no offense."

"Fine with me."

Jack watched through the binoculars as Juanita shredded the center chest of the silhouette, the bottom half finally tearing away and floating to the ground.

Jack watched as she packed the guns away.

"You did good today, Jack. Better than a lot of cadets."

Two agents walked down to take their place, one of them saying "Who's your boy-toy Juanita?"

The other one saying "Asian. Man, the force *shore* is diversifying."

"Fuck you Ottoman. Why don't you learn to think, just a bit, before you speak?"

"That would take all the fun and spontaneity out of it, Juaneeeeetta."

The other guy threw down two cases similar, but longer than the one Juanita had, and the men got down to business.

As they walked away, Juanita told Jack that Ottoman was a privileged narcissist from Woodinville, who happened to be the best shot in their division.

"And his yes-man is T. Theringher Triggs, nicknamed Trigger." Juanita couldn't help but chuckle. "A blue-blood from Connecticut. Crack shot psychopath. The two of them get the real shooting assignments."

"They both seem like assholes."

"Yeah, there's a joke in the force, goes like this. 'What do you get if you add one asshole to another asshole?'"

"Two assholes?"

"Good guess, and mine as well, when first asked. The answer is 'Half a good cop.'"

"Jeez, that's sick."

"Welcome to my world, Jack. Welcome to my world."

43

That night Jack had another dream.

He'd gone to bed around 11:30, after hooking Monique up, via FaceTime, with Li-ne Line, and both of them with his friend Stan, the sound man. Monique had decided, that in addition to broadcasting color when worn by viewers, she wanted her fabrics to radiate sound, and when Jack approached Stan about the possibility of working with a couple of artists, he jumped at it.

It was four a.m. when Jack sat bolt upright in bed, shivering and pale as if he'd seen a ghost.

This dream was different.

An older man, bearing a shock of white hair and a cane, was walking down a street Jack knew all-to-well, NE 175th, directly in front of his condo. Other than the older man, who Jack did not recognize, the street was deserted.

Jack watched as the street lamp that always flickered suddenly quit, and the walking man pull up short. Jack saw through his eyes another man approaching. The man was dressed in a long stylish grey coat. He wore a fedora, rakishly, sand-colored chinos, and running shoes. He walked quickly though easily, as if quickness was his normal gait. Perhaps it was the fact the flickering light blinked out, or that the street had been deserted, that stopped the gentleman with the cane. Jack couldn't know. He watched as the tall man quickly approached, watched the man with the cane raise his hands to shield himself as the tall man withdrew a pistol from underneath his coat. The single shot struck the elder man in the center of his forehead, a small hole blossoming like a night-blooming flower, and the elder man fell slumped to the pavement like a limp rag doll.

Sitting now on his bed, breathing hard, his heart racing somewhat erratically, Jack saw that blue and red light was flashing outside his window. He got out of bed and walked over, looking out. There were five police cars jammed, blocking the street and the Burke-Gilman, and a huddle of cops in a loose circle around the body of the old man. Jack had no more time to look out, grasp the scene, than his doorbell rang.

Of course, he thought, they'd be canvasing the building for witnesses, that thought followed immediately by, 'Am I a witness?' And followed immediately by, "Shit, I just dreamt this and it just happened."

He pressed the intercom button and said "Yes?" his voice thick with sleep.

"Mr. Toyokata?"

"Yeah?"

"This is Gerald Daniels of the Seattle Police Department. Is it okay if I come up and ask you a few questions?"

"What is this concerning?"

"There had been a shooting in front of your building, and we're canvassing the residents to see if anyone heard anything."

"I didn't. The buzzer just woke me."

"That's fine, and this will just take a minute. We're required to physically talk with everyone in the building. May I come up?"

"Sure." Jack hit the buzzer, realizing he was wearing boxers and nothing else.

A few minutes later, the time it took his building's fast elevator to ascend and someone to walk down the hall, there was a knock on his door.

Jack opened it, and gestured the uniformed policeman in, noting that there were other police in the hallway knocking on other doors or talking with neighbors.

The cop, a young handsome black man with a thick well-groomed moustache, held out his badge, then handed Jack a card with his name and contact information.

I'm Gerald Daniels of the Seattle Police Department, and you are Jack Toyokata?"

"That's correct."

"I'm sorry to wake you and interrupt your sleep."

"That's okay."

"I want to ask you about a shooting that happened outside your building tonight, sometime within the past hour or so we think. Is that agreeable?"

"Yes. Do you want to come in?"

"That would be nice."

Jack led Daniels into the living room, and gestured to the cream-colored sectional.

"Boheme. Nice! My father-in-law has one of these."

"Okay." Jack wasn't sure what else to say. The last thing he wanted was some cop in his apartment yakking about his family or Jack's furniture. He hadn't even begun to process the dream.

Daniels sat down. "Sweet hooters too. You build this stereo system?"

"No, a friend designed and built if for me."

"Very, very nice."

"It's a great system."

Daniels sat back in the couch.

"So, Mr. Toyokata, did you witness anything related to a shooting tonight?"

Jack was still not sure how he would answer, but the words bypassed his indecisiveness.

"I was asleep, and when you rang the buzzer, it woke me. I apparently was not awake during the time of the shooting."

"Apparently?"

"Well, if you woke me with the buzzer, that means I've only been awake for five minutes or so. I'm assuming that was after the shooting."

"Do you remember hearing anything that sounded like a gunshot? Sometimes, even when asleep, loud noises register."

"Nope, sorry."

"Have you lived here long?"

"A little over a year."

"And what is your profession? What do you do?"

"I'm a computer programmer. Self-employed."

"You must do well for yourself."

"Well enough."

"So, you didn't get up to piss, get a drink of water, read a book, nothing like that? Just went to bed and woke to the buzzer."

"That's about it."

"About it?"

"That's correct."

Daniels pulled out his phone, clicked a few buttons and handed it to Jack. There was a close-up photograph of a man's face. Jack recognized him as the murder victim, but the hole in his forehead had been hastily retouched. It wasn't evident unless someone knew the wound was there.

"Do you know this man?"

Jack answered quickly, perhaps too quickly, feeling Daniel's eyes registering every nuance of his face.

"I've never seen him before."

"You're sure? He doesn't live in the building? Walk his dog around here? Maybe you've noticed him in the neighborhood?"

"I don't think so."

"Don't think so?"

"I don't recognize him. I haven't seen him before."

"You're sure?"

"I'm sure."

Daniel stared at him for a few seconds, then stood abruptly.

"Okay then, I and the Seattle Police Force thank you for your time. And remember, if you think of anything else, anything at all, please get in touch."

"Will do."

He walked Daniels back through the kitchen and opened the door.

"Goodnight, Mr. Toyokata."

"Say, could I ask you a question, officer?"

"Yeah?"

"What do you think the reason was? I mean, this old man out walking, killed in front of our building. Was he robbed?"

"Too early to say. We're just beginning to investigate, and it could be a lengthy investigation."

"It's just that I run, sometimes late at night. I've never had a problem, but if there's a burglar around who's shooting people, I'd like to know."

"I understand. And the tenants here, and neighbors, will be kept up to date on the case."

"Thanks."

"Take care, Mr. Toyokata."

As soon as the door clicked shut, Jack texted Juanita.

Call me asap

Then he fell back into bed, the dream swirling around his head like shreds of fog he was trying to grab onto and understand. But his adrenaline rush had slacked, and he fell into a deep, soundless, dreamless sleep.

44

Again, Jack woke to incessant buzzing, this time his phone which he'd silenced, but the vibration on his bed table pulled him from the depths of sleep. He fumbled for it, almost dropping it, noticing that the windows were letting in a soft golden light.

"Hello."

"Did I wake you?" Juanita's voice registered surprise. "It's almost nine-thirty."

"Yeah. Rough night."

Jack proceeded to tell her about the dream, the cop questioning him.

"Did you tell him about the dream?"

"Hell no. He wouldn't believe that."

"Agreed." He heard her cover the phone, say something to someone. Then, "I Haven't heard anything about it, but let me see what I can find out. I'll call you back in a few."

"Okay."

He wandered into the kitchen and began making coffee. Today was Tuesday and he had nothing scheduled. Jack was meeting Riordan downtown tomorrow afternoon to scope out SAM. But Monique had called him, pretty excited he thought, and asked if could come over Thursday for lunch. He'd agreed, but worked up the courage to tell her to lay off the "scantily clad" routine. He told her he had a girlfriend, and was monogamous. This met with several seconds of silence, then a burst of laughter.

"You've been talking to Riordan, haven't you?"

"So you'll be decent?"

"I'll dress like a nun."

In fact, Jack was getting excited by the project. He'd never worked on anything like it, and bringing his friend Stan into it would open up some unique potentials. Stan was an amateur sound engineer, and could see possibilities with sound no one else could. And Jack was becoming more and more enthralled by Li-Ne Line's work. There was no doubt that Riordan and Monique were taking him into some wild, fascinating terrain. And aside from paying the bills, the work gave him space from the dreams, Juanita, and the rest of his life.

His phone began broadcasting Eno's *Somber Reptiles*, his ringtone of the week. It was Juanita.

"I talked with the cop in charge, Bill McKenzie, at Seattle PD. He was a pain at first, wondering why the FBI was interested, et cetera, but I told him the case had some similarities to several we were investigating, and that seemed to mollify him.

"They've tentatively ruled out robbery. Which only means nothing obvious was taken, and there were no forcible signs. Ripped pockets, that sort of thing.

"They have two seconds of video footage taken as the killer was walking away from the crime, a hind-shot. Apparently your building has three video cameras. One covering the sidewalk in either direction, and one covering the entrance. The camera covering the approach to the crime was malfunctioning that night. They're looking into how random that was.

"From the rear, the killer matches your description. Tall, long grey coat. He'd removed the fedora however, and was sprinting down the sidewalk. He was out of video range within a couple of seconds."

"Is that it?"

"Bullet hole in the forehead. Nine-millimeter. Probably a Glock, but ballistics haven't come back yet. No one in the apartment heard a shot, so it was probably silenced. A professional hit, so they're focusing on the victim. One Alfred Croshure, according to ID found on his body. Oddly, he was from Santa Monica, California. No apparent relatives in the area, and no one has any ideas why he was walking in that area at that time of night."

"Strange."

"Yeah, but they'll figure something out. There's another thing though. There were three people in your building that the cops flagged as 'suspect,' meaning that they possibly knew more than they were telling. It's typical protocol for these kinds of canvasses, and most of the time it turns out to be people who get nervous around cops. But in this case, you were one of people who was flagged."

"I kind of lied to the officer when he asked me if I'd witnessed the crime. I mean, I did witness it, in a way, in my dream."

"True."

"I was pretty nervous. I had a feeling he didn't fully believe me."

"Well, your instinct was correct."

"What should I do?"

"I think you should get back in touch with him. Tell him you what you saw. Don't tell him it was a dream, just tell him the details of what you saw. Make it seem like you were looking out the window. He's going to ask you why you lied. Tell him you were scared of getting involved. That part's not going to be easy, but you've got to do it. If you don't, they'll come around and question you again, only it won't be some beat cop. It will be two hard-assed detectives who have done this a million times, and they'll crack you in a heartbeat."

45

Jack fingered the card that Patrolman Gerald Daniels had given him, turning it over to where Daniels had scribbled his cell number. Jack had the feeling Daniels knew he'd call back.

The phone rang three times, and Daniels answered in his precise English.

"Patrolman Gerald Daniels speaking. How can I help you?"

"Hi. My name is Jack Toyokata. You questioned me last night. About the shooting outside my condo."

"Oh, hi. Glad you called. What's up?"

"I saw it."

Daniels was silent for a moment.

"Can I swing by?"

"Sure. I'll be here all afternoon."

"Good. I'll be there in an hour."

Jack walked over to the window. He needed to coordinate what he'd dreamed, which he'd seen omnisciently, then from the elderly victim's eyes, with what he could have seen from his window. Luckily, the line-of-sight to where the man had dropped was unobstructed, and Jack could relate the story pretty much as he'd dreamed it.

Jack was coding, working of some information Li-Ne Line and Stan had provided him about hardware, when his buzzer rang. Daniels was early. Jack buzzed him in, and a few minutes later heard his knock.

"Hello," Jack said swinging the door wide. "Come in, and I apologize for making you come back. I should have leveled with you when you questioned me. No excuse, other than I was scared. I've never been near anything like this before."

"Okay, no problem. It happens." Daniels pulled an I-Pad out of his coat pocket and flipped it open.

"Now, tell me what you saw. As exactly as possible."

"Okay. I had to go to the bathroom, so I got up to piss, then went into the kitchen to get a drink of water. I thought I heard something, and glanced out the window when I came back to bed."

"Go on," Daniels prodded.

"At first, I didn't see anything. The street was deserted, and I just kind of glanced around. Stared out at the lake. Then I caught movement, and saw this man, the victim, walking down the Burke-Gilman."

Jack described the victim, as he could, then the killer, seeing him approach, raise a pistol, and shot the victim in the forehead.

"Did you hear a shot?"

"No. I didn't hear a thing."

"What happened then?"

"The shooter took off his hat and began sprinting away. I looked back at the man who'd been shot. He'd fallen to the ground. And when I looked up the path for the killer, he was gone."

"He was travelling north, is that correct?"

"Yes. He was running north."

"Anything else?"

"Not that I can think of."

"Can you show me where and how you were looking out the window?"

"Sure."

Jack positioned himself at the window and Daniels made him go through the scenario once more, pointing to where he'd seen the victim go down, where he'd first noticed the killer, where he'd lost him.

"So the victim was walking south, and the killer north?"

"That's correct."

"You're sure the killer wasn't walking the same way, came up behind the victim? Or that they were walking side-by-side talking? Or maybe arguing?"

"Nope. They passed each other, and the killer raised his gun and shot him as they passed."

"The victim didn't act like he knew the killer?"

"Not at all."

"There were no words exchanged?"

"Not that I could see."

"Look, you're going to hate me, but could you go through it all again. From when you woke up?"

"Sure."

Jack reviewed the entire episode again, and Daniels, taking notes, seemed satisfied.

"Okay. Thanks. I appreciate you coming forward. If you think of anything else, you have my card."

"Sure. I will."

"There is one more thing. I'm going to need you to stop by the downtown station, and give a description to our sketch artist."

"No problem."

"Can you do that today?"

"Sure. I'll squeeze it in. Which station?"

"Downtown. Six-ten Fifth Avenue. Thanks."

Daniels said goodbye and Jack let him out, feeling the sudden need for a drink. He pulled out his phone and called Per.

46

Jack met Per three hours later at The Sandstone Lounge in Bothell. The sketch session had gone well, the artist being extremely perceptive and quick, and Jack had left feeling good about his coming forward.

The Sandstone was a brushed nickel/black leather bar with lots of glass and mirrors, but their deck extended out over a wetland, typically crowded with chatty Canadian Geese. Tonight was no different.

Jack spotted Per sitting on the far end on the deck, and walked over, telling the waiter he'd like a pint of Hefeweizen and some peanuts. As Jack sat down, Per raised his glass.

"Jack, you slacker. What's up?"

"You want the short version, or the long one?"

"Short for starters. If it warrants it, we can go longer." Per looked up from pouring tobacco from a blue pouch into a rolling paper and smiled. "I've been in your immature country long enough to know I can't smoke this here. I'm just going to hang it from my lips. It's a look thing."

"That what a writer looks like, is it?"

"A disaffected European writer."

"Okay then."

Jack filled him in on everything but the dream and murder. Camping with Juanita, his gigs with Riordan and Monique, his life after UniCode. During the monologue his beer and the peanuts came, and Per signaled for a second.

"Sounds like you're a charmed man, Jack. No dark side to all this bliss?"

"Well, now that you mention it, I'll die someday."

"Appropriately morbid."

"Hey, you up for a burger?"

"Maybe some fish and chippers."

Jack signaled the waiter who strode over, and they gave him their orders.

Then he began to tell Per about the dream.

"You've had several of these…dreams, haven't you?"

"Yep."

"They scare you?"

"Not exactly scare. They disturb me, but they also thrill me."

"Thrill? How so?"

"Thrill might not be the exact word. They fascinate me."

"So, you'd prefer to continue with the dreams?"

"Yeah. They're important to me. A glimpse into a different realm. As you said, maybe a cosmic memory bank."

"I said that?" Per snorted a laugh. "I must have been toasted."

"You were a bit."

"The dreams are always correct, aren't they? Someone is really killed?"

"So far, they've been infallible."

"You've seen the crime, the victim, the perps. You've been to the cops and the FBI, yet They've never been able to catch the killers. Why do you think that is?"

"Well, that's not exactly true. The first one, the girl in Chicago, I never saw her killer. Just the car."

"Details. Let me tell you what I think."

Per was interrupted by the waiter bearing food.

"Could I get an extra tartar sauce, please?" Per asked the waiter, then continued.

"If I were writing this, say in a novel, I'd say that whoever is responsible for giving you these dreams is toying with you. Didn't you tell me once that they started happening after you began taking some memory supplement?"

"InSight."

"You still taking it?"

"Yep."

"You try to quit?"

"I did. My memory went to shit. Thinking got muddy."

"Shit, Jack. Doesn't that scare you?"

"Not really. I'm enjoying the benefits. Clear memory, enhanced energy, perceptions."

"And the dreams."

"And those."

"You should quit this stuff, Jack. Cold turkey. I can help, stay with you, feed you and pour whiskey down your throat."

"Thanks. I'll take it to heart. But what were you saying? About a novel? Someone toying with me?"

"Okay. Who makes InSight?"

"Some company named Blu-Pharma."

"You check into them at all? See where they live, who owns them? That sort of thing?"

"Nope."

"Wow. You're a piece of work, Toy. You take some drug that gets you hooked and gives you true dreams about murders and you aren't even suspicious enough to track them down?"

"I found another woman user who had similar dreams."

"And?"

"I asked her to research her dreams, see if she could correlate them to crimes."

"Jack, you are a piece of work." Per took a draught of his pint. "Let me see if I can get to the bottom of this. I work with some top-notch researchers. I'll throw it to them and let you know what they find out. Okay?"

"Sure. But to tell you the truth, I've grown to value the dreams. They've expanded my life, added a dimension I couldn't imagine. And I want to find who's responsible. There's someone behind the dreams. They all tie together."

"There's something you're not telling me, Jack."

"Maybe a few things." Jack sucked ketchup off a fry then popped it into his mouth.

"Okay, that's fair. I don't tell you everything either." Per laughed, "Hey, I don't want to deprive your life of meaning, I just think we should check this stuff out."

"Sorry. I didn't mean to sound defensive. The whole thing is weird."

"Yes, it certainly is."

"Let me know if you find anything out."

"I'll certainly do that."

47

Riordan had arranged a walk-through with SAM's curator, Tish Tosher, who agreed to meet them around one-thirty in the lobby.

Jack lucked out on parking up the hill on Seneca, and caught Riordan a few minutes early in the front lobby. He was talking with a tall, willowy woman with a shock of white hair and heady purple earrings, and waved Jack over. As Jack drew closer, he saw the earrings matched her eyes.

"Tish, my collaborator, Jack Toyokata. Jack, Tish."

Jack took her offered hand, thin as a stick but surprisingly strong. She caught his eyes and smiled. He liked her immediately.

"You're a computer code person, Riordan tells me. How fascinating to be able to work on art. I'm open to learning anything I can."

"Thanks. It's been a very rewarding project so far."

After introductions, Tish showed them the three exhibit rooms, which were a bit smaller than they'd anticipated, but adequate for twenty pieces or so. Jack took photos, and Riordan scampered around with a tape measure, muttering as he went.

After twenty minutes, Riordan said, "Done. Let's get a beer."

They went to Bruno's, several blocks south on First, and ordered two Ballard Bitter Ales, Riordan pontificating on life, love and the pleasures of sex without commitment.

Jack in turn, told him he was meeting with Monique, Stan, and the LA artists Li-Ne Line tomorrow at Monique's Belltown studio to brainstorm some prototypes. Riordan was impressed with the project, the collaborations, how it was all coming together.

"Maybe I'll drop by. Be a fly on the wall."

"Not an apt metaphor for you, big man. More of a hippo in the room," Jack laughed, but fine with me. Better call Monique though."

"Oh hells bells, we go way back. I've been tormenting her with my obnoxiousness and bad manners for years. Why stop now?"

Walking back to his car, Jack began to feel like he was living two distinct lives. One as a coder for a couple of crazy artists, the other as an amateur sleuth. And perhaps a third as Juanita's lover. Though Jack still had no real clue what that meant or where it was going. Sometimes Juanita opened like a door onto summer, yet other times she was unreachable, beyond the horizon. He was patient though, and figured this would change, or not, and they'd continue on from there. Or not. And there was still the apparent fact that she and Rubio were still married. Something he was still struggling to talk to her about. But that too could wait.

His phone rang was he was driving back to Kenmore, and glancing at it, he recognized Juanita's number.

He called her from his condo as soon as he got home.

"Hey," she said.

"Hey yourself. You sound tired."

"I am. I need a great meal at, maybe, Clubbers, then a foot massage, and then…"

"You at the office?"

"I am."

"I could pick you up in an hour."

"That would be absolutely divine, but won't work. I've got a baseball game to attend, then need to help Angel with a school project."

"Want me to help?"

"You're a cariño, but not tonight." "Rain check."

"Indeed." She hesitated a moment. "Hey, are you a kayaker?"

"Kayaker? Not really."

"Yeah. Have you paddled one before?"

"Haven't in awhile, but did a few overnight trips in college and just after. Why?"

"I think kayaks are the best way to get into Lightfoot's port. I'm thinking of Thursday night."

"That's tomorrow."

"Indeed. I've already borrowed two from a friend. They're on my car as we speak."

Jack whistled softly. "You don't take baby steps, do you?"

"Why would I? I'm not a baby." She laughed, but it sounded hollow.

"You've got this planned all planned don't you. Where we put in? All that?"

"I've got some ideas. I'll have it nailed down by then."

"How about the boys?"

"I told them I'll be working late. I'll leave them some tamales in the fridge. They'll be fine."

"How do we work it?"

"Could you swing by here around six-thirty? We can eat a leisurely meal, then head out."

"You make this sound like a vacation."

"We can call it that if you like."

"It's light until ten you know. We'll have a lot of time after dinner."

"Get to know each other better."

"Mess around in the back seat. Where are you thinking of launching?"

"Pier 48. We've got access there through a Coast Guard port. It's roughly a mile paddle. Should take about an hour. We need to paddle to the West Duwamish Waterway, then another half mile. We'll leave around ten, catch daylight for a half hour or so, but the last couple miles will be in the dark. You a good swimmer?"

"The best. Didn't you see me in the Sauk?"

"That seems ages ago."

"Yeah." And it did.

"So, swing by tomorrow evening around 6:30. The building will be locked, but text and I'll come down. Think about someplace nice for dinner. It might be our last."

"You're joking, right?"

"One never knows."

48

Jack drove Stan to the meeting with Monique and Li-Ne Line at her Belltown studio, a fourth floor loft off Second near Battery. Monique, Li-Ne Line and Riordan were already there, kibitzing like old friends. Li-Ne Line was Korean, in his mid-forties, five-eight, rotund, and sported spiky hair and a three-day beard. He wore black jeans and matching T-shirt and wore bright red Converse All Stars. His smile was constant and contagious. He'd brought a leather case of smart cloth, and had spread much of it on a large work-table.

They met for almost three hours, and Jack was excited about the direction this was taking. It would be fully cooperative, Li-Ne Line and Stan equal partners. To Li-Ne's knowledge, this was totally cutting-edge. Nothing like it had ever been done. Jack would be responsible for writing programs governing the behavior of the smart fabric, and the sound/musical responses.

After the meeting, Jack headed over to Japantown to shop at Uwajimaya. Certain Japanese foods, and a particular brand of sake, were still difficult to find in the grocery chains. He spent some time wandering the neighborhood, one he'd spent plenty of time in while at the UW. The area was definitely more vibrant now.

49

They went to Derby on 6th, where they shared a Cobb salad and a brisket platter. Juanita allowed one beer each.

The Coast Guard facility was locked down, but Juanita knew the code, and they were inside in a flash. Juanita pulled her pickup adjacent to an aluminum ramp dropping to a thin square floating dock. The deep evening light washed soft on the array of docks, the boats rocking at moorage.

They got out of the truck, and Juanita walked around the front over to Jack.

"Here," she said, her voice low, in command, all the gaiety and sweetness of dinner gone. She handed Jack the 9mm.

"Keep it next to you on the seat, and when we land, tuck it into the small of your back like we demoed. Safety's on, so don't forget. Hopefully we won't have to use these. But..."

Then she grabbed him, and hugged him hard, then kissed him equally hard on the mouth. Jack wondered what an observer would think, him holding a gun at his side while a woman attacked him with passionate desperation.

Juanita pulled away as suddenly as she'd begun, quietly saying something Jack found unintelligible.

"*Que dios esté con nosotros.*"

"What's that mean?"

"Nothing," she said, shaking her head, staring deeply into Jack's eyes. Then she took his hands.

"Follow my lead, Jack. You'll be okay."

"We'll be Okay," he replied.

She walked to the rear of the truck. "Grab one," she told Jack, lifting one of the kayaks out of the bed.

Jack grabbed the other, surprised at how light it was, then two paddles, and followed her down the aluminum ramp and dropped the kayak lightly alongside hers.

"Wait here."

She jogged back to the truck, pulled it forward alongside a long narrow building and parked it. She emerged a minute later with a small black backpack slung over her shoulder, and trotted back to the dock.

It was just after sunset, the water of Elliott Bay tranquil and gilded. Jack suddenly wished they were simply out for a romantic paddle.

They dropped the kayaks into the water, Juanita steadying Jack's, then settling into her own. She slipped the pack into the cockpit in front of her. "Let's go."

Juanita pulled away from the dock with muscular strokes, and Jack followed, falling into the rhythm and posture of the stroke naturally, memory emerging out of his muscles. One of his college girlfriends had been obsessed with paddling, and they'd gone out every chance they had. Lake Washington, the Sound, the San Juans. The pull through calm water was soothing yet invigorating, his arms and shoulders rising into each stroke, letting go.

Surprisingly, there were several other boats out, and they passed two couples in tandems, and a group of five single kayaks, each of the occupants wearing large binoculars around their necks.

"Bird watching?" Jack asked, as they passed close.

"Orcas," one of the women paddlers said, almost whispering. "They've been spotted down here the last several nights." "This close to the city. Isn't that unusual?"

"Very rare," one of the young men said, his voice tenor and reverent.

Jack wished them good luck with a half wave. Again, he had the desire to escape, slip anonymously into the group. He'd been crazy to agree to this.

They stuck to the shoreline, cutting across shipping inlets, edging around the tips of docks and piers.

Juanita had told him over dinner that she'd flown a drone over the area yesterday.

"The good news is there are no dogs. Dogs are bad news. And all the gates are high security, but there are several ladders and docks that allow easy access from the water."

"What about security cameras?" Jack had asked.

"Who knows? We'll have to be careful." She reached into her purse. "But I've got toys." She placed a small chrome cylinder on the table in front of her.

"A laser pointer."

"Looks like it doesn't it. It's a high-end infrared laser. It can permanently disable a security camera. We'll only use it if necessary."

"Like the guns, right."

"Like the guns."

Light had been leaking out of the sky as they paddled, and behind them and to their left, the brilliance of the Seattle skyline irradiated the darkening sky. They'd paddled steadily for nearly an hour and Jack's shoulders were beginning to ache.

They reached the East Duwamish fork and cut west, skimming the edge of Harbor Island. It was getting seriously dark now. The only sounds were distant traffic, sirens, and the slight splash of their paddles. There were infrequent lights on shore, but no signs of activity.

When they reached the West fork of the Duwamish, Juanita turned in and sculled her kayak to a stop. jack pulled alongside.

"Another quarter mile and we'll be in Lightfoot's turf," she whispered. "You good?"

Jack nodded, and Juanita pushed off into the night.

They'd just passed a monstrous freighter, when Juanita pivoted left into a narrow slip. Jack could see a ladder dropping into the water just ahead. Juanita tied the kayak off on the ladder, and eased out of the boat. She flashed Jack a smile, and disappeared up the ladder and onto the pier. Jack tied up next to her boat and followed suit.

When he topped the ladder, he saw Juanita standing across the pier against a wall, in shadow from a mercury vapor lamp. Jack sprinted across and joined her. She held a finger to her lips, then slid along the wall toward the end of the building. It looked to Jack like a single-story warehouse that had seen better days. Paint had dropped off in patches revealing weathered fir.

At the end of the building, they paused, standing for several minutes. The lighting, largely mercury vapor, and the occasional bulb or LED next to a doorway, were infrequent and sporadic. Juanita broke across a clearing and gained the side of a larger warehouse. She seemed to have a target in mind, and Jack followed. She'd told him at dinner only that there were two structures of interest she wanted to check out.

Jack's focus and awareness had sharpened, and the night seemed their friend.

They moved quickly, smoothly, around a couple more buildings, cutting through a parking lot. Giant cranes towered like mechanical heron waiting to seize an unsuspecting fish. In the next area, well-lit, newer, containers were piled like LEGOS, deep and high, and small fleets of semi-trucks congregated in lots, symmetrically aligned. There was a tension in the air now that was palpable. Once they heard voices, a burst of argument, and they'd frozen, then after a break of silence, moved on.

Time had frozen for Jack. He'd no idea how long they'd been sneaking through Lightfoot's property, which was far more extensive than he'd imagined. They'd spotted two security cameras, but were able to skirt each. Jack was six feet behind Juanita when she held up her hand, then motioned him to join her. In front of them was an opening where several roads intersected. The attenuated light of three mercury vapor lamps raked the area naked.

On their left, next to a mammoth docked cargo ship, squatted a well-lit building with two security vehicles parked outside. They could hear the throb of a bass vibrate the air. There were no curtains on the window, and a security guard sat sideways to them at a desk, staring at a computer screen. Juanita motioned to the right, toward a narrow ill-lit alleyway between two substantial two-story warehouses.

"Follow me," she whispered, then crouched and loped into the alleyway, immediately flattening herself against the wall. Jack joined her a few seconds later. He realized he was panting, and was suddenly scared shitless. The guard was still staring at the computer screen, and they watched as a second man walked behind him, pointed at the screen, and both of them laughed. Juanita slipped further into the alleyway, hugging the warehouse wall, and Jack followed.

They emerged from the alleyway into another open area, less well-lit, also with several intersecting roads and alleyways, two large semi-trucks parked off to their left. Juanita pointed to three weathered shipping containers directly across from them.

"Let's have a look."

Juanita sprinted across the opening and Jack followed. She stopped at the door of the first container, shone a flashlight on it, studied the locking mechanism, a padlock restricting the movement of a bar, that when slid left and lifted, would open the metal door. She moved on the second container, again illuminating a similar bar-lock.

The third container was a bit removed from the other two, and appeared the oldest of the three, its grey paint eroded by weather, a few scraggly clumps of Scotch broom and weeds bordering it. Jack, several feet behind Juanita, watched her splash the flashlight on the door and heard her exclaim faintly, "Hah!"

As he joined her, she pointed at the door. The lock-bar mechanism on this door had been replaced with a thoroughly modern keypad. Juanita was grinning as if she'd found the motherlode, and Jack was more nervous and in the dark than ever.

"Now what?" he whispered. "You think you can crack the code?"

"Don't have to." She swung her daypack onto the ground, unzipped it, and dug out a small grey plastic tub, similar, though smaller, than a margarine container. Opening the lid, she reached into the tub, and Jack watched as she smeared a pea-sized glob of putty onto the keypad. Then she extracted a small remote, and motioned to Jack to back away.

There was a feeble "Whump" and the pad shattered into metal bits and smoke. Juanita stepped up, lifted the door lever, and swung open the container door. Jack crowded up to the opening and stared inside. The container was empty.

Juanita swung her light around the inside. Jack noticed that she was paying particular attention to the roof. "Notice anything?"

Jack whispered "No," but then it dawned on him. He'd seen this room before. On one of the photos that Michael had stashed with his friend. In the photos, elephant tusks had been stacked against the wall, and two men had grinned back at the camera.

"They're gone," he said.

Juanita ignored him, entering the container, slipping the door closed, then crouching and moving slowly, combing the floor and lower walls with the flashlight. Every so often she'd pick something up, place it in a baggie, and move on. Jack watched her and her light disappear into the rear of the fifty-foot container. After several minutes he watched her slow return.

Juanita was roughly two-thirds back when Jack heard a vehicle approaching. It stopped near the first container, and Jack knew if the occupants saw the destroyed keypad he and Juanita were trapped. Panicky, he looked around for something to jam the door.

Ten yards in, there was a pile of scrap wood randomly stacked against the wall. Jack began digging through it looking for a piece large enough to wedge the door shut. As he moved wood out of the pile to the side, he noticed a large square of tar-paper under the pile. He removed the remainder of the wood then kicked the tar-paper out of the way. There was a three-foot square of newer wood with a large metal ring on the right side. Jack reached down and pulled up, and the square of wood swung open revealing an angled metal ladder descending into the gloom.

Simultaneously, several things happened.

Juanita appeared like a ghost at his side, a look of amazement on her face; they heard two car doors slam in quick succession, and two hurried urgent voices. The guards, or whoever it was, were starting their search at the first container, which gave them a few minutes.

Juanita signaled Jack to descend, then climbed down after him, managing to grab the tar paper and slide it back over the square of wood as she let it drop back into place. It wasn't perfect, but would possibly give them a few extra seconds. There was no apparent way to lock the door from within.

Jack was waiting for Juanita at the bottom.

She kissed him briefly.

"Glad you came along?" followed almost immediately by, "C'mon. Let's go!"

She handed Jack another Maglite, and they set out jogging down the tunnel.

Jack had never been in a coal mine, but he imagined this tunnel was like one – timbers every ten feet, heavy beams holding up the earth. The walls looked like they were some sort of sprayed grey cement. The air was damp, thick and musky. Jack sensed they were heading west, but then the tunnel jagged sharply to the left, straightened for a distance, then turned sharply left again. Along the way, other ladders angled up to trap doors, maybe five in all. Several small side-rooms interrupted the continuity. All were empty except two. The first held twenty-two huge elephant tusks leaned against a wall. Juanita whistled and snapped photos.

The next room they came to held around fifty boxes. Slicing one open, they could see it was jammed with shrink-wrapped bundles of white powder.

"Drugs," Jack said.

"Maybe." Juanita sliced through the shrink-wrap and withdrew a bundle. It weighed maybe a quarter of a pound. She slid it into her pocket.

"C'mon."

They jogged another block or so, came to a sharp corner, turned right, and the tunnel ended in a flight of stolid wooden stairs, which they bolted up. At the top was a conventional door. Juanita turned the steel knob and pushed. The door swung open.

They stepped cautiously onto a mammoth empty dock. The area was poorly lit, and Juanita glanced around, killing her flashlight. Jack followed suit.

"I know where we are," she whispered. "The kayaks are that way," pointing.

She pulled a padlock out of her pack, opened it with a key, slipped it into the hasp, and locked the door they'd just exited.

"Buy us time if they're still in the tunnel."

"They know where it ends," Jack said. "They'll probably drive here."

"They'd need to check out all the other exits. I counted seven of them."

"I guess."

"Let's get the hell out of here."

Five minutes later they heard revving engines and shouting several blocks away. But by then, Jack and Juanita were descending the ladder to the boats. Juanita unhooked the kayaks, steadied Jack's while he got in then got in herself. They began paddling awkwardly through the pilings under the pier, and were almost to the end when they heard engines, and the screech of brakes above them. Juanita stopped instantly motioning to Jack. Car doors slammed, and they heard frantic voices, then saw beams of strong light dance quickly out over the water. Then the doors slammed, the engine roared, and the vehicle took off.

"Holy fuck," Jack intoned.

"That was close," Juanita whispered. "Got my adrenaline up, for sure."

Jack could see her gun held ready in her right hand. He started to say something but was shaking so badly he couldn't speak.

"Come on. Let's get you home safe. We'll head across to the other side, then back. I'll buy you a drink."

50

Jack woke groggy and sweat-soaked from a nightmare. He had been kayaking, but lost his paddle, and a brisk wind was blowing him out into the ocean. He tried paddling futilely with his hands, only to watch shore recede further and further away. He was leaving not only the shore, but his life behind. He tried to let go, but his fear was too great. He couldn't stop fighting for his life, paddling futilely with his hands.

Emerging from dream, Jack came back to lying in bed, trying to slow his breathing, steady himself. He was soaked in sweat, and a sheet entangled him like a serpent. His heart was thudding like an overwrought engine. But he took deep breaths, letting them out slowly, and gradually he calmed. Sunlight streamed through the cracks between the curtains, lay in slats on the duvet. And through the fog of sleep and dream the realization came to him. It's day, I'm in my bed, I'm okay.

And then it all came crashing back.

The paddle back had been scary. They paddled furiously to cross the West Duwamish channel, and hugged the far shore, twice stopping as eruptions of commotion, followed by shouting, lights raking the water. But they finally made it to Elliot Bay.

Juanita insisted they paddle out into open water, then diagonal across to the coast guard dock. Once they thought a boat was pursuing them, but it swerved after sweeping them with a searchlight, and giving a blast of its horn.

Jack's muscles felt like over-tuned guitar strings by the time they pulled into the Coast Guard dock an hour-and-a-half later. They took a rain check on the drinks, and Juanita dropped him at his car, then headed home. Enough was enough.

As the memories drifted off like tatters of mist, and he began to regain equilibrium, the phone rang. He picked it up and saw it was Juanita.

"Hey."

"Hey. Get any sleep?" Her own voice sounded drowsy, sexy.

"I slept like a rock."

"Me too."

"What time is it anyway?"

"Did I wake you?" She sounded concerned.

"No. Caught me on the cusp of coming out."

"On the cusp of coming out. I like that. Saliendo del sueño. It's three something in the afternoon Jack."

"Holy shit! I *really* slept."

"You *really* did." She laughed. "So, got a minute?"

"Sure." Jack sank back into the mattress.

"Here's where we are. Unofficially. I took several samples of ivory slivers and elephant hair from the container we busted into. I'm pretty sure it was the same container featured in one of the photos we got from Michael.

"I snapped several photos of the tusks piled in the underground room, and submitted a sample of the white powder to our lab. Won't get any results for a few days. But it's not dope. It tastes and smells like ground up bone. Wild animal bone, depending on the species, is extremely valuable on the black market."

"Wow, you've been busy."

"That's not all. I took the drone up again, and Lightfoot's site is a flurry of activity. Lots of expensive cars, most of them black with tinted windows. Looks like we got the attention of the brass."

"Okay."

"I don't think they'll suspect law enforcement. It's not our typical MO. The FBI would go in with a warrant and a multi-personnel raid. Which, and it's the reason we did what we did, would have taken weeks, if not months to organize. And some judge would have to give the okay, and odds are, would have tipped Lightfoot off."

Juanita hesitated. "No, they'll think this was a competitor, or free-lance operation trying to rip them off. Whatever, it will disrupt normal activity, and quite possibly force an erratic move."

"I was scared last night." He immediately felt like an idiot. A little kid confessing to his mom.

"I know you were, but you did fine. Better than I did when I was a rookie. I had nights when I swore I was not going to get out of bed in the morning." She paused. "Why did you come with anyway?"

"You're pretty difficult to say 'no' to."

She laughed. "So I've been told."

"Okay then, I think I wanted to prove something to you. And I was curious. I have a stake in this by now. But that was way more intense than I…"

"We didn't even get shot at!" Juanita laughed again.

"Thank God for small favors."

Juanita hesitated for a moment. "I'd say you have a big stake in this Jack. You're the one who's having the dreams. If not for that, we wouldn't be anywhere near this. And you don't have anything to prove to me. Nothing. You did fine. And I respect you as a man."

"Are you letting your colleagues in on this? What you found."

"What we found, Jack. And yeah, but not in the way you're thinking."

"How so?"

"I'm going to tell them these photos and samples were given to me by an informant. Someone who wants to remain anonymous. Maybe someone inside Lightfoot. I'm going to tell them the suspected location of the evidence. Then we're going to hand this over to the U.S. Wildlife Service, and let them and Interpol decide how they're going to handle it. Interpol already has a solid global schematic of Lightfoot's international operation -- subsidiaries, partners, customers, that sort of thing. There's a whole flow, a whole system to this Jack. And all we know is a tiny piece."

"What then?"

"Of course, if Wildlife or Interpol wants our involvement, they'll get it. We're a good team player."

"I guess."

"By now, those tusks, and the boxes of bone dust, or whatever it is, are nowhere to be found. Maybe on a boat to Rio or somewhere. And every container, warehouse, office, tunnel, room, and vessel that contains any animal residue is being vacuumed and washed down with commercial detergent. Even if we stormed the place this afternoon, the likelihood of finding anything relevant would be virtually nil. These are pros, Jack. They already made a mistake, letting someone get those photos to Michael. They won't make another one."

"They made two mistakes, Juanita."

"Yeah?"

"They allowed us to traipse around their site, find things we shouldn't have."

She said nothing.

"So where are we now, Juanita? You go hot and cold on me."

Again, the phone was silent, then Juanita spoke.

"It's complicated, isn't it?"

"Life's complicated."

"I got Angel asking about you. When can you come over and help him with his homework?"

"How about you? How do you feel?"

"Look, Jack, this is never going to be normal. Never. I'm a cop. You're not, and you don't know that world. I'm separated, but still married. I'm a single mom of two high school boys. Sometimes I think I'm way too busy to be in a relationship. Then I think I'm too selfish. Then I think it's wrong, since I'm still married. It's making me crazy."

"Get a divorce."

"It's not that simple, Jack, and I'm not sure I can fully explain it to you."

"You don't want to?"

"Maybe. Maybe not."

"You're not sure?"

"Let's leave it at that."

Jack said nothing, mulling over her words, then he blurted out something he immediately regretted. "You need to be in charge, Juanita. Last night, God, you hardly told me anything about what we were doing, where we were going. I just followed you blind. I think you like me being subservient, but I think it pisses you off too. I'm not sure you want a lover. Sometimes I think you want a competitor."

It was Juanita's turn for silence, so long a pause that Jack wondered if she'd hung up.

"Maybe you're right Jack. Maybe you're right. But with respect to last night, that was your choice, Jack. You could have demanded to know, acted more forcefully. That's what I'm used to. And I admit power is a fault of mine. And I get lost in work. I become obsessive, riveted. And I never talk much on the job. Never have. I just clam up so I can get more focused."

"Look, I know this is complicated, difficult, all that. But we had, have something, Juanita. And if we want to keep it alive, at all, we need to communicate. We need to work at it."

"You're a good man, Jack. I don't want to hurt you."

"Do you want to continue to see each other?"

Juanita was quiet for a long time.

"Why not just keep going. See what happens. I don't think we've played this thing out yet. Are you willing to keep going?"

"Yes. And if that's all I can get of you right now, I'll take it."

51

Life for Jack went on, and he managed to immerse himself in Riordan's project and forget everything else.

Riordan had purchased thirty LED screens of various sizes, and Jack was wrapping up the programming. Each contained a different approach to collaging Riordan's portraits. He'd hung ten of them on his living room wall. The resultant collages were striking. A collage of eyes, a flowing abstract of patches of skin, mouths that skittered across the frame, talking in unknown tongues. It was September, and Jack was a good month ahead of schedule. Riordan was already thinking about next projects. And he'd brought Jack a new client.

Jarvis Nome was another photographer, but worked totally with abstractions of landscapes. He and Jack hit it off immediately, and began discussing possible projects. Jarvis liked what Jack had done for Riordan, rather, he was a bit in awe of it, and wanted to explore something similar.

But he also wanted to work with three-dimensional images projected into a gallery space. Jarvis came from a generations-old Seattle family, old money. As far as Jack could tell, Jarvis had spent much of his life playing with art, and sailing. Jarvis was a passionate sailor, and had circumnavigated the globe three times, twice with his wife and two children.

Work with Monique, Li-Ne Line and his friend Stan continued to intrigue him. Li-Ne Line was a genius, a font of ideas, but also grounded in practicality. The son of a carpenter, he'd learned to build things early on. And he enjoyed it. When Jack was around him, Li-Ne struck Jack as an overgrown kid, enthusiastically bustling about, fitting pieces of a puzzle together.

The target for this project was Monique's gallery, *Gallery Strasse*, in Los Angeles. And since Li-Ne lived in LA, it made sense that Jack, Stan, and Monique would all fly down and put the show together. Monique's show was scheduled for early October, and they were working on staging several of her pieces in the Bell Town studio. Jack loved getting feedback from other resident artists. To these people, outside the box was the norm. And he could sense by their interest level, he had several other potential clients.

He met Juanita for lunch and coffee several times, never at her house. Things had cooled noticeably. Jack tried to analyze it, but Juanita refused to go there. At their last get-together, she'd let it slip that her ex, Alex, wanted to get back together.

"The boys need a father."

"Is that what you want?" Jack asked.

"What I want is to not be bothered with men, love, or relationships right now. Terminado." Then she smiled at Jack and he practically melted. This was one of the most beautiful women he'd ever had the pleasure of knowing.

"I'll stay out of your hair till you figure out what you want. But…"

"But?"

"But if you want to try again, I'll still be here."

She reached across the table and took his hand.

"Thank you, Jack. I know this isn't easy, that I'm not easy."

"Aren't you going to say 'But I'm worth it?'"

"Aren't you?"

52

Several days after he'd last seen Juanita, Jack had another dream. This one was different.

Jack inhabited an elephant, a large male boar, massive tusks yellowed with years in the Tanzanian sun.

He watched as the battered green Land Rover slowed to a crawl. The eyesight he'd inherited was blurry, but the Jeep was deliberate in its approach, and his vision cleared as the jeep stopped thirty feet across the small elbow-shaped slough. There were three men inside, a black driver in dungarees and safari hat, a brutish white man, blond, bare-headed, and a black man in the rear, shaved head, diamond stud in each ear. The men not driving held large caliber rifles.

He watched the white man get out, walk around the jeep, and level the rifle across the hood. The man had a small scar on his lip. The scar twisted as he talked.

"Remember me?" the man said. "I took your friend, you motherfucker. Now I'm going to take you." The day was windless, and the man's words floated across the distance. The elephant remembered the man, his voice. He had seen the man kill his brother. He had managed to escape, but not before the man had carved a furrow across his back with his rifle.

Jack heard the sharp metallic click as the man pulled the bolt and locked it into place. The other man slipped out, crouched, and raised his rifle to his shoulder. He whispered something in a language Jack didn't comprehend.

Somewhere in the elephant Jack inhabited, emotion erupted. The bull elephant bellowed, and began to wrench awkwardly in the thick mud, trying to turn, but a succession of barked shots caused dust to pop from his leathery hide, and Jack saw sky reel as the mammoth beast tipped and fell, and sky darkened to night with no stars.

Out of this night, Jack rose towards consciousness, then descended again, finding himself in the back yard of a suburban home. He was now inhabiting a man bending over a rose bush with pruning shears, a Mozart sonata swelling from oversized headphones. Jack watched through the man's eyes as he looked up suddenly.

A wooden gate blew open, and before the man could react, one of two intruders was upon him, hurling liquid into his face. Jack experienced a raging burn, saw jagged erratic light, and again a starless night descended.

Jack came to on the floor next to his bed. He was drenched in sweat, and his heart bucked erratically. He could see through the window it was still night, and when he managed to pull himself up onto the bed, the digital alarm read 3:13 in fluorescent red. His mind continued to reel from the sounds and images that had invaded him. Without thinking, he grabbed his phone off the end table and dialed Juanita's number.

She answered on the third ring.

"Hey," Jack said, "I had another dream."

"Jack, your speech is shaky. Tell me." There was genuine concern in her voice.

He recounted what he could of the first dream, the distinct description of the elephant poachers, the description of the Jeep, the slough, the open forest of thirty-foot trees around the slough.

The second dream was more difficult. It had happened so damn fast.

"The man who threw the acid in my face was white, mid-thirties, stocky, fast. Black hair, wide face and thin lips. Bad acne scars. He looked cruel."

"Any tattoos?"

"Not that I could see."

"How was he dressed?"

"Jeans. Black T-shirt."

"Anything on the T-shirt?"

"A design. Like a Celtic design. A labyrinthine circle. It happened fast."

"What about the other guy?"

"I only caught a glimpse of him, but…"

"But what?"

"I think he was the same man who killed the elephant. They were both blond, and there was something distinctive about him."

"What?"

"I can't remember. I just remember recognizing him. In the second murder, his hair was longer."

"But you're not sure?"

"Not entirely."

"Did they say anything?"

"No."

"Any unique characteristics of the yard, house?"

"I didn't see the house. The man was turned from it. The yard was expansive and ornate. Almost like an English Garden. Boxwood hedgerows, circular flower beds, stone paths. I remember a fountain."

"What did it look like?"

"European. Three white marble figures spouting water into a center pool. There were two ducks in it. Real ducks. Mallards."

"What about outside the yard? Anything distinctive that you noticed?"

"There were large trees behind the back fence. Cottonwood and fir."

"Okay. Any structures?"

Jack closed his eyes, running through the scene, freezing it, running it.

"Part of a house to the left. Stone. Leaded windows."

"Okay, good. Now this might be important. Did you get the sense, as the guy was running up, that your host knew him?"

"No. I mean, I couldn't say. It happened so fast."

"Okay."

"Sorry."

"Let me know if you think of anything else."

"Sure." Then he gasped.

"Jack. You alright?"

"I just realized something."

"What?"

"That elephant. I thought it was terrified, trying to get out of the mud and escape. But it was turning the wrong way."

"I don't understand."

"The elephant wasn't scared. It was enraged. It wanted to kill those men."

53

Jack was lying in bed, listening to the Keith Jarrett solo concert, Tokyo, 1984, letting the music wash over him, through him. Trying to escape or erase the experience of last night. He was a ragged bale of nerves. But he also knew something was coming to a head. It was just a feeling, a glimmer of a feeling really. But he knew it was true.

After a tumbler of Scotch, he'd managed to drift off. And now, he had another day to face.

When his phone rang, the Annie Lennox ringtone clashing momentarily with Jarrett, he nearly jumped out of his skin.

"Jack," Per said, "What's happening?"

"Hey Per. Can I call you back? I'm in the middle of something."

"I'll be here."

Jack eased himself out of bed. Ever since the kayak excursion his arm, shoulder and upper back muscles burned like fire. He'd tried ice, heat, and even a massage that he had to walk out on because it was too painful. Thankfully, the pain was finally mollifying.

A hot shower and a cup of strong coffee later, he sank into the couch and called Per back.

"What's up?"

"Well remember I told you I was going to research that company that manufactures your memory drug, InSight?"

"I do."

"I found out a few things."

"And?" Jack took a sip of coffee and set it back down.

"Blu-Pharma is in turn owned by a Singaporian company named Roydun Industries. Roydun also owns Panex, a Swedish pharmaceutical. Roydun is in turned owned by a Chinese conglomerate called YibinNuCo."

"And this means?"

"Hell if I know, but YibinNuCo is apparently the patriarch company."

"Did you look into what they do?"

"Mostly pharmaceuticals, but neither I, nor my librarian helper Jan, read Chinese. So it's a bit vague. Both Panex and Rondun, as well as Blu-Pharma, specialize in "all-natural" life enhancing products that improve everything from brain-power to staying power. Anything that will make aging boomers think they've found the fountain of youth."

"What's the word on these companies? Are the products legit? Do they work?"

"Lots of good product reviews by users. Even some Medline articles, which I didn't read. Roydun is very big, however. They grossed over seven billion last year. We couldn't find financials on YibinNuCo. But I'm guessing they're much larger."

"Well thanks, Per. Not sure this gets me any closer to anything, but thanks for digging."

"Not a problem. One other thing. YibinNuCo has been investigated several times for using illegal animal parts as ingredients. Rondun, once. Your memory drug might just contain tiger gall bladder, or something like that."

Jack felt a jolt of electricity. "Interesting," he said.

54

Jack was eating breakfast when Juanita called.

"Hey, just wanted to let you know that we haven't found anything yet on that murder. You didn't give us much to go on though."

"I know."

"We don't know when it happened or where."

"Sorry, can't give you any more than I did."

"You couldn't think of anything else, huh? No other details?"

"Nope."

Juanita was silent for a minute, and Jack listened to himself chew granola.

"Maybe something will turn up."

"Hope so. Hey, I've got a possible lead on something. Could you check and see if any of these corporations has a connection to Lightfoot?"

"Shoot."

"Roydun Industries of Singapore, Panex, a Swedish pharmaceutical, and a Chinese company, YibinNuCo." Jack spelled them out for her.

"I'll send these back to a DC researcher we're using on the case, Ariel Linnett. She's top-notch. I'll let you know what I find out." Juanita was silent for a moment.

"You want to grab some lunch soon?"

It was Jack's turn to pause.

"I'd like that very much."

"Good! Good." Then, "Jack, you take care, okay. I know these dreams are rough on you." She hesitated for a moment, then added, "and how I've been acting."

"Thanks. And I will. I'll be in touch about lunch." He almost said 'I love you'. Instead,

"Take care yourself."

"I will," and the line clicked dead.

55

Jack was in line at Whole Foods when the memory hit him. He was back in the head of the pruning man in the backyard, watching a dark-haired man run at him.

And then he was positive. The blond man in the backyard was the same as the blond elephant hunter. Older by ten years or so, but Jack had no doubts now. He froze the image of the blond assailant. Although he'd been riveted on the man with the acid running at him, there was a split second when he'd looked beyond the charging man, and saw a second man with a knife in his right hand. The man's hair was longer than it had been in Africa, he was a bit heavier, but his glacier-blue eyes with their depth of cruelty, and the scar that bisected his upper lip, were unmistakable.

"Hey, mister. Your turn," the clerk said in a bored voice, jerking Jack out of memory.

"Sorry."

He called Juanita from the parking lot. There was no answer, so he let a message.

"Jack here. I remembered something important. Call me."

Jack was driving when she called back, and swung the car abruptly to the curb.

"Hey."

"We found the murder. It happened three hours ago. It happened the day after you dreamt it."

"Impossible."

"This is a game-changer Jack. If you can predict these things..."

"I can't."

"Facts don't lie, Jack. It was Michael's dad. I'm on my way over there now."

"Son of a bitch!"

"You can say that again. They used pure sulfuric acid. His face is burned away, his throat slashed. That wasn't just a murder. It was a message."

"To who?"

"I don't know. Him maybe. Maybe someone he was working for or with."

"Huh."

"Maybe he was double dipping."

"A suburban mid-management guy?"

"What about Marty in *Ozark*?"

"You've got a point."

"The killers left by the rear gate. We're searching the alley and environs to see if there are any cameras. Haven't turned up anything yet. They probably parked at one end, walked the alley, committed the murder, then ran back to the car and took off. The only evidence, if I can call it that, is what's in you dream. We need a miracle on this one."

"Yeah." Jack had never banked on miracles.

"We think now that Michael stole the photos from his dad and was trying to sell them. Maybe someone approached Michael. Set him up to it. Offered Michael serious cash. Or drugs. We think Michael was into opioids."

"Seriously?"

"We took some tissue samples from his corpse. Had them analyzed. Michael was high the night he was killed. Had significant Oxy in him. He'd built quite a tolerance to be able to walk from his house to where he was killed.

"Lightfoot staged Michael's murder. They somehow found out Michael had the photos and were trying to buy them back. Maybe his dad found out and told his bosses. Anyway, Lightfoot approached Michael through these faux gangstas, the Benz Brothers, offered him drugs or money for the photos. But when Michael didn't produce them, they killed him. They would have anyway."

"That means his dad was complicit in his son's death."

"It looks that way."

"Maybe he didn't think Lightfoot would go that far. Kill Michael."

"Doubtful. He knew who he worked for."

"Jesus. And now the dad. Serves him right in a way."

"Poetic justice. I think they figured out he was double-dipping. Or maybe he was just starting to crack from the pressure of his son's death. Either way, he was a liability. Faber and Magic are trying to question his wife, she's the one called it in, but she's hysterical. Will probably have to be hospitalized and sedated. There's a seventeen-year-old sister. We'll talk to her as well."

"Damn, this is crazy."

"That night we visited them? Lightfoot? We rattled their cage, Jack. They're on the move."

"The blond guy, who murdered Michael's dad? I'm positive now he's the same guy who killed the elephant. He has a scar stretching into his left cheek from his upper lip."

"You sure?"

"Positive."

"Things happened fast. When I slowed it down, there it was. On the cheek of the elephant killer, and on the man who killed Michael's dad."

"And you're sure they were identical?"

"I'm positive."

"Then unless we have this very wrong, he works for Lightfoot."

"It certainly looks that way."

"Keep in touch."

56

That night Jack dreamt he was inside a bull elephant.

The elephant was alone, bellowing frequently to stay in contact with at least three other elephants, each of whom bellowed in return. The bull wandered through savannah, stopping only to strip leaves from acacia trees and stuff them into its mouth with its trunk, an act that brought him great pleasure.

In the various memory-dreams Jack had experienced since taking InSight, he was always a neutral participant. But now he experienced the emotions of the elephant. There was true joy in the elephant's ambling, the touch of warm sun on his skin, in breathing fresh air and seeing open sky. And Jack experienced joy, a contentment that was unlike anything in his own experience. It was a state of euphoria brought on by the simple acts of living, most of which humans had learned to ignore.

And when, after hearing a distant companion bellow, he returned the vocalization, Jack could feel the strong bond of friendship. But it was markedly different than his own experience of friendship. It was simple, pure, unfettered by any neurosis, competition, or comparison. It was, as Jack later told Per later, as unadulterated as the breeze, the sun, the savannah itself. It was a distinctly non-human bond. And yet it was, oddly enough, the experience of perfect love, one Jack had experienced in his earliest childhood toward his parents, but not since.

57

As Jack was heating tea water his phone buzzed. It was a text from Juanita.

You up for lunch? We could meet around noon at Soy Haus. I've got some info.

Jack typed back, *Sure.*

He called Riordan about a few things, then went for a run, showered, and headed down to the city. Puttering around Broadway, picking up a few books at Elliott Bay, Jack arrived at Soy Haus a little after twelve. Juanita had snagged a table in the rear, and was studying her phone and sipping tea when he arrived.

"Hey."

"Is for horses," Jack replied, sitting down.

"Well look who's in a good mood."

"Why not. I had a good dream for once."

"No one shot or attacked with acid?"

"Nothing like that."

"Anything you want to share?"

"Nothing of interest really."

The waitress, the daughter of the owners from the looks of her German-Vietnamese features, took their orders, Pho for Jack, Bratwurst with sweet chili sauce for Juanita, and disappeared.

"So, you have info?" Jack asked.

"I do. You know that sketch Seattle PD drew based on your description of the killer? Well, we loaded it onto a bureau-wide alert system and had a hit. It belongs to a known hitman used by the Irish mob in California. His name is Karl Turner, lives in Van Nuys. We're watching him, and will pull him in for questioning soon."

"Great! What about the victim?"

"Didn't I tell you?"

"No."

"Damn, I thought I did. His name is Devon Bridges. He's a retired security analyst for, you'll never guess, Lightfoot. Got into a bit of a tussle with them awhile back. Quit and filed a lawsuit. It was still pending when he was killed."

"What was the lawsuit about?"

"We're working on that." Juanita smiled. "Shit's happening."

"It often does when the tree gets shaken. I wonder what the hell he was doing in front of my building?"

"We don't know yet, but I'm very suspicious of coincidences."

The waitress brought their dishes and refilled their tea.

"What about the company names I gave you?" Jack asked, after slurping up some noodles. "Did your researcher come up with anything?"

Juanita slid a manila folder across the table.

"You'll find this interesting reading, but in a nutshell, the Chinese parent company, YibinNuCo, has a solid link to Lightfoot. Turns out that Lightfoot has a subsidiary based in Singapore called MarsX Transport. MarsX has a large presence in Shenzhen, a major Chinese port, and MarsX is YibinNuCo's primary transport company. The other two companies, Roydun and Panex are both solidly linked to YibinNuCo. So all these companies are linked."

"And Lightfoot is tied to illegal ivory, and possibly other illegal wildlife smuggling; YibinNuCo has been charged with using illegal wildlife parts in its products. It looks like a case.

"Far too big for us though, as you know. I hand everything over to Wildlife, and they can involve Interpol and whoever else they want. Multinational cases like this take years to mount, and rarely achieve much. The companies involved are usually tipped off by some paid player, and evolve new strategies and operations. But we'll remain optimistic cause that's what we do."

"Good. I'll give this a go-over. Thanks for keeping me in the loop."

"You're my dreamer."

Jack chuckled.

Juanita started eating, then abruptly set down her spoon.

"Alex came over for dinner last night."

"Alex." Jack was silent for a moment. "How did that go?"

"I have to tell you Jack, it was wonderful. There was one point where I was watching my two boys and Alex laughing, eating, and I had my family again. My heart just about flipped. Alex is seeing a counselor, a HUGE step for him, and he just seemed so happy to be back with us. I think our separation taught him something about himself. He may be a tough guy, but he's also a family guy. He needs it. I think he's ready to give it a second try."

"And you're ready to let him?"

"Yeah, I am." She reached out and touched Jack on the arm. "Look, I know how you feel about me, and I have feelings for you too, but this development with Alex is right. It just is right."

"Well that's great, Juanita. I'm very glad for you." Jack hoped he looked glad. He certainly didn't feel it.

"Are you going to be alright?"

"Yeah. I'll be okay."

They finished their lunch in relative silence, and as they were leaving the restaurant, almost as an afterthought, Juanita asked Jack if he'd be willing to describe the blond killer he'd seen in his dreams to another sketch artist.

"Of course," Jack said.

"This would be off the record, since you didn't really see him in person. We're going to keep the dream part of this hush-hush. You good with that?"

"Sure. Where do we do this?"

"How about we come by your place early next week?"

"I'll be around. Just let me know when so I can synch up."

Will do." Juanita leaned over and gave Jack the softest kiss on his lips. "Take care Jack." He watched her cut across Broadway and get into her car, his vision starting to blur, and he realized he was crying.

58

Jack went for a long run that afternoon, running blind, as if he didn't care about anything. Somewhere around Sand Point Country Club he collapsed onto a bench sobbing.

Jack had never considered himself emotional. To the contrary, he'd been extremely steady, rational, able to withstand the pressures and whims of a rapidly evolving tech market with a cool head. Some of his former colleagues had called him "Cool Head Jack." Additionally, he'd not fallen in love since college. He hadn't the time or energy. Casual hook-ups, few as they were, were the limit of his involvement with women. And those breakups fazed him for a day or so before he shed them.

But now a crack had opened in his armor, and like a fool, he'd let the light come storming in. And it had blinded him and his rational, cool-headed mind. His heart, well hidden, was now flopping on the surface waiting to be picked apart by scavengers.

Early after meeting Juanita, when his feelings for her first emerged, he'd stared into a mirror after emerging from the shower and stated the obvious. This wasn't going to work.

She was a cop, and lived in a world he could barely imagine. An edgy, dangerous world. Juanita needed to be hard. Her work demanded it. She was a risk-taker, a maverick when she needed to be. And she was highly competitive. She'd try to suck him into her world. And she'd probably succeed. He actually did some Google searches on the success or failure of relationships with cops by non-cops. The results were dismal.

Furthermore, Juanita had two kids, high school boys, one of whom wanted nothing to do with Jack. Juanita was separated, but not divorced, from her husband, a jealous cop with anger-issues who still considered them married. He'd already threatened Jack once.

And finally, Juanita was extremely committed to her work and family and crazy busy. Crazy busy as he'd once been. Which left very little time to grow a relationship.

He spoke to his just-showered image that day, pointing his finger at him for emphasis. "There is no way you should get involved with this woman," he told his dripping reflection. And then he'd conveniently ignored his own guidance.

"Are you all right?" A woman's voice broke through his darkness.

He sat up, backhanding the tears from his face. A woman was sitting on the far edge of the bench. She was older than Jack by some, beautiful, her blond hair commingled with silver. Dressed fashionably in designer jeans, a white silk blouse, Cartier watch on her wrist, small pearls around her tanned neck, she seemed an intrusive anomaly.

"No," Jack muttered. "I'm not the least okay."

"What's wrong?"

Her voice was soft, warm, soothing yet strong. An invitation for him to talk.

He resisted.

"Nothing." He sat up straighter, looking around. Three seagulls were on the path screaming at each other over a discarded sandwich. The woman was staring at him, concerned, yet not worried. Calm and resolute.

"Here," the woman said, unzipping her fanny-pack. She reached in and extracted a card which she handed to Jack. He took it, digested the printed information, regarded her closely.

"Is this how you find your clients?"

"Always on this bench." She smiled, and though he hated himself for his lack of control, Jack smiled as well.

"Call me if you need to, okay?"

Jack turned the card over, read her name, Clara Deans, then slid it into his pocket.

"Sure. I will." Jack watched her walk away, looking simultaneously sexy and regal.

After the woman had left, Jack walked over to 35th, found himself a tucked-in deli, and had some lunch. The voices in his head went back and forth until they quieted, replaced by the buzz of conversation and a pleasant Jack Johnson groove. He punched Per's number into the phone and left a message, then took an Uber back to his place. When he got home, Jack forced himself into Monique's project and promptly lost himself. Emerging hours later, he checked his phone. Nothing. He pulled some leftover noodles, tofu and broccoli out of the fridge and re-heated them in the microwave. While he was eating his phone buzzed. It was a text from Monique,

telling him they were heading to LA next Wednesday. She'd taken the
liberty of getting him a ticket. They'd be flying down with Riordan
and Stan. They were staying in the Dorian Hotel, which Jack checked
out online. White, Romanesque, nice swimming pool. She'd booked
them for four nights. Expect long days, she'd said.

'God, would it take that long to set up?' he thought then decided
it probably would. Monique was OCD about her art, and they still
had a few bugs in the computer/sound interface. Then Per called.

"Talk?" Jack asked.

"Sure."

"In person?"

"Still sure."

"Come over?"

A bit of hesitation. "Sure. Twenty minutes?"

"See you." Jack began streaming Zeena Parkins' *Captiva*, brewed
a pot of Oolong tea, and sat down with a Scientific American to wait.

Per arrived with a brown paper bag, which he held aloft as he
entered.

"Not too early to do a bit of drinking, is it?"

"Never. What are we drinking?"

"Scotch. Bowmore, from the Isle of Skye."

Jack got up and fetched two squat glasses. "Want ice?"

"Yeah, I'd take two cubes. Thanks."

Jack returned, placed the glasses on the table. Per poured an
inch, then a tad more, sat down.

"Now we're ready."

Jack raised his glass to Per's.

"Skol," Per said.

"Is this how you and Marla do it? When you talk."

"Hah, I wish. Now what's on your mind my friend. On the
phone, you sounded like you needed a stout drink."

Jack spent the next half-hour spilling his heart to Per, and Per,
bless him, sat, drank and listened. Then Per talked, for he'd had his
share of heartaches, and in fact, he told Jack, the liaison with Marla
may be reaching a premature conclusion. And Jack sat, listened, and
drank. And the golden liquid in the bottle went down, down, down,
and some hour or two later Tool's cover of Zeppelin's *No Quarter*
detonated through the array of pre-amps, dacs, and sub-woofers, and
the two men danced a chaotic stagger, and later still an enormous
laughter erupted and did not end easily.

Jack made it as far as the sofa, a soft Paul Bley piano solo wafting through the room. Per blew him a kiss, let himself out, and the elephant found him in his muddled sleep, and carried him away.

Waking the next morning, tongue like sandpaper, head splintering, what occurred to Jack immediately, was not grappling for a drink of water, downing three Tylenol, or jackknifing over the toilet. It was the bull elephant, who he discovered was named Peho. The dream unreeled like an old film as he sat on the side of his bed, head between his knees.

Peho was traveling with a family group of twenty or so elephants. They walked steadily, with purpose to their direction, yet unhurried. Again, a sense of great peace come over Jack, a feeling of such security for his place in life. There was no need for introspection, all was here as it was. A completeness he'd perhaps never achieved, or achieved only as a very young child, a perfection that included nothing other than what existed within and without the body.

Ambling across the savanna, Jack watched the clan through Peho's eyes, heard their trumpeting and snorting through Peho's ears, felt Peho's movement through Peho's nervous system and cere-bellum. As ungainly, at times, as the beasts appeared, Jack experienced the fluidity of Peho's movement, a liquid flow of a coherent anatomy unfettered by either pain nor self-consciousness.

Jack watched with joy as young elephants climbed each other, chased and mock-fought, head-butting, stumbling, running for cover under a mother's belly. How careful the mothers were, how sensitive to their children's every need. How delicate even, these giant creatures. They crossed dried grassland in blistering heat, tails swinging, trunks lifting food to mouths, spraying dust over themselves. They did not seem to know fear.

The goal of their migration became apparent to Jack as they broke through a barrier of thorn-infested shrubbery, waded across a border of lush chest-high grass, and entered a seemingly infinite expanse of shallow water, where they bathed, drank, lay down and rolled on their backs, blowing water out of their trunks like the explosions of spouting whales.

Jack had no sense of time in the dream, as if it happened without that cognitive awareness of past and future. And even now, hunched over in human pain, he knew the remnants of great peace, vast completeness. It was a feeling as close to the spiritual as Jack had ever experienced.

It resonated, even after a shower, a light meal of oatmeal with bananas, and a long run. Sitting on a bench overlooking the slow curling of the Sammamish River, the feeling was within him, and for a moment he wondered if he'd been visited by a god?

59

Over the next number of nights Jack dreamed he inhabited Peho. These were largely uneventful dreams, the daily wanderings of an African elephant, yet were an important bonding experience. Jack knew his relationship with Peho deepened over the course of these dreams. And every morning he woke feeling he'd been blessed, full of what he could only foolishly describe as grace.

The flight to LA was uneventful, and the remainder of their first day in the City of Angels was spent settling into their hotel, visiting, scoping the gallery space, lounging by the pool, and meeting up with Li-Ne Line for dinner.

Gallery Strasse was located on Washington, in the Culver City art district, but had inadequate space to handle a show of the magnitude Monique and Li-Ne Line were bringing to it. The owner, Trish Sherwood, had rented a commercial space off National, three blocks from the gallery. That space was a 3500-plus square foot rectangle, fifteen-foot ceilings with hanging fluorescent lamps. Trish had the walls and ceilings painted white two days before, and the space reeked of new paint. It had a funky vacant feeling to it that Monique tripped out on.

"I'm going to make this place MINE," she exclaimed when she first entered.

Stan and Monique had both shipped equipment down to the gallery, and they spent several hours the next day moving it over to the new space and unpacking. Jack had brought two identical MacBooks, one for backup, just in case.

The four of them spent the next three days planning and hanging the show, assisted by Li-Ne Line, and a carpenter named Daniel Blaine that Trish had secured. They built cubicles, hooked in ceiling wires for the hanging fabric pieces, set up plexiglass pedestals and display cases, and installed sound equipment under Stan's guidance. Jack installed a modem and linked all the pieces, reviewing and testing code, while Riordan wandered around pontificating, and giving largely unheeded advice. Evenings were dinners, drinks, and more pool time.

Jack couldn't believe how much went into setting up the show, but by the morning of the last day, work was completed, and the fabric pieces field-tested. There were shawls, light coats, gloves, socks, hats, and scarves. All of them reacted to various metabolic data, stimulating alterations in color and triggering an array of wild sound effects. One of the sound challenges had been to segregate sound around particular pieces, which was solved by installing baffling. On completion, the entire gallery space looked like something out of a mad-scientist's nightmare. The opening was set or five that evening. They were due at 4:30.

Jack spent the remainder of the day swimming, sunbathing, and reading a Clive Cussler novel he'd picked up at the hotel's book exchange. It was his first art opening, and he'd brought a Calvin Kline sports coat for the occasion. He met up with Monique, Stan and Riordan in the lobby. It was immediately apparent that Monique was nearly hammered. Art show nerves, Riordan later told him.

Trish and her partner Anne greeted them, showed them wine and hors d'oeuvres tables, which both Riordan and Monique dove into, and at 5:00 sharp Trish opened the front door. Jack was immediately amazed. A line of people stretched down the block as far as he could see. He later found out the door count was over 300. And while Jack was not a social creature, he enjoyed wandering the floor, watching people's interactions with fabric art, and speaking to more than a few Los Angeles natives. A few who expressed interest in future collaborations.

The next morning he flew back to Seattle.

60

Jack had been ignoring most texts and emails, but Juanita had written several times, updating him on events, the most relevant being the arrival of an FBI mob specialist from Chicago who would stay a week or so, training her in mob-related behavior, and assisting her with the Lightfoot case. There was no invite for Jack to join them, just the statement. He was stung again, shut out as a colleague as well as a lover. Juanita was apparently closing doors, one after another. He needed to forget about her and move on. He needed to talk with someone other than Per. He found the card the woman therapist, Clara Deans, had handed him on the bench at Sand Point, in what seemed ages ago, and dialed her number, leaving a message at the voicemail prompt. She called back two hours and some minutes later, her voice soft yet forceful.

"Jack, this is Clara. How can I help?"

No niceties, no bullshit, straight to the point. Jack respected that.

"I'd like to make an appointment to see you."

"Ahh. I was afraid you'd ask that. My next opening is in November."

"November? That's two months. I was hoping to get in right away."

"I'm sorry."

"Damn."

The line was silent, and Jack thought Clara might have disconnected.

"Tell you what," she said slowly. "Why don't we meet informally, for a glass of wine. That would be cheaper and easier."

"Seriously? Is that, like, legal?"

"Seriously. And ethical would be more to the point. And no, it probably isn't. But look, you're in pain, and maybe I can help. We'll do it off the books, off the record. We'll kill all the witnesses."

Jack snorted a laugh.

Did that feel good?"

"Yes. I don't laugh much these days."

"Sorry. Maybe we can turn that around a bit. Do you know Sand Point?"

"Not at all."

"Can you meet me at Baxter's next Thursday, say 5:00? It's on 95th. Put it into your maps app."

"Sure. That should work."

"Good. I was hoping it would. We can talk then, and I can see if you're a good candidate for the type of therapy I do."

"What type is that?"

"We'll talk about it then, okay?"

"Okay, and thanks! I'll see you then. Thanks very much. I really need this."

"I can tell. Until then, be gentle with yourself."

"Thank you."

61

Jack had been thinking about a get-away when he got back from LA, a few days on his uncle's land up the Skykomish. Between the stress of the exhibit, and the collapse of his relationship with Juanita, he needed some space.

His uncle answered on the third ring. "Sora speaking," he answered in a voice that always made Jack think of a pair of worn leather gloves.

"Uncle Sora, it's Jack."

"Jack! So good to hear from you. How's things in Washington?"

"They're okay. How's things in Santa Clara?"

"Life goes on Jack. That's the thing. Are you well?"

"A bit stressed." Jack didn't go into detail, just that he'd been in LA working on an art project.

"That's crazy-land down there," his uncle said laughing. "I did my time and won't go back."

"Hey uncle, I was hoping to stay at your land up the Sky for a few days, but I remembered you said you and Marla were coming up for a few weeks. I don't want to intrude."

"No intrusion even if you did come, Jack. But we're not arriving until the twenty-second. You have until then to isolate." Uncle Sora knew Jack's needs. "But even so, come up for a night or two when we're there, okay? We'd love to see you."

"I will, I will. But I'll probably head up there tomorrow as well, and spend a few days decompressing."

"You sound tired Jack. Everything alright?"

"Yeah, Uncle, just work."

"That tech stuff is stressful. Gardening, much better."

"I look forward to that someday, Uncle." Jack laughed in spite of himself. He remembered how Uncle Sora could make any hurt and pain seem minor.

"And do come up after we get there on the twenty-second. Any day. We'll be there for two weeks, just messing around."

"I will, and thanks, Uncle."

The following morning Jack gathered his camping equipment, enough food and clothing for four or five days, his fishing equipment, then loaded the car and drove north out of Seattle. It was still early, and he listened to NPR awhile, then slipped in a disc of Haydn's London Symphonies, and reveled in the music that swelled into his car. Hadyn had a special place in his heart dating back to early college, and an UW orchestra viola player named Tomoko.

The drive up the Snohomish, then the Skykomish, or Sky as it was called locally, was relaxed, and it wasn't until he pulled into the narrow drive that led to his Uncle's land, that Juanita ghosted into his mind. He pictured her as she'd sat in the car, deft and beautiful, smiling, sun-washed, as he'd walked back from opening the gate. There was promise in the day, in her eyes. They were going somewhere together then. What had come of it?

This time he gunned the car through the gate, forcing her out of his mind again as he locked the gate behind him.

He drove past where he and Juanita had camped, following the river upstream this time on a faint tire-track, which wound through a mixture of alder and spruce. The track ended in a small egg-shaped clearing of thick grass and bracken ferns. To the right the bank dropped steeply to the river. But the channel had shifted since he'd been here last, and rather than dropping into a deep slick, there was only a trickle separating the bank from a long dog-leg of cobble, and the main channel on the other side of that. Jack had learned that rivers were living things, and they constantly shifted and evolved. It was no error that Lao Tzu, the author of the Tao Te Ching, had written that those who understood water understood the Tao.

Jack parked the car by a pair of ancient cottonwoods, and quickly set up the tent, flattening the grass, clearing the few sticks. Once the tent was erect, he blew-up his air mattress, spread his sleeping bag over it, and placed a pillow at the top. His bed for the next few nights. Above the bed from a hanger he hung an LED lantern.

That finished, he slid the bank to the river, waded the shallow riffle, and walked out onto the dog-legged cobble bar, stripped and dove into the icy water. The electric shock took everything away, even his breath. It was exactly what he needed. After floating thirty feet, he scrambled out, found a narrow sand beach tucked into the cobble, and lay down in the arms of the sun.

Over the next few days Jack slept, hiked, ate, fished, swam, sobbed, screamed, howled, and pecked at the several books he'd brought with him. The nightly fire and a bottle of whiskey became ritual. Juanita was always present in one way or another, leaking into his consciousness when he least expected it, hovering barely submerged the remainder. But as Jack slowly surrendered to the water, wind and sun, and let them erode him, he relaxed. He began to let go of fighting, suppressing, holding on.

Jack lived with the male elephant Peho every night in his dreams, and this was truly the highlight of his time up the Sky. The experiences deepened each night, his consciousness becoming more expansive, more fluid. A dynamism engulfed him, sweep him along in this vast current called life until it was impossible to say whether he was within it, or it within him.

As his consciousness expanded, he realized that Peho was a teacher who'd been mysteriously sent to him. Jack, this person, was no longer an isolated being. Surfaces were fluid, his inner and outer worlds were infinite. Energy was ever changing, shapes were ever changing, consciousness was ever-changing. Nothing remained as it was. Even the bare stone that protruded from the grassland was continually eroding, exchanging matter with its immediate environment, taking in sunlight as heat, sloughing off infinitesimal grains of sand. The line from Blake's, "To see a world in a grain of sand," was suddenly obvious, but in fact ill-written. There was no "world" to see, no concept to understand.

Jack would awake after these dreams entirely refreshed, cleansed and utterly at peace. It was such a foreign experience that he wanted to lay there and revel in it. But then the day would catch him. The first birdcalls so crystal-clear, they often shattered his thoughts, leaving only vast silence.

When he emerged from his tent, and gazed around the small meadow, the large trees ringing it, the oval of pale sky, he saw it all with wonder. Grace descended on him and engulfed him in its clarity.

It was on the night before he'd planned to leave, that he experienced two dreams.

Jack had stayed up later than usual staring at the fire, listening to night sounds, thinking about his life, where it was going. The whiskey had run out two nights before, so he drank only river water, snowmelt from the Cascade peaks towering above, the icy crystal blood of mountains.

In the first dream he was again with Peho, but the elephant and his tribe were agitated. It was unclear to Jack why, but they behaved restlessly, given to snorting, grunting, nervous movement, and erratic sprints. A sensation of dis-ease permeated Jack as well, foreboding, as if some great evil was hatching from an egg hidden beyond their ken. Peho was given to pacing, raising his mighty trunk, and sounding it like a trumpet of alarm. Yet the day was clear, and a mild breeze stirred the leaves.

Waking from the brief dream there was no peace, rather a great apprehension. Despite this, after hours of restlessness and monkey-mind, he managed to fall into a ragged sleep near dawn.

He was in Juanita's head this time. He caught her reflection as she slammed her car door, and sun caught the window and framed her there.

She was not alone.

She walked around the car and joined a man who stood with his hands on his hips surveying the wreckage.

They stood in a cu-de-sac of a partially built, then abandoned, subdivision. Blackberry and knee-high weeds grew from scraped soil, the rows of planted maples on the parkways were dead. A few weathered goose-necked street-lamps stood like stark metal birds, and skeleton houses squatted on plotted rectangular lots. The man glanced over his shoulder, spoke to Juanita.

"Come on, over here." Jack read his lips. Then he turned and walked toward one of the derelict houses, and Juanita followed.

As they began climbing the driveway, already cracked and veined with weeds, the man stopped to pick something up. Juanita walked to his side, but he motioned her on, ahead. She continued walking up the drive, and Jack was suddenly trapped by his knowledge of what would transpire. He watched helplessly as the house drew closer. He strained to scream a warning, to shake her awake. For he knew she would never reach the partially framed house at the end of the driveway. And then it all went black.

62

Jack left his uncle's land immediately, driving like a madman to Gold Bar where he found cell coverage. He sat in a parking lot and dialed Juanita's number repeatedly, but there was never an answer. He finally gave up. It was barely seven, and the chances of anyone answering at the FBI were slim, still he called. No one picked up, and he left a message that he was looking for Juanita Hernandez, and to please have her call him. He left his number and clicked the phone dead, feeling the wash of horror and resignation surge through him. He knew he was too late.

When Jack pulled off I-5 at around 9:10, he slid onto the shoulder of the exit ramp and dialed her again, listening to the ring echo hollowly, then the message kick in. He left another. Then he called the FBI. This time they were open, and he asked the receptionist to talk with either Michel Faber or Christine Magic. He knew Juanita hadn't mentioned his dreams to anyone, at least that's what she'd told him, so he'd have to tread lightly as how to play this. He couldn't come across as a kook.

"Which one?" the receptionist asked curtly.

"Christine," Jack said without thinking.

Jack listened impatiently to soft jazz, then a voice cut in.

"Magic here."

"Christine, this is Jack Toyokata. I was doing some research for Juanita Hernandez. We met a couple of times."

"I remember."

"I can't seem to get in touch with her. Do you know where she is?"

"No, I don't. Have you called her cell?"

"Several times. All I get is her message."

"And you've left messages?"

"Of course."

"Then I can't help you."

Jack knew she was close to hanging up.

"Wait! What about the agent from Chicago, the mob specialist?"

"McCormick."

"Is he around?"

"No. He returned to Chicago. His daughter had some soccer thing this weekend."

"Was he with Juanita yesterday?"

"He told us he was supposed to meet her to check out a lead, but she never showed."

"Didn't that bother you?"

"Why? Juanita's a big girl."

"Would it be too much to ask you to text me his photo?"

Silence, then, "Yeah it would. I think we're done here, Mr. Toyokata."

The line went dead.

63

Jack was unsure how he ended up in his parking garage, much less his apartment. He remembered standing in the elevator staring at a silver panel with two rows of black numbers, not having a clue what to do.

He managed to stumble through the day, taking a run, forgetting to shower, heating a package of noodles in the microwave then forgetting them. He'd called Juanita every hour, but there was no change until nine that evening, when the message told him her mailbox was full.

The dread he'd known since the dream was growing heavier, thicker, turning to something other than dread, turning to certainty. He knew she was dead, lying on the driveway of a deserted subdivision somewhere outside Seattle.

He tried calling Christine Magic again, but the receptionist wouldn't connect him. He asked for her partner, Michel Faber, but the receptionist said he was gone for the day, and refused to give Jack his cell number. He'd been cut out. Probably by Juanita herself, warning them that Jack might pester her, then by his own actions. He was coming across as a stalker, a harasser.

He poured himself a thick glass of whiskey, turned on the Bach violin partita No. 3 in E major thinking it would raise his spirits, but its deft joy depressed him all the more, and he clicked it off.

He was working on his second glass of whiskey when there was a sharp knock on the door. He picked himself out of the couch with a sudden surge of hope, walked over and swung it open.

The man who stood there was familiar to him from a photograph he'd seen in a hacked police file. Officer Alex Rubio, Juanita's husband.

Rubio looked beyond Jack into the apartment as if he expected someone else.

"Is she here?" Jack heard anger in his voice. And something else. Fear.

"No. Come on in." He turned his back on Alex and walked into the kitchen, retrieving another glass. When he walked into the living room, he saw Rubio collapsed onto the couch taking a pull from the bottle.

"Fuck!" he said. "Fuck-fuck-fuck. Where is she?"

Jack handed him a glass.

"I should kill you."

"A lot of good that would do." Jack sat down heavily.

"She never came home yesterday. Not today. We had plans tonight. We were going to a movie. Told the kids they were on their own."

"Did you meet that FBI agent she was working with? The one from Chicago?"

"Only heard about him."

"Could you get a photo of him?"

Rubio looked at Jack as if he were crazy. "Why? What's he got to do with this?"

"I think he killed Juanita."

"What? You're crazy!"

"Maybe. They were supposed to meet yesterday to check something out. He said she never showed up."

"How do you know this?"

"I talked with one of her colleagues. Christine Magic. She told me."

"Huh." Rubio stared into the whiskey. Swirled it.

"Did she tell you about the dreams I have? About murders."

Rubio looked up abruptly.

"Yeah, she did. I told her it was bullshit."

"She didn't think so."

"No, she didn't. But I do."

"I had one. I was in Juanita's head. We were in a deserted subdivision. A man was with her. I think it was that agent. Then it all went black."

Jack could see a nightmare of emotions flowing through Rubio's eyes. After a long minute he said, "Know what I think? I think YOU killed her. You couldn't have her so you killed her."

"You're crazy. I..." He almost said he loved her. "I didn't kill her. You have to believe me."

"I don't necessarily believe you. Prove it to me."

"How?"

"You want to see a photo of that FBI agent? McCormick? You

describe the man who killed her."

"Late forties, early fifties. Six foot, two hundred pounds. Square face and jaw with dimple. Mole near his left cheekbone. Eyes hazel-grey. Salt and pepper hair. He was wearing a sand-colored sport coat. Is that him?"

"I never met the man. Never saw him. You got a computer I can use?"

Jack led him into his study, hit a button, and pulled the desktop out of hibernation mode.

Rubio slid into the offered chair, began typing, entering a different password at three separate prompts.

After the last password, an FBI personnel database opened, offering different search options.

"How'd you do that?"

"I'm married to an agent in case you forget."

Rubio entered the name Douglas McCormick, and a second later a page loaded with his photo and a bulleted list of personal information.

"Shit!" said Rubio.

The man Jack had described was staring out at them. This time his coat was powder blue, and he had more pepper than salt, but it was the same guy.

"You swear you haven't met this guy? Seen his photo somewhere."

"Swear it. I didn't even know it was him until now. I just know the man I saw."

"Tell me from the start."

Jack closed his eyes and started talking, started with Juanita getting out of the car, him seeing her reflection in the car window, stopping finally when everything went black.

"Damn," was all Rubio said, then lifted his glass and immediately set it down. "You look for that place?"

"I used Google maps, but it was futile. Seattle area is huge. I had no idea where to look."

"Anything at all you saw that could matter? Street signs? Anything?"

"The only possibility is the streetlights. They looked like upside down Js painted black. Older. The place had to have been abandoned fifteen or twenty years ago."

"Hmmm. I'll send out a query. We've got this interagency listserv. See if anyone might know where it is."

"What about you? Did Juanita say anything?"

"Just that she'd see me for dinner."

"Yesterday."

"Late morning. Said she'd be home for dinner," repeating himself.

"Do you know those agents she worked with, Christine Magic and Michel Faber?"

"Only by name. Never met them."

"Could you call them tomorrow, ask if they know anything?"

"Sure." Rubio exhaled heavily, put his hands on his knees and pushed himself up. "I gotta go. I'll call you as soon as I know anything."

"Thanks."

Rubio barked a laugh and shook his head. "If anyone had told me I'd be working with you to find my wife, I'd have hauled them off to the funny farm."

"I hope I'm wrong. I hope we can find her."

Jack was still staring at the door five minutes after it closed.

64

Jack had a meeting with Riordan the next morning to review the exhibition, but couldn't keep his mind in it. He hadn't slept, was hungover, and jittery from too much coffee. Luckily his work was largely done, and it was Riordan trying to figure out what hung next to what, which screens were grouped in the same room. Jack killed another double espresso and nodded a lot.

"You really tied one on last night, didn't you?"

"Someday I'll tell you about it," Jack said, trying to rub the sand out of his eyes. His body felt like he'd been run over, and his heart and soul? He couldn't even go there.

Rubio finally called around eleven.

"Got a hit. Want to take a ride?"

"Sure. I'm in Belltown."

He gave Rubio the address, and five minutes later a black Ford SUV slid to the curb in front. Jack exited the coffee shop and climbed in.

"Where?"

"Maple Valley. Ever been there?"

"No."

Rubio studied him then spoke. Jack caught the flicker of hysteria in his voice.

"It could be the one. The cop I talked to said the project was shuttered seventeen years ago and it's been tied up in a legal battle ever since. He was up there for a drug bust five years back. The black upside-down Js rang a bell."

"Let's go."

Jack was grateful that Rubio showed tact on the drive south. He did not try and pry into intimate details of Jack and Juanita, which Jack figured he'd do. Rather, he became maudlin, telling Jack all the things he'd done wrong in the relationship. Several times he seemed near tears, which didn't help Jack any. He could see them on the shoulder of I-5 bawling. But Rubio never cracked, just kept talking, and Jack was feeling like his shrink by the end of the drive.

Rubio followed the GPS through a well-maintained subdivision named GreenVille, the serpentine road ending at a turn-around. Across a field of weeds and tall grass he saw the straight line of another road. Rubio figured it out at the same time.

"Fucking navigator, he spat. Jack could tell he was more on edge now.

He punched the gas, sending the SUV plowing into the weeds, which topped the windows in places. It reminded Jack of driving through a corn field in California when he was a kid. He remembered being scared that it would never end, that they'd get stuck there.

The SUV broke onto the asphalt, and Rubio skidded a turn left and uphill. The road cut through a swath of forest then broke again into the clear, and Rubio braked hard in front of a rusted steel bar-gate that blocked the road.

Rubio got out and yelled at Jack to do the same.

"Don't touch anything! Just look." He pointed to the right of the gate. Fresh tire tracks showed a vehicle jumping the curb and driving around the barrier, then re-entering the road. On closer inspection there were two sets of tracks. One traveling up, the other coming down and out. Rubio's mood, which had alternated from confessional to sentimental on the drive down, turned stony.

He pulled out his phone and took several photos of the tracks, then got back into the car. Jack followed suit. He bolted the curb on the opposite side, swung around the gate then skidded onto the road.

Jack stared out the window with sinister premonition. The studs of partially-built houses stabbed the sky, cracked sidewalks were choked with weeds, and the same streetlights Jack had seen in the dream stuttered along the road.

Jack was nauseous and breathing deliberately, trying to keep the licks of bile at bay.

They tried three dead-end streets but Jack didn't see anything he recognized. On the fourth, he saw the skeletal house Juanita had been walking toward when everything went black.

"There."

Rubio pulled into the drive and inched toward the house, stopping suddenly. A chocolate-carmine stain, shaped like a lop-sided star with a downhill tail, rested on the left side of the drive. The only new thing around.

They got out and walked toward it, Jack realizing he was holding his breath. He glanced up to steady himself, and saw four vultures circling lazily on the gyres of wind.

"He dragged her somewhere," Rubio said. He could have been talking to himself.

Rubio started searching off the driveway, making larger and larger circles, Jack following like a stooge.

They found her in a tangle of blackberries. She'd been shoved or thrown several feet in, and the pain he got from the thorns pulling her out sharpened Jack. But when they turned her over, he lost it, vomiting into the weeds. Juanita's face was blown nearly off from the shot, which had entered the base of her skull.

"Fucking magnum," said Rubio.

And then something broke in him. Rubio grabbed Jack and slammed him to the ground, leapt on him and began pounding him wildly with his fists, shouting over and over again, "You did this. You killed my wife."

And somewhere, in the abandoned subdivision named GreenVille, Jack lost consciousness for the second time.

65

Over the next hour or so Jack had flashes of consciousness, emerging from oblivion in an emergency room cubicle, tubes and wires running out of him into an array of intricate machines. He vaguely remembered answering some questions, then drifted off again.

Over the next five days he was sequestered in a fifth-floor private room, and visited by an array of doctors and nurses. He learned he'd suffered a severe concussion, had two broken ribs, a collapsed lung, some internal bleeding, and numerous bruises and cuts. His left eye was swollen closed, and his tongue found a gap where two teeth had resided. Among his other visitors were Per, Riordan, Monique and Miguel. To the obvious and initial question "What happened to you?" He answered, "I was beat up." To the second obvious question, "By who?"

He answered, "I don't know."

On the afternoon of the third day, he woke from a nap to find Rubio sitting next to his bed. For a long time neither of the men said anything, then Rubio said, "I'm sorry."

"Well that makes me all feel better," Jack said, his voice cracking.

"I fucked up."

"Yeah."

"You're not going to report me are you?"

"No."

Rubio breathed an audible sigh of relief.

"I found something out that you'll be interested in hearing. Told your FBI friends Magic and Faber too. Lightfoot owns that fucking subdivision. Has for over fourteen years. The Feds are searching it now."

"Lightfoot? Shit! Did you find McCormick?"

"He's back in Chicago. I talked with him briefly. Says that he was supposed to meet Juanita to check out a lead, but she never showed."

"Where were they meeting?"

"He didn't say."

"You believe him?"

"No."

"Why not?"

"Cop sense. He knew it too."

"Now what?"

"We got lucky. We canvased the subdivision below the abandoned one where, you know, and found a lady who was watering her yard. She saw a car go up there Thursday with two people in it. We showed her some photos. She IDed Juanita, but couldn't see the driver. She told us the car was a grey Dodge Durango. Only reason she knew that is her son-in-law drives one. She caught three numbers on the plate. We checked McCormick with all the rental companies and got a hit at Budget. They rented him a dark grey Dodge Durango with a plate that matched those three numbers. Which puts our boy up there in a car with Juanita on the day she was killed."

"He was working for Lightfoot. That's how he knew about the subdivision."

"Seems that way."

"So, again, what now?"

"Well, it's outta my hands for one. My captain is talking to McCormick's admin in Chicago. And apparently IA has been building a case on him for several years. This could be their big break."

"God, I hope he goes down for this."

"Don't get your hopes up. If he's mobbed up, which he apparently is, then he'll disappear before the shit hits. They'll either wack him, or if he's valuable enough, move him to another country with counterfeit ID."

The humming, whirring, and clicking of machines replaced any conversation until Jack awkwardly asked, "Do you have funeral plans?"

Rubio looked at him strangely and said, "You're not invited."

Jack didn't respond.

Rubio stood up, started to pat Jack on the shoulder then pulled back.

"I beat you up pretty good, didn't I?"

"You over it?"

"Yeah. I blew up. What can I say?"

Jack said nothing, then, "You didn't really think I could kill Juanita, did you?"

"I've seen a lot of weird shit, Jack. There were moments I believed it."

"I see. Well, I'm glad you no longer do."

"That doesn't mean we're going to be friends."

"Fuck you Rubio."

Rubio laughed.

"Heal fast," he said, turning heel and walking quickly out of the room.

66

Jack remembered his meeting with Clara Deans hours after the fact, and called her at home. She answered on the third ring.

"Hi," said Jack. "It's me, Jack, your date."

"I wouldn't have used that word." She sounded mildly amused.

"Anyway, something came up."

"Apparently."

"I hope you didn't wait long."

"Au contraire. I stayed for an hour or so, enjoyed a nice glass of Syrah and a lamb chop."

"Good. And sorry."

"So what came up?"

"I'm in the hospital."

"Hospital?" Concern entered her voice.

"It's not what you think. I was beat up."

"By who?"

"It's a long story."

"You have time, I have time. I'll come visit."

"No, you don't have to do that."

"No, I will. What hospital?"

"Harborview. Room 578."

"How about this evening? We can resuscitate our 'date.' When are visiting hours?"

"Seriously?"

"When?"

"Until ten. But they don't seem overly strict about kicking people out."

"I'll come down. It's almost seven. I can leave in a few minutes. I just have to feed the cats."

"Wow," was all Jack could say.

Fifty minutes later Jack was finishing his over-cooked broccoli, rice and a piece of Salisbury steak smothered in gravy, when the room door opened and Clara Deans walked in, and over to his bed.

"Looks good."

"Thierry Rautureau's special."

Clara laughed. "I didn't know he was working at Harborview."

It probably was the morphine, but Clara's laughter sounded like celestial bells.

Jack dabbed his mouth with the napkin and set the tray aside.

"Thanks for coming. I'm... I have to say I'm surprised."

"No need to be. I do this for all my future clients."

"Am I to be a client, then?"

"We'll see."

Her smile, her face, came as close as anyone's to Helen Mirren, Jack thought. She was that beautiful.

"So, tell me about everything. Start with this." She waved her hand over his battered supine sheet–covered body.

Jack gave her an abbreviated version that, with Clara's questioning, led to a more complete version, one that broke through Jack's already feeble defenses like a stone through rotted spring ice. And somewhere amidst his bouts of sobbing, shaking, and cursing, the nurse stuck her head in to make sure everything was all right. And when she saw Clara snugged in bed next to Jack, holding him as gentle as a child, she eased the door closed.

67

That night Peho came to Jack in a sequence of three dreams.
Peho stood sideways to Jack, the vast crescendo of African sky soaring above him. After a moment, he raised his mighty head and gave a horrendous bellow, which echoed across the plains like a sonic boom. As the roar faded, Jack stared in shock at the many ruptures in Peho's hide, where large caliber slugs had torn through and burned into muscle, bone, and organs turning them to slush. Immeasurable sorrow and grief flood him.

In the second dream, Peho faced Jack and stared profoundly into his eyes, and Peho merged with his consciousness, and the wind of his thoughts, saying, "Find my killer, but do not kill or hurt him. Teach him."

Jack started awake, the dream churning in his waking mind. What did Peho mean? "Teach him how?" And how was Jack to find the killer, the blond murderer.

As he lay on the narrow bed analyzing this strange message, the machines that surrounded him were suddenly, overwhelmingly unnatural, terrifying, and Jack wanted to flee for his life. He began to sit up, then stopped, remembering Clara. She was gone, but her scent, that of lily-of-the-valley, lingered on the sheets, the pillow. It comforted him immensely, and he lay back again, falling back asleep and entering the third dream.

He was walking a narrow pathway along a tall stone building. It was night, clear, the sky awash with stars, the air tropical. He could hear his footsteps echo off the structure, which seemed to continue forever. The night was flooded with the scent of frangipani and ginger.

After walking for what seemed like hours, a doorway appeared on his right, emanating light, and Jack was drawn to enter. He found himself in a courtyard. In the center of the courtyard, across a trimmed lawn, was a sculpture of Ganesh sitting in lotus posture on an onyx plinth. Spokes of light radiated from his head illuminating the small courtyard.

Approaching the statue, Jack saw it was Peho, his now-human arms and hands, four of them, raised to his sides and held in mudras, with the exception of his front right hand which held a lotus. Standing there before him, Jack knelt without thinking, and Peho gazed at him with great benevolence. And then the mighty beast, no longer animal or human, but god, slowly extended his trunk and placed it gently on the center of Jack's forehead, and light flowed into him and irradiate his entire body. And then he slept.

When Jack woke the following morning, he was entirely healed.

68

Per picked Jack up early afternoon.
  Jack's doctor, Dr. Stefens, was more than puzzled at Jack's improvement, and commented over and over again, "I've never seen anything like this." No one had.

"You healed fast," Per said, after Jack had thrown a small bag of clothes into the back seat of Per's Audi. "Ridiculously fast. What did they have you on? Some miracle drug?"

"I have no idea."

Jack was tempted to tell Per about the dream, but Per was chatty, and wanted to run an idea for a new novel by Jack and get his input. Twenty minutes later Per dropped Jack off at the front door of his Kenmore condo.

"Take care. Don't jump into things too quickly."

"I won't."

But as soon as he'd settled a bit into his apartment, Jack dressed in shorts, put on his running shoes, and took off on the Burke-Gilman towards Bothell. He ran with ease, feeling not only energetic, but radiant. He could still feel the enormous sublime energy that Ganesh/Peho had transferred into him in the dream courtyard. It had not only healed his body, it had healed his soul. He still knew enormous loss for Juanita, but he experienced it with a higher level of understanding. It existed, but it was simply a part of something much greater than either of them.

As he ran, he thought about Lightfoot, the blond murderer, and what Ganesh/Peho had told him. To find the blond man, but not to harm him. Rather to teach him. He wasn't sure what it meant, but he knew the first step was to find him.

Jack ran by a mother shepherding a toddler, and half-chasing a slightly older girl on a bike with training wheels. He absorbed their gaiety, their energy and casual love. He thought back of his visit to Chicago, his cousin Kaito. How he'd known such a strong desire to have a family. He'd thought about that when getting to know Juanita.

Maybe it would work, and he'd win Angel over. Maybe then he'd feel the same sense of belonging he'd sensed in Kaito's house. But it wasn't to be, and thinking about it, he realized he wanted to experience having a baby, raising the child through all its ages. He was hopeful despite everything. Hopeful it might still happen.

At Sammamish Park Jack turned around and headed back to his condo. The running was so effortless, he decided to push it, see how fast he could go. He steadily increased his speed until he was sprinting, running at least fifteen miles an hour. It was effortless. He passed several bikes, laughing at what was happening, then feeling hubris, he slowed to around ten miles an hour. Still incredibly fast for a steady run. When he arrived back at his condo, he wasn't the least bit winded, and decided to bolt the stairs. Even then, standing in front of his door he was barely panting, his hand was steady inserting the key.

There was only one possible way Jack knew to find the blond man, and that was to hack into Lightfoot's personnel files, which meant hacking into Lightfoot. And the more he thought about it, the more obvious it became. That was the next step.

He took a quick shower, then selected Holst's *The Planets* and cranked the volume. One of the things he really loved about his condo, aside from the stunning views, was how well-built it was. It had been one of his criteria. He was a music buff, and he liked to play music loud at times. He didn't want hassles with the neighbors. And vice-versa, he didn't want their TV shows or spats interrupting his work. The walls and floors of his condo were impenetrable. He'd yet to have a complaint, or hear a sound from any of his neighbors.

He sat down in front of his computer screen and went to work, feeling his way around their Unix-based system. locating firewalls, wandering hallways, ducking out of the sight of patrol bots.

Hacking was analogous to breaking into a building or compound on the physical level. There were locked doors, hidden spaces, burglar alarms, tricks, cameras, and guards. All of these had to be outwitted, evaded, and conquered. And to do that meant continual evolutionary coding. One created the tools needed as one went.

Jack had a copy of the sketch the artist had drawn for Juanita of the blond man. It had been broadcast across the FBI and numerous police agencies to no avail. He'd dumped the digital image into facial recognition software and run it against Lightfoot's extensive personnel files, over three thousand people. There were no hits. Either the blond man's file didn't have a photo, unlikely, or it was somewhere else, most likely behind a locked door. In poking around further, Jack came to the conclusion there was a lot of hidden content.

Several hours went by, and Jack conceded initial defeat. The going was much tougher than he'd thought. Lightfoot was a legitimate company harboring illegal operations. The legit stuff was easy to access, but there were vast areas that were password guarded or more.

When he called Miguel, his old colleague at UniCode, Jack had five windows open on three monitors, with streams of numbers and code flowing across them. He was making headway, but not enough, nor fast enough.

Miguel was a Red Hat hacker, and Linux was hiding much of the material Jack was after. Miguel could also disable password security, the pesky programs that shut down retries after three failed logins. And these needed to be shut down before a password cracker like

Aircrack, or John the Ripper, could do their work. And even then, there was no guarantee of getting in. The most reliable way of getting into password-guarded territory was to find a list of them in someone's drawer. Which was not an option.

Miguel showed up twenty minutes later. Opening the door, Jack made no mention of his cobalt-dyed hair, nor the fine lines starting to radiate out from his mouth and eyes, irrigate his forehead. Miguel was twenty-nine.

"Light traffic," Miguel said, giving Jack a bear hug. "Been awhile."

"Too long," Jack agreed. "Make yourself at home."

Jack steered him to another Mac desktop that mirrored what his did.

"Want something to drink? Pepper, Coke, Dew, Bull?"

"Nah, man. Gave that shit up. I'd take some water though." Then he whistled, staring at the complex computer screen. "This is a fortress, dude."

"Tell me about it. There's at least three pass-worded areas that need breaching."

Miguel swung into the chair. "What are you going to do with the info behind them?"

"Store it. I built a website. I just need to dump it there then study it. However, of special interest, is a personnel file or equivalent.

I'll get you that water."

Three hours passed in the timeless zone. They'd managed to breach two of the three areas, pulling what information they'd found, and copying it to Jack's storage website.

"You want something to eat?" Jack asked Miguel.

"I could go for that." Miguel stood up and stretched, following Jack into the kitchen. "How you been anyway? It's been what, four, five months?"

"Oh, up and down. Having fun with the artists."

"Is that what this is for?"

"No, and the less you know about it, the better off you are. Seriously."

"Got yourself into some deep shit?"

"Let's just say I saw some things I shouldn't have, and now some people want me to un-see them."

"Hah! Good luck with that. You want an insurance policy."

"That and I need to find a guy that's hiding out here." Jack pointed to the table. "You want to sit?"

"Nah, I've been sitting long enough. I'll stand."

"Noodles and tofu? It's about all I eat anymore. Got some bananas and hard-boiled eggs too."

"Sure. Sounds good."

Jack scurried around getting the eggs out of the fridge, putting the noodles and tofu in a pan, turning on the stove. He retrieved a moderately brown banana out of an otherwise-empty fruit bowl on the counter, and laid it in front of Miguel. Then he placed the eggs in a bowl, and brought salt and pepper over from the table. When the noodles boiled, Jack poured them off into two bowls and set them on the counter next to a bottle of Sriracha hot sauce.

"Chopsticks?"

"Never did get the hang of them. Fork and spoon should work."

Jack retrieved them from a drawer and set them in front of Miguel.

"How's life at UniCode?" he asked.

Miguel blew across the noodles. "Hot." he said, then, "Better now that they moved Ken to a different position. That asshole. You know that you leaving swung a spotlight onto Ken Billetts, and they didn't like what they saw." He dipped the egg into a heap of salt and pepper, then took a large bite. "The new guy, Roger Jay, is older, about your age."

They laughed.

"Got these white streaks through the hair on his temples."
Miguel laughed again. "But he knows the score. Tries to keep a
balance. He's funny, always has a joke or two. But you know how it is.
There's no letting up. Deadlines getting tighter, competition more
frantic. You're lucky you got out."

"I thank my god every day."

They stood around the counter, ate, talked, caught up. But Jack
cut it short. He was itching to get back to it. And he'd had an idea.

"What if the login is fake?"

"I looked at the source code. It looks standard."

"Look again. I think it's a trapdoor."

"Okay, I'll take another look."

A few minutes after they began working again, Miguel yelled
"Bingo."

"You were right. It's a fake password request. There's a link
that's composed of distributed lines of text. I just need to find them
all, connect them, and I should be able to get in."

"I think this is the motherlode Miguel. I've got my fingers
crossed."

Another hour passed, and Jack heard Miguel yell "Shit!"

"What?"

"I found all the pieces, but they're encrypted. These guys are
like, super-paranoid."

"As they should be."

Silence, humming computer fans, breathing, and a lyrical ECM
medley were the only sounds for at least another hour. Time by now
was fluid and relative. But then Miguel was in, and Jack knew it when
he heard him intone "Holy shit!"

"Who are these people, man?"

"You don't have to know, and you don't want to. Just copy
everything and dump it into the website."

"Yes boss."

It had taken them another hour to clean up and cover their
tracks, and when that was done, Jack ordered a large pizza, delivered.
They drank some beers until it came, then wolfed it.

When Miguel hugged Jack as he was leaving, warm energy
flowed through him. He knew Peho's presence. And at that moment
he knew with certitude he had Lightfoot's nuts in a vice. But that was
for later. Now he had to find the blond man's identity.

A supplemental "personnel" file hid in the folders Miguel had
found behind the fake password door. Jack began flipping through

the entries, noting photos, cryptic bios followed by symbols, and contact information. It looked to be a criminal goldmine, one the FBI could play with for years.

When Jack searched it using facial recognition software, and the sketch of the blond man, he had two hits. The first hit was false, but the second was right on.

The blond man stared back at him defiantly with glacier-cold eyes, and Jack shivered. Here was the man who'd killed Peho, and Michael's father, and God knew who else. But Jack guessed, from the nine bullet icons after his bio, there were at least seven others.

His name was Lance Demmert. His current address was 1050 Harwood St #1906, Vancouver, BC. His cell was 604-986-3782. His email, ldemmert@gamil.com.

Jack skimmed his short biography.

Lance Demmert was an Afrikaner, with dual citizenship in South Africa and Canada. He'd been arrested three times, once for wildlife smuggling (dismissed), attempted murder (dismissed), and assault on a woman (dismissed as a domestic issue). Jack whistled to himself. Lightfoot kept him lawyered up. He must be valuable property.

So now that he knew where to find the blond man, what?

Jack poured himself a couple fingers of Scotch and retired to the couch, chose Bach's second cello suite performed by Eva Lymenstull, and as its somber haunting notes ascended into the room as he sat back and took a sip of the Scotch. Then he let the music take him. The question of how or what he would teach Demmert simply dissolved, and for the next twenty minutes he was simply filled with beautiful music.

He finished his whiskey around midnight, and before he retired, he sent FBI agent Magic a URL to the clandestine website where he'd stashed the secreted Lightfoot information. The website had been created by a fictitious Bulgarian named Stefan Bogachev, and was routed through nineteen proxy servers in the Middle and Far East. The email came from a radical Israeli group called Kahane Chai. There was no chance either could be traced back to Jack.

The website contained all the clandestine folders and files he and Miguel had found behind the hidden door. All except one. What was contained in that one had taken Jack's breath away. It was his get-out-of-jail-free card in case this all went south.

69

Riordan woke Jack around nine with a rowdy guffaw. "Haven't had your coffee yet, have you?"

In response Jack yawned loudly into the phone. "Late night."

Riordan was ready to hang the show and wanted Jack's help. The opening was Friday at four-thirty, and Riordan, very well known on the Seattle art scene, was expecting several hundred people.

After a run, shower, and light breakfast, Jack drove downtown.

Riordan was in a joyous, gregarious mood, and had several Cornish art students in tow. The hanging went smoothly, although they switched a couple sections for dramatic effect.

Jack was most taken by the shifting collages of eyes. There was something haunting about seeing them hung on white walls. A paranoid would freak out in here.

Afterwards, Riordan took Jack and the students to Julie's DamnFino Diner for burgers and beer. Jack enjoyed hanging out with the students, and conversation varied from art theory to politics to relationships to the best dope for creativity. It was after three when he got home. Per called shortly after.

"Jack, I have news."

"Yeah?"

"You know that memory stuff you're taking? InSight? Why didn't you ever have it analyzed?"

"Well, to be honest, I thought about it. Then I decided I'd keep taking it regardless. I don't know what's in Tylenol either, but I know it works. I did quit it twice, but the memory problems stormed back. Besides, I felt really shitty, so I began taking it again. Haven't really looked back."

"Didn't you wonder why it gave you those dreams?"

"I wondered a lot."

"And that didn't provoke you to get it tested?"

"No," Jack laughed, "I was comfortable with the wondering."

"You're a strange guy, Jack Toyokata."

"No doubt I am." He laughed again.

"Well, I'm a bit more skeptical than you. I bought some, and sent it to a chemist at the University of Puget Sound that I know, for analysis. He called me this morning with the results."

"You found out what's in it."

"I did. You want to know?"

"I'm not sure. Now I'm a bit scared," he laughed. "Should I be?"

"Maybe."

"Damn it, Per."

"Why don't I just tell you."

Jack sat down, gazed out the window at some seagulls wheeling over the lake.

"Okay."

"Well, the stuff listed on the label, Hericium erinaceus, Ashwagandha, Gotu kola, Kelp, Gingko biloba, Seakale, all seems to be there. But it's hard to know if they do anything at all."

"How about the Aesther compounds? I know I spent some time trying to figure out what those were."

"My chemist friend tells me that was bullshit. A red herring. Nothing like that exists."

Jack knew Per was enjoying this.

"So, you're telling me basically what I already know."

"Not exactly. He found something else."

"Oh? What?"

"Have you ever heard of Ibogaine?"

"Never have. It's in there?"

"A tiny amount."

"What is it?"

"It's an African hallucinogen. A psychedelic substance derived from the roots of Tabernanthe iboga, an evergreen bush that grows in West Africa."

Per paused for dramatic effect.

"You, my friend, have been micro-dosing ibogaine."

70

That night, Jack had another dream.

In it, Peho had come to him blazing with flame, his ivory tusks brilliant gold. Jack's spirit opened, and Peho's spirit entered him. There were no words, only boundless experience, as if Jack were traveling through a kaleidoscope of morphing shapes, sounds, colors, sensory and non-sensory experiences. He understood clearly where the art he was coding, fit into a larger picture, and how that picture fit into a frame, and how that frame was surrounded by sky, the same sky that now framed Peho, back to his original elephant form, in a savanna clearing. And perhaps more importantly, the darkness that surrounded all.

When Jack woke, he understood one thing. That Peho would handle Demmert. His only responsibility was as a change-agent. He needed to give Demmert the drug Ibocaine. Peho would take care of the rest.

After dealing with some emails, a run, and a smoothie of vanilla yogurt and Tuscan melon, Jack made several phone calls.

There were three guys and one woman he knew in the Seattle tech field who had, or currently micro-dosed psychedelics. He reached three of them, but none knew anything about Ibogaine. LSD, psilocybin, and Ayahuasca seemed the drugs of choice. The woman, Theresa, recommended he get in touch with a man named Rand Lewis. She gave Jack his phone number.

Jack had known Rand Lewis only peripherally. He'd been an early Microsoft coder, and had made a small fortune on stock options. Enamored of micro-dosing, he'd gotten into psychedelics quite heavily, traveling extensively and internationally to sample different biologics. Rand had dropped out of the tech world around four years ago. Jack had met him only twice. Once at a birthday party for a friend of his who worked at Microsoft, six or seven years ago. And more recently at a retirement party. Each time they'd had interesting conversations. Jack remembered that Rand was interested in biological computing, an area Jack knew little about. Rand had a powerful aura, or as some would call it, charisma, and spoke passionately about the subject of altered states of consciousness. Jack doubted Rand would remember him.

But Rand, answering on the second ring, and after a bit of context, did in fact remember Jack.

"How's life at UniCode? I hear that bastard Billetts was removed."

"Yeah, he was, and that's a blessing. But I left UniCode. I'm working with artists now. Coding. It's fascinating work."

"That sounds far more fulfilling than fixing some glitch in a gang-rape video game.

What can I do for you, Jack? Want to heighten the artistic and imaginative consciousness?"

"I was hoping you could get me some ibogaine."

"Ibogaine?" Jack could see Rand's eyebrows rise. "That's different. Why Ibogaine exactly?"

"I have my reasons."

"That's a very powerful psychedelic."

"I know."

"This the best number for you?"

"The only one."

"Give me a bit. I'll get back to you. How much do you want?"

"Not much. Five hits."

"It's a root you know. The root of Tabernanthe iboga. It will exist as dried, ground-up root in large gelatin capsules. Is that ok?"

"What's it taste like?"

"Bitter. And it's a tough root. It won't dissolve in liquid. You'll have to swallow the caps."

"Hmmm. And the synthetic? That will dissolve?"

"Yeah. It's a powder, or I can get it pressed into tablets."

"You don't think the synthetic is as good?" "They never are. How important is this dissolving part?"

"Critical. I've got esophageal issues, and can't swallow anything larger than ground pepper."

"There's a chemist in Switzerland who makes pretty accurate synthetics. It's chemically identical, but that's never exact. The organic always differs, and to my mind is preferable. But given your limitations, I'll text him and see what he's got." "That would be great. How much will this cost?"

"He'll want $30 per tab, so $150, plus shipping. He'll FedEx it directly to you. He'll want payment in crypto. That okay?"

"That sounds fine. Let me know when you know anything."

"I will. A pleasure talking with you."

71

Jack was accompanied by Clara Deans to Riordan's opening.

They arrived a half-hour after the opening began, but had to wait nearly twenty minutes to get in. The gallery was stuffed to the point of discomfort, and the art was barely viewable. Jack spotted Riordan across the room holding court, but he was separated from Jack and Clara by at least thirty people, and Jack didn't feel like mashing through.

"What say we get something to eat, and come back when it's thinned out."

"If it thins out," Clara said.

"Yeah. Well let's give it a try."

They walked over to Dragonfish, a trendy Asian fusion restaurant in the theater district, and after a short wait, were seated. They ordered an array of sushi and a bottle of Saki. "S and S," as Clara put it.

Jack had talked with Clara every day since getting out of the hospital, long meandering conversations touching on nearly every facet of life and existence. Jack found Clara was extremely easy to talk to. She was exceptionally open and honest, and as a therapist was skilled at getting people to open up, and supporting them when they did. Her technique certainly worked on Jack.

Early on, Clara had told him she couldn't take him on as a client. She admitted she was attracted to him, and that could lead to difficulties maintaining a neutral client-patient relationship. But if he still wanted a therapist, she could recommend someone very good. Jack was thrilled. He wasn't feeling the least need for a therapist, and he declined that. But the need to be in a relationship with this fascinating and beautiful woman? That was another matter. And it looked possible.

Clara was eleven years older than Jack, but retained a coltish spirit, which Jack loved. She was tall, possessed crystal-blue eyes, and her silver hair was stylishly cut, framing and complimenting her lovely face. Clara was intelligent, witty, and at times, bawdy. She was beautiful, lithe, and dressed with casual elegance. Her tastes were understated. A hint of excellent perfume, a simple white gold necklace in the V of a white silk blouse.

Clara was a widow. Her husband of twenty-one years had surrendered to an aggressive prostate cancer a little over two years ago. She'd been a psychotherapist her entire adult life with several shifting areas of specialization. She was currently a generalist, but specialized in working with vets and PTSD. Regarding their age difference, she'd told Jack, "The spirit of the heart is ageless." It sounded like a 'new age' cliché, but with her he had to agree.

After hanging up one night after a four-hour call, Jack lay in bed and contrasted his feelings for Clara, with those for Juanita. It was like comparing serenity with passion, simplicity with complexity, order with chaos. Juanita had had so many issues – power, parenting, relationship with her ex, work – whereas Clara was centered, self-aware, and at peace with who she was. Mature would be the summative word, but Jack found it too limiting. And while Jack didn't want to commit to anything too quickly, he was happy, and optimistic about where this was going.

After a protracted dinner and enlivening conversation, they walked slowly back to the gallery, holding hands, stopping every so often to kiss. Clara had the softest lips, and there was no desperation, no frenzy in her kisses. Yet they were far from lethargic. It's just that her energy was soft and sure. It reminded Jack of readings he'd done many years ago in the Tao Te Ching, how he'd initially been confused, but then understood. The feminine, the yielding was not weak. It was an alternate form of strength.

The scene had thinned considerably when they returned, and Jack and Clara were able to wander, and view the art in a relaxed manner, Clara asking insightful questions. It became obvious to Jack that she possessed extensive, though unassuming knowledge of art. And innate curiosity.

During their rounds Jack caught Riordan's eye, and when they were finished viewing, he steered Clara over. Suffering a staggering bear hug, Jack introduced Clara to Riordan, and Riordan in turn introduced Jack to three artists who claimed to want his services. One of them, Roscoe Albee, was interested in robotic art. The other two, a painter and a sculptor, were simply fascinated in what Jack and Riordan had achieved, and wanted to explore some ideas of their own with Jack. He took their contact information, gave them his, and they agreed to touch base soon.

While he was chatting with Roscoe, he noticed how comfortably Clara was conversing with Riordan and a lady friend Jack hadn't met. She seemed entirely poised and at-ease with social interactions, pride swelled as he watched her.

As they left the gallery around 10:30, it was apparent another, wilder crowd was moving in. Lots of tats, nose-rings, dyed hair and bizarre clothing. It would be fun to stay, thought Jack hesitating near the door, but the slight squeeze of his hand Clara gave was enough to keep him walking.

He drove her home, her house a small brick, L-shaped neo-Tudor, with a roomy front porch and a view of Lake Washington.

He sat on the swinging porch bench while she went into the house and retrieved two tumblers of brandy. Then they sat in the quiet night, talking softly, sipping brandy, staring out at the dark lake. Clara had her legs tucked under her, and occasionally rested her head on Jack's shoulder. He found himself stroking her hair. It was comfortable, relaxed, and natural. And then suddenly they were kissing, more firmly than before, Clara's tongue plying his lips, slipping into his mouth, entering, for the first time, his body.

"Let's go inside," she said huskily, pulling away, taking his hand and pulling him up and through the front door. Inside, it smelled of flowers.

He followed her through a small but well-conceived living room, cream walls adorned with art, some of which he recognized belonged to the famous Northwest mystic, Morris Graves. A rich cobalt couch, white cushions, marble coffee table with a vase of yellow lilies, antique wooden rocker on a narrow Hopi rug. They ascended the carpeted stairs, Clara turning and giving him a seductive smile, still holding his hand.

At the top of the stairs a lit hallway stretched both ways.

Clara led him to the right, to a single doorway. She entered first, flicked on a table lamp. The master bedroom was expansive. There was a desk, several bookcases, more art, a large closet, the sliding door half-open. The bookcases were jammed with books of all sorts, and noted Jack, in several languages.

The king-sized bed rested in an alcove that fully contained it. It stood level with a bay window. Clara let go of his hand, walked over, and pulled opened the curtains. Below, was a brocade of yellow light from houses and the black of the Lake. It was exquisite. Two of the windows were open, and Jack heard the furious chirping of crickets.

Clara turned down the covers.

"Take off your clothes and get in. I'll be back in a moment." Then she turned and disappeared into the bathroom.

Jack stripped and slid under the cool crisp sheet and light blanket. A few moments later the bathroom door opened, then the bathroom light blinked out, leaving only the room lamp. Clara sashayed out wearing only ivory panties. It was the first time Jack had seen her in any state of nakedness. She was truly a beautiful woman, and in this room, this night, Jack thought she looked like a goddess.

Mimicking a stripper, she slowly inched the panties off, and tossed them to the side. Then she turned off the lamp, but Jack could still see her body, incandescent in the afterglow.

A few moments later, Clara slid in beside him, snuggling.

"You are such a gift," he whispered, beginning to run his hands over her body.

"Watch out, I'm ticklish," she laughed.

"Hopefully not where I'm going."

He grazed her peach-sized breasts with his fingers, then cupped them, feeling her nipples harden under his hands. She gave away a groan of pleasure. He lightly fondled her erect nipples, and they resumed kissing. Clara, her hand lubricated with lotion, fondled then stroked Jack's cock until he was fully erect.

They were kissing more passionately, frantically now, their bodies trying to consume each other, to achieve that impossible unity. Jack abruptly slid into her, and a gasp escaped her, a gasp they both owned. She began gliding, up and down, holding Jack's shoulders as anchors, and Jack moved counterpoint, deeper, then nearly withdrawing, then burying himself again. They were like waves in a dark bottomless ocean, bodies connected to a much larger truth. Between the whisk of the waves, the sound of the crickets intensified.

Several times they nearly climaxed, but at each, Clara froze, held herself still until they could start again. After three times it couldn't be withheld, and they both came in quick succession, and the sounds of their animals drowned out the crickets. Then there was silence.

"Oh God," Clara said.

Jack couldn't speak.

They held each other a long time without talking, listening to rise of night sounds, crickets, a distant car accelerating, fragments of music. Sometime in all that they fell asleep.

Jack woke to feel Clara's hand on his penis, soft but firm, riding up and down the shaft, waking him in several ways.

"I want more," she said with a small growl.

This time was slower, more inventive. They explored various rhythms, shifted positions, Clara's tongue finding Jack's nipples, licking, and sucking them erect. Jack's tongue finding her slickness that smelled of salt and sea.

After they finished, Clara said quite unabashedly, "I love sex. You should know that about me."

"And I love that you love sex."

"No. I *really* love sex. It was one of the things I missed the most when Bill became ill. I would dream about it, fantasize about it. It was a hunger."

"You turned to yourself for satisfaction?"

"Yes. And it helped. But it's nothing like this. Like sharing my body with another man."

"I agree." He kissed her nose.

Clara smiled then sighed suddenly.

"I came to learn in my heart and soul that life is made up of loss, of things, people. People you love leave you. There is no way around this."

Jack thought of Juanita and sadness entered him.

"I haven't made love in nearly three years. It's as if I've been fasting all that time."

Jack didn't know what to say, so he remained silent.

"I hope that doesn't bother you, that I'm candid about my pleasures."

"No, not at all. I find it refreshing. People don't often talk about it."

"Or they do so pornographically. Without love, emotion, affection, passion. The physical mechanics of pleasure only. So shallow, so transitory."

They were propped on their elbows now, faces inches apart.

"You're quite the analyst, aren't you?"

"I believe in honesty. It's what I teach as a therapist. It's what penetrates our skin, our eyes, our sex. Without it, we are superficial, unreal beings skating a flat world of our own making. The world. Hah," she laughed. "So vast, no one can know but a fraction. I love that sense of infinity, chaos, uncertainty. Sometimes I think the best we can do is reside comfortably in uncertainty. That and love. But then, they are the same."

"I don't know what to say."

"Say nothing." She touched his lips with her finger. "I'm going to take a shower. Then while you shower, I'll make you breakfast. And I make a mean breakfast."

72

The Ibogaine arrived three days later in a small white box with a Zurich postmark, and Jack's name printed neatly underneath. He removed the newspaper, with its foreign text, that wrapped a smaller box containing a folded piece of tin foil. Unfolding the tin foil, Jack saw five tiny white tablets. He took one out and stared at it. Incredible that this tiny pill had the power to entirely alter one's perception of reality. Or perhaps that was wrong thinking. Perhaps there were numerous realities, and this pill simply allowed us to experience a different one.

Staring at the tiny pills, he wondered if five were enough; if the synthetic would render the same reality as the root itself; if Peho would be capable of moving through this realm into Demmert's psyche. Then his worry dissipated like mist from foothills in strong sun. He had done his best, and would continue to. For Peho.

Jack found an AirBNB just two blocks from Demmert's Vancouver condo, and booked it for six nights, with the proviso of adding more nights if needed.

He and Clara had been inseparable lately, and she suggested accompanying him to Vancouver, but Jack told her it was a working trip.

"Even the dinners? Even late evening?" She fixed him with a bemused eye.

But Jack was firm, and she accepted that she'd see him on his return, and hadn't pried. And while Jack respected her desire for honesty, he hadn't told her anything about the dreams, Peho, or Lightfoot.

Jack packed a small suitcase and left early Sunday morning, driving up I-5 through Bellingham, where he stopped for coffee, then on to Blaine, and the Peace Arch border crossing.

Crossing the border was a breeze. The border patrol guard had asked him a few questions then waved him through. Just another American tourist heading up to Vancouver to shed Canadian dollars on Robson Street. A tourist with 5 Ibogaine in his Dop kit.

Jack found his AirBNB building on Burnaby, parked in the adjacent parking lot, and walked around to the rear, per the AirBNB instructions. He opened the mounted lockbox by the rear door with the given code, extracted the key card, then returned to his car, retrieved his suitcase, and used the key card to access the lobby.

The building was older but well-kept, the lobby windowed with a heavy splash of Arica palms and Ficus on perches of decorative tiling. The air smelled faintly of flowery disinfectant.

He took the elevator to the 8th floor, walked down the carpeted hallway to 857, and used the same card to open the door.

Looking around, he saw the one-bedroom condo was up-dated and spartan. It had an artificial "fresh" smell that came from an aerosol. There was a sheet of instructions on the counter, a chilled chardonnay in the fridge, and a vase of flowers next to the bed. He tossed his suitcase on the bed and left.

Jack spent the next three hours getting the lay of the land.

He first walked over to the building that housed Demmert's condo, 1050 Harwood St.

This building was a circular ultra-modern affair of blue cement and glass that ascended twenty-eight floors. Jack thought it must have pissed a lot of neighbors off when it was built, eclipsing their views of False Creek and Georgia Strait. But that was the game of development. Build in front of and higher than the pre-existing structures.

He tried the lobby door but it had the same arrangement as his building. A key card was needed to get into the lobby. However, like his building, there was inherent weakness in the row of doorbells and the intercom. As a child in California, Jack and his friends had wagers of how many building lobbies they could enter, simply by pushing a bunch of doorbells, and saying "Delivery" or "Pizza" to the first person who responded.

Demmert was in number 2606.

Jack stood in the street and counted up. The twenty-sixth floor was two floors below the roof, and the apartments, and balconies, were substantially larger than those on the floors below. Jack could imagine the stunning views. The man obviously had money. Lots of it.

Each unit claimed floor-to-ceiling windows, roomy balconies, many adorned with plants. Would Demmert keep plants? Jack thought not. Jack suspected he was gone too much, and wouldn't want someone else coming around to water.

He walked around the block studying the building with a pair of small binoculars, finally focusing on one unit. The pale gray shades were drawn. On the balcony, one metal chair angled under a small glass table that appeared to hold an ashtray. No plants. That could be the unit Demmert lived in. But it probably didn't matter. His plan didn't require entering Demmert's condo, or even knowing where it was. That was a distant plan B.

Then he walked the neighborhood attending to restaurants, sushi places, take-out Mediterranean counters, coffee houses, and pubs. There were a large number as he spiraled out in further and further from Demmert's building.

After he had a basic lay of the land, Jack walked the steep hill down to False Creek. He sat on the grass in a wedge-shaped park, and watched the boat traffic flow by, the bikes, runners, and walkers on the asphalt path, kids and parents playing on the beach. His purpose here seemed mis-aligned with such casual life. But then he pictured Demmert, looking out over the same scenes with an entirely different eye, and it strengthened his resolve.

73

Six o'clock the next morning found Jack sitting in his car just down the street from Demmert's building. He'd found a classical radio station, and was listening to a Liszt piano concerto, its dark foreboding melodies infusing an ominous patina on the otherwise sunny day.

It was a walking neighborhood, and Jack was hoping Demmert was a man of habit. That he'd walk to get coffee, breakfast, a paper, whatever. Jack wanted to learn his routines.

Over the next three hours Jack moved the car three times, and watched a number of people enter and leave the building. But Demmert wasn't one of them. He was giving up hope, thinking this gumshoe move idiotic, not to mention the leg cramps and distending bladder, when Demmert walked out the front door and turned right towards Thurlow. Jack got out of the car and followed him on the opposite side of the street.

Demmert crossed Thurlow and continued onto Burrard where he turned left, crossing thirty feet in front of Jack, who ducked his head briefly.

Demmert walked quickly, slaloming artfully around pedestrians, but Jack, twenty feet behind now, was able to keep him in sight. At Robson, Demmert crossed the street, stopped briefly to study a beautiful Asian woman in tight white pants, who was herself studying the window of Lululemon. Then he continued down Robson to the City Centre Sky Train station, where he entered, disappeared down an escalator, and Jack abandoned the tail.

From the Sky Train station, Jack wandered toward Gastown, where he lunched at Jules' Bistro, then wandered through the numerous antiques, thrift, and novelty shops, buying Clara a lovely apricot silk scarf, then strolling back to his place. He took a brief nap, did some work, then returned to his lookout in from of Demmert's condo, finally leaving at seven to get some sushi.

The next morning, he was again parked near the entrance to Demmert's building, but this time he was luckier.

Demmert exited a little after eight, and turned left. Jack got out of his car and followed him, again sticking to the opposite side of the street. Demmert walked west to Jervis, turned right, walked a block, and entered a small coffee shop just west of Davie.

Jack paused in front, studying the sign, Mocha Heaven, and the building, a blue wooden two-story, with a massage and chiropractic office inhabiting the top floor. He gave Demmert a couple of minutes, then entered.

Demmert was just leaving the counter with a porcelain cup of coffee balanced on a saucer. He headed toward the rear of the room and settled into a corner table. Somewhere he'd picked up a Vancouver Sun, which he unfolded and began reading, sipping the coffee.

Jack stood for a moment and looked around. The tables and chairs were all sizes, styles, and colors. It looked like the owners had backed a truck up to a thrift store, loaded all the furniture, moved it to Mocha Heaven, and set it up. The walls were adorned with amateur artworks. A large window was jammed with well-tended plants. The café was moderately busy, and there was a nice buzz. Keith Jarrett's Koln Concert drifted from unseen speakers, merging with the conversations.

Jack walked up to the counter, and ordered a latte from a dark-skinned woman of Mediterranean descent, wearing a lot of embedded silver. A silver moon glistened on her tongue as she spoke. It was strangely sexy. He picked up a copy of the Georgia Strait, paid for the latte, and settled himself at a small table near the center of the room. He read and drank coffee for nearly two hours, keeping an eye on Demmert, who made several phone calls, hit the bathroom twice, then scraped the chair back, stood up, and left. And he noticed, and was pleased, that Demmert liked his sugar, spooning it freely from a pale blue bowl. Rand Lewis had told him Ibogaine was bitter.

The next two mornings were a repeat performance. The following day Demmert again walked to the SkyTrain. But the next morning he returned to Mocha Heaven. Jack extended had his lease for two days, and decided tomorrow was the day.

But tomorrow of course, was different.

Demmert was picked up by a black Escalade a little after 8 am, and the driver left the curb with a squeal. Jack didn't bother to follow.

He spent the remainder of the day working on code, reading emails, and wandering Vancouver, which he was slowly falling in love with. It was a melting pot of cultures, languages, containing both glamor and grit in nearly equal doses.

The following day, Jack guessed right, and was again seated at Mocha Heaven, flipping through a *Maclean's* and nursing a mug of coffee, when Demmert entered. Jack watched him take his coffee and settle into his usual table with the paper.

Demmert was indeed a creature of habit, which played in Jack's favor. Each morning Jack had watched him in Mocha Heaven, he'd taken two bathroom breaks, the first far longer than the second. The first break occurred a half-hour to forty minutes into his coffee, the second just before he left. Jack had already planned to make his move during the first break.

Twenty minutes after Demmert arrived, Jack found the words in *Maclean's* start to blur, his hands sweat, his heart jump tempo. A poor time to get a case of nerves. And the coffee wasn't helping. He'd drunk it faster than usual. The pressure in his bladder was building.

Finally, Jack could hold it no longer. He got up and walked to the rear.

The bathrooms were located in a short hallway, across the long rectangular room from where Demmert sat. Jack shot him a glance as he walked by, but the Demmert was absorbed in his newspaper and didn't look up. Still, Demmert's cruel eyes bored through the paper and stared into his soul. Demmert knew. His hands were cold now, sweaty, and he suddenly felt like prey. The man sitting no more than eight feet away was a professional killer. And Jack was going to slip him a hallucinogenic mickey.

Jack opened the bathroom door. It was empty, and he walked over to the first urinal and began relieving himself. He began counting five for his inhales and exhales, something a yoga teacher had taught him once as a way of calming down. It didn't seem to be helping, then the door opened, and Jack's urine froze in mid-stream. Trying for nonchalance, Jack zipped himself up, then turned to walk over to the sink, and nearly ran into Demmert who stood blocking his way.

Jack experienced a chill emanating from the man, and when he raised his eyes to meet Demmert's, he saw only emptiness that neither judged nor cared to. An executioner. Then suddenly, Demmert brushed by him and entered the stall.

Jack left without washing his hands.

Even though he'd planned this out, gone over it again and again, he almost balked. Banking on the fact that most people in coffee houses were immersed in their own pursuits, Jack walked over to Demmert's table and sat down. He took a glassine envelope that now contained the Ibogaine out of his pocket, his hand shaking so badly that he almost dropped it. Then he did, onto the floor, and had to bend over and rustle around until he found it, banging the table with his head as he straightened.

Glancing around, ready to abort, he saw that no one was paying him any mind. And suddenly he was totally calm. Peho's presence held him like a mother's arms.

Jack poured the five pills into Demmert's half-full mug of coffee, picked up the spoon that sat next to it, and stirred the coffee a few times. Then he stood up, walked back to his table and sat down. Still calm, he glanced around the room but no one seemed to have noticed.

Five minutes later he saw Demmert exit the washroom and return to his table. He immediately picked up the mug of coffee and took a drink. Jack saw him grimace, then pick up the cannister of sugar and pour a liberal helping in. Jack continued to sit, read his magazine, and sip coffee—a refill—until Demmert left. He had no idea how long it would take for the drug to act, or even if it would. Demmert seemed perfectly sober when he had walked past Jack's table and out the door. Despite the confrontation in the bathroom, he didn't bother Jack a glance.

Jack gave him ten minutes, then slid the chair back and stood up, leaving the magazine on the table. He was walking over to the busing station with his mug when someone yelled at him.

"Hey! Hey mister!"

Jack almost kept going, but turned, feeling like a kid who'd been caught shoplifting.

A man with a Yaletown sweatshirt and dreads was walking toward him too fast for it to be casual.

"Mister." The man raised his hand and Jack came close to hitting the floor, thinking Demmert had a partner who'd been watching him the entire time.

"Mister, you forgot these." He held out Jack's sunglasses. "You left them on the table."

Jack reached for the glasses, thanking the guy in a shaky voice, while another voice, this one inside his head, said, "*I gotta get out of here.*"

Jack left for Kenmore that afternoon.

74

Rubio called him as he was passing Ferndale.
He pulled off I-5 at Slater Road and onto the shoulder of the exit ramp. Rubio had left a short message. "Call me."

Jack dialed him back, and Rubio picked up immediately.

"It's Jack."

"Yeah. Good. You should know this. I'm pretty sure Juanita was killed because she broke into Lightfoot's operation at the Port. They knew what she found out."

"How would anyone know that? How do you know it?"

"She told me. She kept me appraised of a lot of what she was doing. I think she wanted to know I had her back. In case something went wrong."

Jack didn't answer immediately. "Okay. So how would anyone else know she was there?"

"Besides you?"

"Oh, come on Rubio. You don't seriously think I had anything to do with what happened to her?"

Now there was silence on the other end.

"No, no I don't. But you might be in danger. I wanted to warn you. There were security cameras out there. She disabled a couple, but might have missed some. And she told me that one of them captured her before she lasered it. You were still around the corner of a building, so she didn't think it got you. But it got her. It wouldn't take too much for an organization like Lightfoot to find out who the woman in the photo was. And they knew how to deal with her."

"Shit. She never told me."

"No. That's Juanita. Played by her own rules, and kept a lot close to her chest. Hey, on another note, you wouldn't know anything about a bunch of electronic files that fell into the laps of the FBI, agents Magic and Faber to be exact. Files belonging to Lightfoot?"

"Not a clue. But that's a good thing, right?"

"I heard it's going to sink Lightfoot's boat for a long time."

"That's by far the best news I've had in a long while."

"So, you had nothing to do with that, right, computer guy?"

"Nope. Don't know anything about it."

"You're a piece of work, Toyokata. Breaking and entering. Hacking. Yeah, I know about my files. Juanita told me. And now maybe Lightfoot. You stay safe now, okay?"

"Okay."

"And stay the fuck out of my way." The phone clicked dead, and Jack was left staring across of field of dying lupine, the pale sky above it seeming to ache.

75

Back home, Jack fell into a rhythm of work, exercise, primarily running, and spending time with friends. Especially Clara. It was almost as if the horror of the past three months had never occurred. As if he'd been able to press *reset*. Yet every-so-often the elegy of those months descended on him, and Clara was his solution.

Working with Monique and Riordan, and now two other artists, Manuel Gomez and Sandra Keating, kept him busy and fulfilled. He loved learning new things, in this case robotics, and something called *smart paint*, acrylics that contained coded nanoparticles.

His relationship with Clara was blossoming. She was a woman he could truly talk to and cry with. Her skill as a therapist was also her skill at communicating deeply, something Jack had never liked to do, and he realized now it was because he was afraid of himself. What he would find if he looked into himself too deeply. Clara was giving him a safe foundation, and a parachute, to find out.

Clara loved to dine out. She frequented several north Seattle restaurants where she knew the staff, and they were friendly with her. Chefs would visit her table, and she introduced them to Jack. They were always interested in what Clara and Jack thought of their meals, and Jack could tell it was sincere. Clara knew food, and her opinion mattered. And Jack was treated to the finest, and most unusual dishes he'd ever eaten. Clara was a pescatarian, and ate vegetables, fish and seafood. No red meat or poultry. It was a diet that Jack had flirted with from time-to-time, and loved. Diet and exercise were now central to his life. He thought back on his later years at UniCode, when he lived largely on fast food and stress. He had traveled far.

One evening after they had made love on the rug of his apartment and were sitting by the window, staring out into the night across the lake with a glass of Pinot Grigio, he told Clara he loved her. The words just fell out. She was silent, and he was afraid he'd scared her. But then she smiled at him, the most beautiful smile he'd ever seen, reflected back at him in the window glass. And it was enough.

A few days later, Jack received a text sent from a phone number he didn't know. It stated simply, *Check your email.* Which he did, finding an email with a link to *Dharma Tibet Vancouver.* Usually suspicious of email links, an unusual flush of warmth flowed through him when he saw the link. It was Peho. He clicked the link, which opened the newest edition of the Dharma Tibet Vancouver's newsletter. On the first page was an article welcoming their newest monk trainee, an older man named Lance Demmert. But what was most remarkable to Jack was the recent photo. His eyes were no longer vacant. They held life, like a dying candle fanned back to flame. His hands were held at his heart in prayer. Jack let out a laugh. Demmert a Tibetan Buddhist monk! Peho must have taught him a profound lesson.

The article went on to say that Lance had joined *Dharma Tibet Vancouver,* wishing to atone for a life of "evil." His word. He'd experienced an event that opened his heart "so vast I thought I would die of wonder." After that, Demmert had sequestered himself in his condo, crying for days, not eating, not sleeping, simply crying out of pure agony for the crimes he'd committed, the pain he'd caused others. When he finally came out, seven days later, he walked the city, somehow ending up outside the Dharma center's doors. A young monk invited him in, and he was filled with such peace that he decided to stay. He'd turned over his condo and extensive savings to the Buddhist center where he now resided.

76

It was now late November, and the grainy grey of the Seattle area, the rain and wind that occluded perception, invited depression, and enervated the spirit had descended.

Jack had largely been impervious to it in the past, but this year was raw.

One factor was his relinquishing InSight.

Once Per had revealed its primary actor, Jack had decided to quit. He couldn't justifiably continue taking a hallucinogenic, even in miniscule doses. But he remembered succinctly what had happened the two times he'd tried to quit. The crippling lethargy, memory loss, mild disorientation, sleeplessness, anxiety. The temptation to continue was great, but Jack resisted it. He was in a very different place now. He no longer knew the need.

The night he quit, he had one last dream.

Peho, the majestic bull elephant came to him in a mist-enclosed field surrounded by frangipani. Drum beats filled the air like a swarm of birds, arcing one way, then another. A giant python wound lethargically through Peho's legs, and several egrets perched on the arch of his spine. As before, there was a feeling of enormous peace and surrender, and the giant elephant began nodding his head up and down, his trunk curled like a horn ready to sound. His eyes glowed like a warm smile, and Jack felt something hold him so securely that he remembered his mother before he could remember, and smelled the richness of her hair and skin, the spicy tang of her breath.

He had many questions for Peho, but only one was transmitted. "Why me?"

What Jack heard were not words, but their translation was "Because I knew you would find me."

It was enough of an answer for Jack

And then the great elephant faded, and Jack was alone with the mist.

He was compelled to lie down in the exact center of the field, the very spot Peho had stood, and when he lay down, he dissolved into something so much greater than his piddly ego it was indescribable. But he knew with certainty it was true, and unceasing. And as he lost his self, he became part of something else, something boundless, vast and peaceful.

And the next morning, Jack left InSight behind.

77

One night around four-thirty Jack returned to his condo with Clara. She was driving her Prius and he was staring somewhat vacantly out the passenger window. Dusk was coming earlier, and the street lights hovered in the darkening air. As they drove past the entrance of his condo to turn into the underground garage, Jack saw a familiar figure sitting on the cement ledge jutting from the building. The man was smoking, and his sudden inhale as Clara's car was passing, illuminated his face just enough that Jack was certain. And Jack's heart quickened, though he said nothing to Clara.

Once upstairs, he asked Clara to fix them a couple vodka tonics. Entering the living room, leaving it dark, he walked over to the window and stared down. The man was still sitting, and Jack watched him. He reminded Jack of a predator, one of great patience.

Then suddenly, Jack saw the arc of the flicked cigarette and sparks as it hit the pavement some distance away. Simultaneously the man stood, turned, and stared up in Jack's direction, then ambled off. There was no doubt in Jack's mind now. The man was tall, and dressed nearly the same, in a dark greatcoat. He wore a fedora tipped at a rakish angle. It was the killer who'd shot Devon Bridges, the retired security analyst, outside his condo. Karl Turner from Van Nuys, California.

Jack shook his head. He thought the FBI had picked Turner up. Maybe he'd bought an alibi as well. It seemed there was a market for them.

"Fuck," he thought. "What am I going to do?" But he instantly knew.

Clara walked into the room with two drinks, and Jack walked over and kissed her, lifting one of the glasses out of his hand.

"Romantic," she whispered. "Shall we sit?"

"Yes. Let's."

And for the next few hours Jack told Clara everything he'd been withholding from her, answered her many questions, giving his own analysis. At times they were moved to tears, laughter at others. And at the story's end, he explained that it hadn't really ended. Yet. That the man sitting in front of the condo when they drove up was the hitman named Karl Turner. And that he was here because of Jack.

"But I thought you said the FBI were closing down Lightfoot."

"That's my understanding. But it doesn't mean they don't want me dead. I'm a loose end, or maybe it's motivated by vengeance. Or I know too much. Or all of those."

"God Jack, you should go to the police. Or the FBI. Tell them."

"That's one way. But it would only buy me time, if that. I have another way."

And he told her.

78

Jack drove to Olympia the next morning, fighting rush hour traffic, cycling through the first two Mahler symphonies.

Olympia was in the news a lot lately, due to a battle between Governor James Remnick and congress over several transportation and budget bills. The Governor had cancelled a DC trip, and was hunkered down tweeting out fighting words left and right.

Remnick was an ex-Huskie football player from Moses Lake, known for his no bullshit country style. His politics were conservative, but he was known to break ranks. Previously a state senator, he'd been investigated for several possible scandals, one sexual, the other three involving money. Nothing solid had shaken out of any of the investigations. Remnick was known as a good friend to business. The larger they were, the better friend he was. It had led to some dubious allegiances.

Traffic was light, and Jack parked in a public lot off Union and walked the four blocks to the Capitol building. He wore a cotton shirt and khakis, and sought out the sunny side of the street. It was a brisk morning and he walked quickly, carrying only a thin manila folder.

He'd only been to the Capitol once before, when his father took him on a "historic tour" of Olympia. He remembered the huge rectangular limestone monolith, lined with columns like erect soldiers, and a crowning dome. He remembered that the dome was one of the tallest in the country. He must have been ten or eleven. He remembered his dad had introduced him to a senator, a tall man with a bald pate and a mustache. Jack had given a slight bow to the man, and both the senator and his dad had shared a laugh.

Jack took the stairs to the second floor, and found Governor Remnick's office without trouble. The Governor's administrative assistant was on the phone, and Jack waited for her, scanning the various framed accoutrements hung around the room. Beyond the assistant's desk, an oak door with inset frosted glass was shut. The light was on.

"Can I help you?" The assistant's voice was already weary and sharp. She'd hung up the phone and was staring at Jack expectantly.

"I'd like to speak with Governor Remnick," Jack told her.

"What time is your appointment?"

"I don't have one."

"Then it's impossible. The governor is terribly busy."

"Call him. Tell him it's about Lightfoot. I think he'll see me."

"Lightfoot?" She looked puzzled. "You have a lot of nerve."

Jack was silent.

The assistant turned away, ignoring Jack, picking up a pile of papers and sifting through them.

Jack stood his ground.

The assistant glanced up at him, frowned, then threw the papers down and picked up the phone. Jack heard a man's voice answer, then the woman tell the Governor what Jack had said. There was silence, then a muted reply.

"What is your name?" the woman asked.

"Jack Toyokata."

The woman repeated the name into the phone, listened, then a moment later turned to Jack.

"He said he can give you five minutes. No more."

"That will do."

"Wait over there," she said curtly.

Jack walked over to a cluster of heavily upholstered chairs and took a seat.

Less than a minute later the oak door swung open, and Governor James Remnick stepped out.

He was a large man, very large, and silver bled into blond on his sizable head. He wore jeans and a crisp white shirt, sleeves rolled up, collar unbuttoned. When he saw Jack, he smiled widely. A practiced smile.

"Mr. Toyokata. Come on in."

Jack stood up, and walked over to the Governor, who shook his hand, squeezing it like a WFW wrestler, then letting go sharply.

"Follow me."

Jack was oddly calm following him into his office. Two flags, one American, the other Washington state, flanked a massive oak desk that was piled high with paper. An enormous computer monitor stood in the midst of it, like a ship cutting through rough seas.

Remnick shut the door behind them, gestured Jack to sit, then walked around his desk and settled heavily in a worn chocolate-colored leather chair.

"Now what's this about Lightfoot?"

"They want to kill me, and I need you to make it go away."

"Now wait a minute. You're not making sense."

Jack opened the manila folder, slid out a sheet of paper and handed it across the desk to Remnick, who took it, studied it then frowned.

"I have in my possession an electronic Lightfoot file which they have aptly named "The Guv." I've scanned enough of it to know you have an intriguing relationship with them, and there's some very damning material in there. Material that could cause you to lose this office, and get you arrested."

Remnick stared at Jack coldly.

"I've given a copy of this file to my lawyer with the instructions that if anything happens to me, she sends it to the *Seattle Times*. I've also given copies to two of my friends with the same message. I have another copy in a safe place, and the original in a web vault. When I came home last night, there was one of Lightfoot's hired assassins outside my building. His name is Karl Turner. I want him, and anyone who intends to do me harm out of my life. Do that, and none of this will come to light."

Remnick sat extremely still, saying nothing for nearly a minute. Then he cleared his throat.

"Mr. Toyokata. If I had any idea what you were talking about, maybe we could reach some agreement, but...." He turned his hands up in a gesture of "what can I do?"

But Jack had seen something shift in Remnick's eyes, and knew he'd get what he'd asked for.

He stood up.

"I appreciate your time, Governor."

"And yours." Remnick stood as well. "Visit anytime. And don't forget to vote."

"I never do."

79

It was a rare sunny day in mid-November, temperature hovering around fifty degrees, and Jack and Clara were taking advantage of it. They'd driven over to Saint Edwards Seminary, parked, and hiked down the steep trail to Lake Washington. Wandering along the cobble shore, they found a convenient sitting log and settled themselves. Clara laid out crackers, cheese, pate, and slices of tart apple on a linen cloth. Jack had carried down a bottle of sparkling Kava and two plastic wine glasses. Sunlight danced on petite waves, and the worries of the world seemed far away.

Jack's mood was expansive, and he marveled to Clara on the remarkable transformations of the past year. Lightfoot was in total lockdown, their entire site quarantined and crawling with federal agents. Their operations worldwide, and that of several auxiliary companies were also shuttered. Over thirty people had been arrested, with more arrests coming daily.

Governor James Remnick had suffered defeat on November 4th in an upset that catapulted a progressive woman, Tia Meins, from Bellingham, into the Governor's chair. He'd decided to quit politics altogether, and return to a quiet life outside of Moses Lake raising quail, pheasants, and guinea hens. Remnick had been true to his word, and Jack had seen neither Karl Turner, nor any other threatening persons around his condo, nor did he expect to. For one thing, Lightfoot was taking so much heat worldwide, that interest in Jack had most likely disappeared.

And Jack had been fair with Remnick, holding the electronic file "The Guv" at bay. Although sometimes it seemed he was letting a big one get away. But that was life. Full of Faustian bargains.

After they ate and cleaned up, Clara lay back against Jack and he cradled her, and they lay staring out over the Lake, enjoying the rare sunshine, and talking softly and randomly.

Jack was working nearly full-time now, with three additional clients giving him eight, but despite the workload, he was largely stress-free, and thanks to his experiences with Peho, he was able to enter into extraordinary states of relaxation. He was feeling one of these now, holding the woman he'd grown to love above all others.

They'd discussed selling their places and moving in together, and a recent decision had made that more likely. Because of Clara's age it was impossible for her to bear children, and she had none with her previous husband. But Jack's visit to his cousin's in Chicago had affected him greatly. He wanted a family. He wanted a child to crawl up on his lap and call him daddy. And Clara was willing. So, they decided to adopt, and had just completed the copious paperwork and interviews required. Now it was simply a matter of time.

And they'd talked of marriage. They'd made lists of who they'd invite, where they would do it, what vows they would say. But they were in no rush.

A bank of clouds appeared to the southwest, and drifted slowly toward them, and the chill of wind flicked spray from the waves where they struck the rocks. The temperature dropped precipitously.

"Wow, that was sudden," Jack said as they roused themselves off the log and stood up.

Holding hands, they began walking back toward the uphill trail.

"It reminds me of something I read recently," Clara said. "It was by one of the Desert Fathers."

"Who are they?"

"Monks who sought the solitude of the desert in order to deepen their insight."

"What did the monk say?"

"Life is weather. It changes quickly. One minute, sun, the next rain. One minute, wind. The next, calm. If you favor one over the other, you will resent half your life."

"I don't want to resent anything," Jack laughed. "When we get back to my place, I'll make us hot chocolate."

"And I will have a large glass. With marshmallows."

"Definitely with marshmallows."

And they began climbing the steep hillside back to the car.

Acknowledgements

Thanks to the clan of early readers, editors, muckrakers, inspirers, and benign critics: Joan Piper, Frank Haulgren, Dan and Susan Hahn, Gregory Frost, Charles Luckmann, Tim Pilgrim, Sherwood Smith, Jennifer Stevenson, Maya Kaathryn Bonhoff, Marissa Doyle, Stan Goto, and David Bass. Thanks to TK Palad for the terrific cover art. And special thanks to anyone I've forgotten and will remember as soon as this goes to print.

About the Author

Paul S. Piper is the author of two novels, *The Wolves of Mirr* and *The Soul Loves Best What Is Lost*, and five books of poetry. He has also co-edited several collections of essays. He recently relocated to Northern Westchester County, New York.

About Book View Cafe

Book View Café is an author-owned cooperative of professional writers, publishing in a variety of genres including fantasy, science fiction, romance, mystery, and more.

Its authors include New York Times and USA Today best-sellers as well as winners and nominees of many prestigious awards such as the Agatha Award, Hugo Award, Lambda Literary Award, Locus Award, Nebula Award, RITA Award, Philip K. Dick Award, World Fantasy Award, and many others.

Since its debut in 2008, Book View Café has gained a reputation for producing high quality books in both print and electronic form. BVC's e-books are DRM-free and distributed around the world.

Book View Café's monthly newsletter includes new releases, specials, author news, and event announcements. To sign up, visit https://www.bookviewcafe.com/bookstore/newsletter

www.ingramcontent.com/pod-product-compliance
Lightning Source LLC
Chambersburg PA
CBHW072206170626
46813CB00003B/815